Catching
Fire

ALSO BY ROSE SENEHI

Catching Fire

Rose Senehi

K.I.M. Publishing, LLC

KIM

Published by

K.I.M. PUBLISHING, LLC
Post Office Box 132
Chimney Rock, NC 28720-0132

Cover Photograph: John Cayton, Canton, NC

Published in the United States of America.

PUBLISHER'S NOTE

This story of the Party Rock Fire is told in novel form by the weaving together of information from the North Carolina Forest Service's twice daily press releases, daily incident status summaries, and various internal reports as well as personal interviews with members of the incident command, chiefs of the various fire departments, and a host of people who were involved with the fighting of this fire. With the exception of the four fictional main characters, the real names of most of the Forest Service and fire department personnel have been used; however, their narratives and quotes are solely derived from the author's imagination.

PUBLISHER'S CATALOGING-IN-PUBLICATION DATA

Names: Senehi, Rose, author.
Title: Catching Fire, A Novel / Rose Senehi.
Description: First United States Edition. I Chimney Rock, North Carolina : K.I.M. Publishing LLC, 2018.
ISBN: 978-0-692-17805-8 (trade paperback edition)
Subjects: Party Rock Fire—North Carolina—History—Fiction. I Family and relationships—Blue Ridge Mountains—Southern—Fiction. I Henderson County (N.C.)—Fiction. I Buncombe County (N.C.)—Fiction. I Rutherford County (N.C.)—Fiction. I Women—North Carolina—Fiction. I Nature—Bats—North Carolina—History—Fiction. I BISAC: FICTION/LITERARY
Classification: LCC PS3619.E659 D36 2018 (print)

Library of Congress Control Number: 2018910762

*For the Men and Women who fought
the Party Rock Fire*

The most essential element of successful wildland firefighting is competent and confident leadership. Leadership means providing purpose, direction, and motivation for wildland firefighters working to accomplish difficult tasks under dangerous, stressful circumstances."

—Incident Response Pocket Guide, National Wildfire Coordinating Group

ACKNOWLEDGEMENTS

The Party Rock Fire was a momentous event in the history of western North Carolina, and I have attempted to tell its story in novel form. I have woven together information from the North Carolina Forest Service's twice daily press releases, daily incident status summaries, and various internal reports in order to secure an accurate timeline. In addition, I conducted personal interviews with members of the incident command and chiefs of the various fire departments, as well as a host of people who were involved with the fighting of this fire. With the exception of the four fictional main characters, I have used the real names of most of the Forest Service and fire department personnel; however, their narratives and quotes are solely derived from my imagination.

In a novel of this length, I couldn't begin to include all the heroic, generous and kind acts that were carried out in November of 2016 in order to save the communities of Lake Lure, Chimney Rock, Shumont and Bat Cave, or, for that matter, depict the groundswell of love and gratitude that came from the community for those who came from near and far to help. However, I have tried to put in as many vignettes as I could to reflect the spirit of this overwhelming support for a common goal.

I would like to thank some of the people without whose help I couldn't have written this book. Dan Brandon, who was the NC Forest Service Incident Commander for most of the fire and has since retired; Ferrell Banks, Chase Payne, and Doug Thompson, NC Forest Service; Ron Morgan, Retired Chief, Lake Lure Fire Department; Gary Wilson, Chief, Fairfield Mountains Fire Department; Richard Barnwell, Chief, Bat Cave Volunteer Fire Department; Brent Hayner, Chief, Broad River Volunteer Fire &

Rescue Department; Chris Melton, Chief, Chimney Rock Volunteer Fire Department; Jim Howell, Chief, Bills Creek Fire Department, and James Ledgerwood, Park Superintendent, Chimney Rock State Park. I would like to give a special thanks to Bruce Cook, the assistant chief of the Broad River Volunteer Fire Department, who drove me all over the Shumont Mountain wilderness, without which sights I never could have grasped the enormity of the challenge of defending the homes up there or fighting a wildfire on that treacherous terrain.

I am grateful to Katherine Caldwell, Mammalogist with the N.C. Wildlife Resources Commission and Kat Canant of the Lake Lure Police Department and a volunteer firefighter with the Lake Lure Fire Department who were the inspiration for the character of Annie Simms. Adam Warwick, the Stewardship Manager of the Southern Blue Ridge Office of The Nature Conservancy was a big assist and the inspiration for the character of Mike McNeil. I thank my editors Jackie Price, Jamie Stanton, and Annie Pott, who have given me immeasurable professional support and personal encouragement, but most of all, made this book better. Finally and foremost, I want to thank my researcher, LuVerne Haydock, for sitting at her computer for hours during the fire and weeks afterward, diligently gathering data I would need to write this account.

North Carolina's over 52,000 highly-trained and well-equipped firefighters, of whom approximately 42,000 are volunteers, come from 1,940 fire stations sprinkled throughout the state's 100 counties. This force, along with the 650 men and women of the North Carolina Forest Service, are part of the brotherhood that makes up the state's awesome and confidence-inspiring network of emergency response and management entities. It has been an honor to come to know the people I have met while researching this book. It left me with the conviction that, due to this almost invisible force of well trained and equipped men and women who are committed to helping their fellow man, anyone can go to sleep in North Carolina knowing that if there's a fire, everything that can be done, will be done to keep them safe.   R.S.

PART ONE

The Family

THE WIND SPUN THE pink plastic pinwheel and made it sing a clicking, snappy tune as the little girl held it aloft. The mountain air felt cool and silky against her sweaty skin. Annie closed her eyes and enjoyed the feel of the steady breeze swirling her flaxen hair away from the stickiness of her neck.

She was just six, but knew the wind could also be capricious. In the winter she'd chase it as it barged into the cabin through all the cracks in the window frames. No matter how much they stuffed them with old rags, the bandit would keep stealing its way in, and she'd have to hug her brother under the covers to keep warm. But mostly, she hated when it roared like a train for days at a time—what a woman who lived nearby told her the Indians called "the long winds."

Living on the side of a mountain that jagged its way down into a gorge, it seemed natural to her to always be going either uphill or down. Upon returning from one of the rare occasions when her mother would take her and her big brother, Jack, off the mountain, she would race to the bluff and look down the valley. Sheathed in a hardwood forest and crowned with massive granite balds, it seemed to stretch on forever before disappearing into the back and beyond. The sky was big up on Bluerock Mountain, not pinched like in the tar-covered, car-jammed towns where hard-edged buildings punctured the horizon.

She picked up the small cage she and her brother had found in the pile behind their cabin and put it on her lap. The little mouse stood on its hind legs, begging.

"You have to be patient like me and wait for Jack to come back," she told it.

Early that morning, they had gathered eggs from the

chicken coop, and her brother, who was four years older than she, had gone on foot to the little village at the bottom of the mountain where he could trade them for milk and bread. Their mother hadn't found work for weeks now and their larder was bare.

She took the mouse from the cage and held it in one hand as she ran a finger down its back. It quickly ran up her arm and onto her neck, making her laugh as she pulled it from her tangled hair. She put it back in the cage and spotted her brother trudging up the trail. Eyeing her, he picked up his pace.

He knelt down next to her, placed the basket he carried on the grass and pulled aside the napkin to reveal a bowl with scrambled eggs and bacon, with biscuits and cookies piled around it.

"Mrs. Reynolds made me breakfast and sent these up for you," he said as he carefully fashioned a sandwich and handed it to her.

"She's nice," said Annie, pinching off some of the biscuit and feeding it to her mouse. "Can you take me with you the next time?"

"I don't think so."

"Why not?" she asked as she munched on the feast.

"She always gets angry when she talks about Mom. Says someone should take us away from her."

"Would they ever do that?"

"Maybe. That's why I don't want you along. She always asks a lot of questions and you might say the wrong thing. They took my friend Billy and his two sisters away from their parents and put them in different homes. The only way we're going to stay together is if we stick with Mom."

"I don't know why we can't go live with Grandpa."

"He's mad at her because of her drinking."

Annie made a face. Finished with her sandwich, she reached for a cookie. He yanked the basket away.

"No. You've had enough. We'll save these for later when Mom gets up." He pulled her up on her feet. "Let's go up to the bat cave. It's cool in there."

He tiptoed into the little three-room cabin, placed the basket on the table, and the two took off for the woods. They scurried up the narrow trail that climbed up the mountain until it turned steep with huge boulders that had fallen from the cliffs above. Jack scaled them, then pulled Annie up. They finally reached the top and Annie ran to the cave entrance. She stood there looking up at the two giant slabs of granite that had slid from the mountain and formed an arch eighty feet tall. She had seen it dozens of times, but it still awed her.

"Are we going to see a bat today?" she asked her brother.

"How many times do I have to tell you, they don't come in the cave until October."

They entered the dark, cool cavern and listened to the sound of falling water echo from somewhere in its deep interior. Something in the air flapped by them.

"Eek!" screamed Annie as she started running toward the entrance, splashing through a stream along the cave floor. She lost her footing and fell down, but quickly got up and ran out. She sat down on a rock and examined a scrape on her knee. Jack, came and sat next to her.

"That's gonna leave a bruise," he said.

"Like Mama's? She always has bruises," said Annie.

"She falls a lot," said Jack.

Annie grimaced.

"Don't worry. When I get old enough, I'm going to take care of her so she doesn't get them anymore." He squeezed her hand. "And I'm gonna take care of you, too."

He smiled the easy sort of way he always did, as if he were dead certain that someday all would be well.

"Jack, can I tell you about my new game?"

"Sure."

"Every time a car comes up this mountain... you always know when that's happening 'cause that poor ole dog Sam keeps chained up makes a big stink... well, I pretend it's my real parents and they found out the hospital accidently gave me to the wrong people and they're coming to get me."

"I get a kick out of you and your imagination," said Jack.

"For sure you're in the right family. We look almost exactly alike."

"It's only a game," said Annie, pouting. "Just the same, when I grow up, I'm gonna live in a nice house like grandpa's and I'm gonna take care of all the animals in the forest."

He reached over and started tickling her. She squirmed and laughed in his arms.

"I'm hungry," said Annie.

"You're always hungry," he said as he stood up and brushed himself off. "Those blackberries should be ripe by now. Let's go get some."

They hollered gleefully as they ran helter-skelter down the trail, skidding to a stop at a huge boulder. Jack lifted her down saying, "After we get our fill of the berries, we can go swimming in the river."

The two didn't get back to the cabin until after four and were surprised to discover the smell of food being cooked coming from within.

"Well, you two are finally back," her mother said as they cautiously entered. "It looks like I'm raising two wild animals."

Pork chops fried in a skillet and fresh corn that had just been shucked waited for the water on the cookstove to boil.

"Sam stopped by and dropped off some supplies for us. My pay for cleaning his house," she said.

Annie noticed the sulky expression on Jack's face. Something that only appeared when her mother mentioned their neighbor.

After they ate, they went out on the porch. Her mother sank down on a rocker and motioned for Annie to come sit in her lap. Mae Simms was thin and bony and always looked like she wasn't going to make it through another day, but she could still conjure up a good story as she rocked on the porch and gazed at the setting sun. From up there on Bluerock Mountain they could watch the blazing orb paint the skies a brilliant orange as it sank behind the rolling Blue Ridge Mountains. Her mother's stories of her carefree childhood in Lake Lure always comforted Annie and Jack. It was good to know she had seen happier days.

Somewhere in the back of her mind, Annie knew she had fallen asleep as she was carefully put in bed. She drifted into deep, dreamless slumber until something woke her. She sat up. The door was ajar and she could see a candle flickering on the kitchen table. She reached over for Jack, but he wasn't in bed.

A siren wailed off in the distance. She rose and went to the door and peeked in. Her mother rocked in her chair chanting, "Please, God, please don't let them come, please don't let them come." The door squeaked open, making her mother turn her head.

"Where's Jack?" Annie asked.

"Go back to bed," her mother ordered.

Her mother's tone frightened Annie, for there was something in it she had never heard before. A sort of terror.

She went to the bedroom window and peered out into the night. A red glow sat on the horizon in the direction of Sam's house. She'd never seen a fire that big, and recalling her mother's eerie chants, she jumped in bed and burrowed her head under the covers.

She woke the next morning as the sun rose at the far end of the gorge. She thought it odd that Jack still wasn't in bed with her. She had to get up and find him. No one was in the main room, so she tiptoed into her mother's bedroom. Seeing Jack in bed with her, she wanted to get in, but didn't have the heart to disturb them. Besides, it was time for her to get dressed and go out and feed the chickens. Yet, she couldn't take her eyes from the brother who always took care of her. Even though his thick blond hair was matted against his sweaty forehead and blue eyes hidden behind lids, he was still beautiful. Everyone said they looked alike, but she could never think of herself as being as easy on the eyes as he.

She got dressed, and before running outside, stuffed two biscuits in her pocket and grabbed the mouse's cage. She went over to her favorite rock and sat down. She took the mouse out and started feeding it crumbs from her hand, raising it almost next to her nose so she could watch it eat every morsel. This small, living creature fascinated her—another heartbeat in the world she was getting to know.

Jack finally woke and came out of the cabin. She ran up and hugged him.

"Leave me alone. I've got to go get Bubba," he said, pushing her away.

"Why do we have to get Sam's dog?" she asked.

"I said *I* was gonna get him, not *we*," he said as he lifted off a coil of rope hanging on the porch.

"You're afraid of him, aren't you?" said Annie.

"Anybody with any sense would be."

"Then why are you going to get him?"

"Sam isn't there anymore, and someone's got to take care of that dang dog."

"Well, I'm not afraid of him," said Annie.

"Like I said, anyone with any sense would be. Now you stay here."

"You better take me with you. Bubba likes me."

He stooped down and looked at her head-on. "Don't tell me you've been petting that cur."

She looked away. "When you were in school, I didn't have anyone else to play with."

He shook his head. "I can't take my eyes off you for one minute. We're lucky you're alive." He started down the trail. "Come on. I gotta see this."

They took the shortcut to Sam's cabin. As they went tripping down the path, the smell of smoke got stronger and Bubba's barking got louder. They reached the clearing behind Sam's place and the sight of its charred remains stunned them. The blackened cookstove and chimney, along with the refrigerator, stood abandoned. Eerie swirls of smoke snaked into the air from out of the scorched earth.

"Is Sam coming back?" Annie asked.

"No. He's dead."

Suddenly, they heard a chain being dragged through leaves. A huge white pit bull came running toward them and lunged at Jack. Reaching the end of its chain, the sudden stop sent it ricocheting into the air. Jack jumped back and fell to the ground. The dog regained its footing and snarled menacingly at Jack.

"There's no way we're gonna get that dog. He can stay here and starve for all I care," said Jack as he slowly got up.

Annie came from behind her brother, and the dog, spotting her, stopped barking.

"Hi, Bubba," she said.

It eyed her. She stepped closer.

"Come away, Annie," Jack said.

The dog strained on its chain. Annie took some left-over biscuit from her pocket and held it in front of her on her open palm. The dog whimpered as she neared.

"You're hungry, aren't you?" she said as she came near enough for him to sniff the biscuit.

She came one step nearer and he gobbled down the morsel, slathering saliva from his floppy jowls all over her. She turned to Jack and reached for the rope, then proceeded to attach it to his collar and unhook his chain.

"Come on, boy, we're gonna take care of you now," she said, as she led him toward the trail.

The whole way back up the mountain, they had to keep pulling the dog along. All Bubba wanted to do was sniff and spray every tree, every rock, every patch of ground.

"What happened to Sam?" Annie asked.

"I don't want to talk about it," said Jack.

Annie knew her brother well enough to know something was wrong. No matter how bad things got, he was always cheerful and looking for a way to make everything better. She decided not to ask any more questions about their dead neighbor.

By mid-afternoon it started to rain, twining a rancid smell in the air as it seeped into the burned remains of Sam's cabin. Annie played with her mouse on the floor of their cabin while Jack read an old, tattered comic book. The only sound other than the rain drumming on the roof was the creaky music of Mae rocking in her chair.

Suddenly, Bubba, who they had put in their shed, started barking and the creaking stopped. Mae got up and went to the window. Annie and Jack ran up next to her. Two sheriff's cars had pulled up. The three watched at the window until, finally, the sheriff got out of one car and a woman in a uniform stepped out of the other. They both ran onto the porch, dodging the rain, then knocked on the door.

"Go to your bedroom. I'll take care of this," Mae told the two children.

Another knock.

"Let us in, Mae Ellen," a voice demanded.

Annie and Jack didn't move as Mae took a moment to straighten her dress, then strode over to the door and opened it.

"Mae, we want to question you regarding the fire at Sam Boswell's place last night," said the sheriff. "Our investigator found a kerosene can with Simms written on it, and he says it's arson." He nervously cleared his throat. "I'm afraid you're gonna have to come with us."

The social worker took Annie's hand, and started to lead her out.

"Leave me alone!" Annie screamed, yanking her hand away.

The woman took hold of her and tried to pull her along, but Annie grabbed the table and wouldn't let go.

"Mama! Don't let them take me away!" Annie screamed as dishes crashed to the floor.

Mae started for Annie, but another officer who just drove up grabbed one of her arms and, along with the sheriff, started to wrestle her out the door. Jack ran and stood in the doorway, barring them from leaving.

"Stop! Don't take her! I did it. I set the fire."

THE TWO-STORY LOG CABIN standing at the top of a winding gravel mountain road in Lake Lure, North Carolina, hardly appeared to be the likely location for the office of the state's mammalogist. But like most of the scientists who work for the North Carolina Wildlife Resources Commission, twenty-seven year-old Annie Marie Simms operated from her home when not in the field—which in the summer was mostly at night, since bats were her domain.

She glanced at the pink gel Baby-G on her wrist with the alarm and stopwatch functions needed for her work. Time to leave for the fire college, she gathered the things she needed for the class that would cost her three of her vacation days, and ran out the door. She waded through ankle deep leaves and climbed into her state-supplied Chevy Colorado. It looked like something a contractor would drive with ten-foot pipes stacked on the roof rack and its camper shell packed with paraphernalia she used in her job.

After all the nights spent recording bat activity, she enjoyed the colorful remnants of the fall leaf season as she made her way to Hendersonville, a half-hour away. This week, she would knock off another course she needed for her Technical Rescue Certification. She was already a certified firefighter and her position with the state didn't require she take these courses, but since her last name would forever be associated with local fire lore, she felt compelled to redeem the family honor by doing her part in fighting them.

On this Monday morning, she dreaded the first day of a grueling three-day course dealing with ropes, anchors and lowers, but, on the other hand, she'd be getting in on the news about all the fires burning in the western part of the state that were sure to be circulating among the firefighters—interesting details that rarely appear in the papers.

She pulled up to the building housing the firefighting college, quickly signed in and found a seat in the crowded classroom. Being the last to arrive, it wasn't but a few minutes before the instructor sauntered over to the chalkboard and scribbled "Mike McNeil" on it before diving into a Power Point presentation.

The instructor interested her more than what was on the screen, for she had always thought of him as more than the nice kid who always helped her and her mom load the trash from his family's three-story lake house into the back of her mother's pickup after they finished cleaning the place. He'd been an enigma all the years she was growing up. She'd pass by the lake and see someone skiing, and wonder if it were him. When she was sent to his room to vacuum, she'd study the framed photos on his desk, and then glance at the clothes hanging on his bedposts and wonder where he had worn them.

Annie's eyes rested on the tall, broad-shouldered silhouette in the front of the class and smiled to herself, for she knew more intimate details about Michael Samuel McNeil than did anyone else in the room.

He wrapped up the morning spent on the textbook version of the course by announcing, "Everyone find a place to eat and be back by one-thirty." He went to the wall and turned on the lights. "The last one back gets to take me to dinner."

Annie gathered her notes along with reams of handouts and started out. Mike, who was chatting with a few firefighters, grabbed her arm as she passed.

"Eat with us," he said. "You can ride with me."

He told the group to meet him at a nearby Thai restaurant, and she followed him to his truck, surprised he had singled her out. She suspected he was just patronizing her after admitting to herself there was quite a gulf between the son of a distinguished state senator and the daughter of the lady who cleaned their summer place—to say nothing about the matter of her brother.

"How's your mom?" he asked as he wheeled the vehicle out

of the lot. "Still makin' a clean sweep of it?"

She forgave his attempt at a joke. He was five years older than Annie and had forged a kind of friendship with her mother during his teen years—one where he could confide anything, such as is the case with a lot of housekeepers—and the familiarity gave him the right to kid around about her.

"She's doin' fine. How's your family?"

"Same old, same old. Mom and Dad spend a lot of their time in DC. Hardly get to the lake house anymore." He shot a glance over to her. "I hear good things about you."

He had a calm good humor laced with an easy self-confidence that came from knowing from his earliest childhood that he was one of the privileged—someone who came from an educated, well-heeled background, yet knew enough not to take it for granted or look down on anyone because of it.

His affable manner snuffed out Annie's misgivings and she hated herself for allowing her old dreaded suspicion to raise its ugly head—a fear she would be judged, not by who she was, but by how others in her family were branded. Funny, she said to herself, how this anguish that she had managed to bury long ago could reemerge as unexpectedly as the moon from behind a cloud on a dark night.

By the time they got to the restaurant and ordered their food, everyone was talking about the forest fires burning in the western part of the state.

"The Boteler Fire over in Clay County is giving the Forest Service a fit," said one of the firefighters.

"Most of our southern Blue Ridge hasn't burned in ninety years," interjected Mike. "So not only are we dealing with a record drought, we've got hardwood leaf litter and pine needles that have been building for all that time on those mountains. Heaven help us if we get some big wind event with any of the fires that are burning right now. The one over in South Mountain State Park in McDowell County looks like it's still spreading."

Their food arrived and the conversation drifted to other subjects.

"What's Bat Girl been up to?" someone chided.

"Nothin' much." She raised an eyebrow. "Just lookin' for Bat Man."

Annie's response drew a chuckle, with a couple of the guys offering up one of the guys who had been sweet on her when all of them were in an incident planning class a few months back. She was still with her boyfriend at the time and never took him up on it.

On the drive back to the college, Annie said, "I don't remember our having this many fires when I was a kid."

"That's why we need more controlled burning," said Mike. "Think about it. We've been investing millions of dollars suppressing fire, but it's been a natural part of the environment for thousands of years. The sooner we go back to using it to improve the health of our forests, the less fuel we'll have to burn from lightning strikes, accidents or arson."

The word 'arson' made Annie purse her lips. How she hated that word. She tried her best to carry on with the conversation— the way most people do when they want to ignore something unsettling that's staring them in the face. In this case, it was the third person in the truck, her brother.

ANNIE STUCK THE MEMORY CARD from the Anabat detector she used to pick up bat sonar into one of the three Mac notebooks on her office desk and glanced at the clock. She hadn't gotten in from a bat survey on the Blue Ridge Parkway until four that morning, but six hours of sleep should hold her.

While waiting for the ultrasonic bat calls she had recorded the night before to load, she studied the large framed print of a big-eared bat with its wings spread wide open that dominated her office wall. She liked it mostly because the furry little body and mouse-like face appeared surprisingly unintimidating—more like confident, as if it were assured it had earned its place in the world.

Her office was sparsely decorated. A baseball cap blazoned with the Wildlife Resources Commission logo hung on the wall along with two framed diplomas. A picture of her cat, Blackie, in a Halloween witch's hat adorned her desk.

She had noticed her new roommate's beat-up pickup outside, and now, wanting to comb her sun-streaked blonde hair into a fresh ponytail, she went in the downstairs bathroom so as not to let the creaky steps disturb Terri, asleep upstairs.

Not feeling a need to enhance her "All-American girl" looks, she didn't linger in front of the mirror. She knew who she was and what she was doing—and that was looking after the bats of North Carolina.

On her way to put on another pot of coffee, she stopped at a big black cat perched on a stool. It rose to an arch and pressed against her, purring while it got a vigorous rub. Footsteps upstairs made her glance at the clock. Two. Terri was finally up. Annie's schedule was peculiar, but Terri's seemed to be even more erratic. She couldn't figure out exactly what the girl did; and the way she instantly produced cash every time she was presented with a bill made Annie wonder if she even had a checking account.

She had liked Terri's bouncy naiveté when she interviewed her, and distinctly remembered her saying she was a landscape designer. Yet, the other day she said she had just gotten a big job staging someone's house.

Annie strolled into the living room and lay down on the couch. She glanced around at the chestnut log walls and ceiling beams and then closed her eyes and let out a long, satisfied sigh. It had taken every dime she had earned since getting her Masters three years ago, along with a hefty mortgage, to wrestle the place from her uncle, but she had promised herself when she was a kid that she'd own it one day, and now she did.

It comforted her to be in the room that was her family's original log cabin. Her very own little homestead. It had been added on to over the generations and sat on the remnants of the 200 acres her great-grandfather bought from the State in 1786. An ancient, framed deed hung above the fireplace, proudly proclaiming the date of the purchase as "in the eleventh year of our Independence."

Her roommate suddenly appeared, trailed by two Pekingese.

Terri slid down into an ancient leather easy chair and looked around before casually asking, "Exactly what do you do every night?"

"Bat surveys."

"Can I go with you sometime?"

Terri's question piqued Annie's interest. "Do you think you might want to be a volunteer?"

"Not really. Just kinda want to get an idea of what it is you do."

Annie held back from saying she would like to spend some time with Terri and see exactly what it was that she did. But she didn't want to discourage what still might be an opportunity to sign up another volunteer.

"Tonight I'm doing a survey on the Pigeon River. You're welcome to come along... around four; but it's an all-nighter. Do you have to work tomorrow?"

"Don't worry. I can handle it."

Annie eyed the two dogs that sat like Buddhist deities in their overly large cushions. The psychedelic patterned pillows clashed with Annie's braided rugs, as did their ragtag toys scattered about. They'd only been in the house a couple of weeks, but she had already tripped on their toys twice in the middle of the night. Her job required so much physical activity, there was no way she could do it with a broken limb.

She began to regret renting the room to the girl. She should've said no when one of her mother's friends who also had a cleaning business called and told her about a girl who needed a place. She would vouch for her, she had told her. That's what you get for not checking things out, she said to herself as she surveyed the clutter that spoiled the homespun character of the room.

Annie spent the afternoon relaxing on the couch and napping until her alarm went off at four. Time to leave for the Pigeon River. Annie looked up to see Terri in the doorway. She had said she was twenty, but the striped tights and frilly skirt flaring out from her oversized sweater, along with her petite stature made her look more like ten.

"I checked the weather and it said the temperature was going down to the sixties tonight, so I dressed warm," said Terri as she swiped a fluffy shock of her kinky blonde hair from her face.

If that was her idea of dressing warm, all Annie could think of was that Terri was definitely not volunteer material, then she pictured her assistant, Johnny, rolling his eyes when he got a load of her getup.

Annie went into the kitchen to pack some snacks and drinks and saw that the dogs were already fed and in their crates. In spite of the fly-by-night impression Terri made, she did seem to attend to business. Annie began to look forward to the ninety minute drive to the survey site. It would give her a chance to get to know her new roommate.

Her assistant and another biologist who was coming over from the US Forest Service were going to meet her on a road under an I-40 overpass on the banks of the Pigeon River just before the Tennessee border. It was late in the season for conducting this kind of survey, but she needed to chart the late fall activity and see what kind of migrating bats they would net.

The two piled into the truck and headed west. Once past Asheville, they settled back for the long drive.

"So, exactly, what is it that you do?" asked Terri.

"I primarily focus on coordinating and conducting bat surveys. Ever since they discovered the first bat mortalities from white-nose syndrome in a cave in New York back in '06, documenting what's happening to our bats has become a priority."

"What exactly is that?" Terri asked.

"It's a disease that causes white tufts of fungus to form on the bat's nose and muzzle. That's how it got its name."

"Is it deadly?"

"Eventually," said Annie. "The fungus grows at low temperatures and high humidity. This makes bats that hibernate in caves the perfect victims. It causes them to behave oddly. They move toward the mouth of caves instead of staying in its depths, and then fly out when they should be hibernating. It's believed this activity uses up the fat that's supposed to sustain them through the winter."

"Is the disease in North Carolina?"

"Oh, yeah. Since 2011. We're talking a mortality rate of 95 percent of the bats that hibernate in caves—the Northern long-eared, little brown, and tri-coloreds. Thankfully, the ones that migrate and the species that roost in hollow trees and man-made structures haven't been affected."

The truck rolled up, down and around Route I-40 as it spun out of the Blue Ridge Mountains and spooled into the Smokies. The fall had come earlier to the Smokies than Lake Lure, and the bare trees revealed the forest's mysterious underbelly littered with huge decaying blowdowns and massive boulders lying on or jutting from the earth. Every once in a while Annie got a glimpse of a creek below with its waters streaming across rocks and mirroring the lowering sun's crimson color.

Annie let a moment pass and then said, "Tell me about yourself."

It didn't take much to get that ball rolling.

"I'm from a little hick town in Florida," said Terri.

"That's nice. I like Florida."

"You wouldn't like this place. At least, I didn't. I took off when I was fifteen."

Annie gave her a quick glance.

"I couldn't handle my mother anymore... even though I was supposed to be the adult in the family. She was either dead drunk or running around with some scary guy. When you have to go to sleep every night with a knife under your pillow, you're not in a good place."

"How in the world did you survive on your own?"

"Slept on people's couches. Did whatever." She threw out a cynical laugh. "Once I got to Asheville, I even begged. Let me tell you, standing on a street corner holding up a sign for hours is a tough way to earn a living. Someone from one of the TV stations interviewed me and ran it on the news as a feature on local poverty. I always dreamed of being famous, *but a poster child for the homeless?*"

"Everyone at the station was kinda nice. They found a shelter for me, and on my way there, I discovered someone had tucked a hundred dollar bill in my pocket."

Terri traced the edge of the window with her finger. "Believe it or not, that was my big break. This kind old lady saw the TV newscast and tracked me down. She said she could tell I was a nice person and just needed a little help. She was going to sell her house, and asked me if I would help her pack everything up. She let me stay in a room in her carriage house; but best of all, she introduced me to a lot of her friends who also needed things done."

Annie found Terri's candidness disconcerting. She had felt the same way about her mother when she was fifteen, but couldn't turn her back on her or Jack. And as far as casually talking about it to a stranger, that was out of the question. She buried it. Erased it. It wasn't going to leave a mark on her. And not only was she determined to come out of the whole mess unscathed, she'd always been hell-bent on doing whatever she could to fix it. Her mother had fallen in the deep pit of accepting she was flawed, and couldn't claw her way out. On the other hand, Jack was harnessed to a cart that someone had made too heavy, and he was having a hard time pulling it.

By the time they reached their destination, Annie had become amused, and at the same time impressed with the various schemes Terri had dreamt up to survive—everything from walking dogs to decorating homes for Christmas. She had filled gardens and grounds with hundreds of flowering plants in advance of a gala party, and even stripped down a house and disposed of its contents for one of her clients after one of their relatives passed away. One thing came across loud and clear—Terri's clients were well off, used to being catered to, and willing to pay for it. That explained all the cash.

Terri made a dramatic sweeping gesture with her hand. "I think of myself as a kind of concierge with a collection of people under my wing who just need things done."

Annie fought off an impulse to stop the car and give Terri a hug. She couldn't help feeling both amazed by, and sorry for this version of Wonder Woman meets Little Orphan Annie. Just like herself, Terri was a survivor. She'd bet anything that those pricey Pekingese of hers were throwaways. One of her clients must've tired of them. Poor little things. She pictured the two abandoned dogs sitting on their gaudy cushions with their inscrutable gazes and had to admit they *were* kind of cute. She'd just have to be sure to turn the lights on when she came home in the dark.

S HE HUNG FROM THE TREE BY ONE FOOT. Her furry tail membrane was wrapped snugly around her like a cape, making it appear as if she were a dead leaf. She was unaware that scientists considered her the most beautiful chiropteran in North America with an ancestry that reached back 50 million years. Soon, the day would become night and she would soar through the dark, feeding on as many as 8,000 insects—for she was an eastern red bat.

With her little rounded ears, pug nose and silky dense fur, she had a somewhat mouse-like appearance, with the white on the tips of her hair adding a frosted edge to her plush reddish brown coat. Only four inches long, she held the distinction of being among the world's only flying mammals.

The two young women didn't notice her as their truck rumbled down the gravel road. But sometime in the middle of that night one of them would be clasping her firmly in a gloved hand.

The truck came to a stop next to two pickups, and after quickly introducing Terri to the two men, and a few words of greeting, Annie and the two biologists got right to work unloading the pipes and equipment from the top of her truck.

Annie dug out some scrubs for the three of them to wear over their clothes. Johnnie would decontaminate them, as well as the nets, outdoors tomorrow with a hot water bath, then hang everything out to dry.

The clicking of cardinals and the soft splashing of water rippling over the river's rocky bed blended with the drone of a plane overhead as they went about assembling six sets of twenty-foot-long poles. The clanking of metal sounded through the forest as they outfitted them with latches, pulley ropes and curtain rings so the nets could be raised and lowered.

Interstate 40 was on the other side of the river, fifty feet above and hidden behind the thick forest of ash and hickory. The far-off hum of semis rumbling down the six-lane highway harmonized with the wilderness song and became part of the symphony of the early evening.

The team proceeded to the bank of the river where they would be setting up the first net. Annie, in waders up to her armpits, ventured into the water pulling one end of a measuring tape, while Bill, the biologist from the US Forest Service, stood on the bank holding the open reel. She gingerly felt her way across the gently flowing, yet icy water that quickly grew to a depth of three and a half feet.

"Sixty feet," she shouted when she got to the other end. Before crossing back over to get a mallet and a piece of rebar, she took a moment to gaze at the eastern range. Dark mountains hovered one behind the other in the distance, turning a glorious green on the facets facing the late afternoon sun.

The ring of mallets hitting rebar into both banks echoed through the narrow canyon. Bill waded across to Annie with one of the twenty-foot poles, and the two stood it up by slipping it over the rebar post. They quickly stabilized it with ropes tied to nearby trees, while Johnny did the same on the other side.

With the poles solidly erected, the three of them sloshed back and forth across the river stringing two cables to the poles. One cable would hold the top of the net and the other the bottom, with the net in between. Next, working chest deep in the frigid water, they brought in the net, attached it to one cable, and raised it twenty feet to the top of the poles; then they secured the bottom of the net to the other cable—a labor that took almost an hour.

Finished, they used the post's pulley system to lower the net.

"Why'd you take the net down?" Terri asked as Annie came out of the water.

"We'll pull 'em back up at sunset," Annie replied.

The three scientists gathered their tools and went about installing a net over the road. Afterwards, they would put up another one over the river downstream from the causeway.

TERRI KEPT A FLEETING EYE on what the three were doing as she ambled along the river. Sprinkled along the banks, the last holdouts of Queen Anne's lace and purple lobelia poked up between rocks and crevices. It was still warm enough for the dragonflies to be out swooping low across the crystal clear, yellowish water.

Terri suddenly screamed. Bill, who was on his way to get materials from the truck, raced over, and recognizing the snake, picked it up.

As it coiled around his wrist, he said, "Nothing to be afraid of. It's not venomous. Just a little northern water snake."

He found a place to put the snake down and left.

She strolled to a small causeway spanning the river and studied the onrushing water when Bill returned holding a roll of rope in one hand and something in his other clasped hand. He let the rope fall to the ground and showed her a small striped lizard.

"It's a *plestiodon inexpectatus*."

She giggled at the mere thought that he expected her to know what he was talking about.

"It's a five-lined skink. I caught him as he tried to skitter under a rock."

He gently let the amphibian down, picked up the rope and the two of them went to join Annie and Johnny.

IT WAS STARTING TO GET dark and Annie was glad to see the last net go up in the three likely bat thoroughfares. She had calculated the twilight hour before she left the house and could see by her watch they should be starting soon. The men got the table and four chairs from her truck and set them up next to the causeway while she toted a big plastic box containing her supplies.

She took out a battery-operated lamp, put it on the table and turned it on and then off again. Next, she pulled out her forms, data sheets, timer and all the paraphernalia needed to weigh and measure the bats. She took her Anabat bat detector out of its case and promptly turned it on. It would beep every time a bat flew over. After she put a pail of crackers and snacks on the table and handed out the headlamps, they all sat down to wait for the approaching night.

Annie munched on a cracker and watched as Johnny put his lunchbox on his lap—in a sort of ceremonious fashion as if it signaled the formal start of an all-night endeavor—then took out a sandwich and ate it. A beefy bear of a man in his early thirties, he was both laconic and compulsively organized.

As usual, he hadn't said one word to her all night except basic responses. In fact, he hadn't said much to anyone. He hunched forward with his forearms bracing his bulky torso on his legs, and gripped his cup with both hands. He looked up at Annie and spoke.

"What've you heard about all the fires?"

She casually started organizing her forms as if the subject barely interested her. She could tell he was stewing about them, or he wouldn't be bringing them up. "Not much. What about you?"

"They say quite a few of them have been started by arsonists."

"Really?"

Annie got a sneaky suspicion that he knew about her brother, then tossed the idea out. Don't get paranoid, she told herself. He probably brought it up since he knew she was a volunteer firefighter. She straightened up the table hoping he wouldn't be going on about fires all night. She checked her watch. Twenty minutes until the twilight hour.

"We better start raising the nets," she said. "Bill, you cover the one over the road." She turned to Terri. "You can go with him tonight if you want. Just don't touch anything, especially the bats."

Then Johnny, with no more than a look from Annie, stood up. As usual, it was up to them to tackle the two over the river.

It was almost dark, but Annie knew the way to her spot blindfolded since she had performed this survey in this location dozens of times. Johnny stayed behind on the bank as she steeled herself for the shock and entered the water. Careful not to stumble, she plodded through the river and pulled herself up on the opposite bank. Quickly, she untied the pulley rope and yelled over to Johnny. "I'm ready!"

The curtain rings squealed on the posts as the net was slowly hoisted. She secured the hoist rope and navigated her way back across, using the net's bottom cable as a handrail.

"I'll take this one tonight," Annie told Johnny. Then the two of them went and pulled up the second net. Finished, they went to help Bill who was having some trouble, then the four of them returned to the table.

They settled back in their chairs, wondering what the evening would bring. It had grown cold and clouds had cloaked the moon and the stars. It was late in the season and the katydids had stopped their rattling. Only an occasional cricket made an effort to be heard.

Other than the river, the hum of traffic was the only refrain as the four sat with their thoughts. There was a constant flow of vehicles on I-40, their drivers shrouded in blackness as they focused on the endless stream of red taillights in front of them. They were oblivious to the primeval forest through which they drove, and equally unaware of the scientists in the darkness below—three committed young people playing their small part in staving off the collapse of the planet's second largest group of mammals.

Annie had put on a pair of gloves and was busy smoothing them.

"Are those batting gloves?" Terri asked.

"Un-huh. The bats' teeth are too tiny to make it through them, yet they're flexible." She let out a short laugh. "Don't want to get rabies."

A look of apprehension washed over Terri's face and Annie regretted the offhand remark.

"Less than one-half of one percent of bats have rabies," said Annie. "But we've got to assume that any we handle may have it. There's no way of telling by just looking at them. Only a laboratory can by checking their brains. Of course, they have to be euthanized first."

Terri shook her head. "I don't know. This looks like a pretty dangerous way to make a living."

Annie patted Terri's hand. "Don't worry. We've taken every precaution. We have up-to-date rabies shots and get a medical examination once a year."

Annie checked her watch again. "Okay, everybody. Here we go." She dialed the timer at eight minutes and would set it every time they returned from a search. She stuffed a few small mesh bags in her pocket, handed some to Johnny and Bill, and the four of them turned on their headlamps and started for their destinations.

Annie reached her station and waded into the river, shining the lamp on the net as she crossed. She started searching from the top and then scanned the net back and forth sideways looking for bats, but there were none.

"We've got one! We've got one!" yelled Terri from afar.

Annie carefully slogged back across the river and went over to Terri and Bill's location.

"At first I thought it was a dead leaf," Terri exclaimed in wonderment.

Annie took a small net bag from her pocket, blew on the slit at the top to open it, then gently grasped the bat. But she couldn't pull it off. It had gotten twisted in the filament. Bill untangled it enough for Annie to finally get it in the bag, then she pulled the drawstring and the three of them returned to the base.

Johnny, who had already made it back, dangled a bag. "I've got a gray."

"Great! So do we," Annie said. "Getting two right at the start is a good sign."

She hung her bag on a small hand-held scale, then grabbed a pen and registered 14 grams on a form. Terri watched with rapt attention as Annie opened the bag and pulled out the bat.

It had a dark gray matted coat with long pointed ears and tiny beady black eyes. The way its little forearms rested on Annie's thumb wrapped across its belly made it look as if it had just come out of a hole and was looking around. However, what the tiny creature lacked in size, it made up for in spirit as it made a slight clicking sound, then opened its mouth wide and bared two small eye teeth.

"It sure is feisty," Terri said, backing up a bit.

"You'd be feisty, too, if you went out to eat and got caught in a net," razzed Johnny.

His teasing her made Terri feel part of the group.

Annie measured the bat's wingspan at 12 inches, then she took a hair sample, put it in a vial and labeled it. An examination determined it was a male, and seeing it was banded, Annie took down the number.

"Does it have that white-nose thing?" asked Terri, a little nervously.

"No. This little guy's migratory. Stays in one cave in the summer and goes to another one to hibernate for the winter. Before they put it on the endangered species list, it was on its way to extinction because people were disturbing its roosting caves. Now that most of their caves are protected, they're starting to recover."

Finished examining the bat, Annie tossed her hand up in the air and let it fly away, then she recorded the data on Johnny's gray and let it go, too.

All night long the team trudged to their stations every eight minutes, capturing two big brown bats and three more grays. By four, with a half hour more to go they began to drag, yet Annie was impressed with the way Terri hung in there. She just might make a good member of her citizen-scientist volunteer army after all.

Traffic on I-40 had been getting sparser all night, and now it was down to an occasional semi. In the distance, a slight gray glowed on the horizon, a sure sign the sun would soon start to rise. Annie was collecting her papers when Terri spoke up.

"What do they do with this information?"

"Well, this bat study we're doing has been going on for fifteen years, and it's telling us their life story."

"So, we're kinda making history tonight?"

"You could say that."

Terri sat mulling everything over. She found the whole evening strange, yet intriguing. Who would imagine anyone making their way into the Pigeon River every eight minutes in the middle of the night to pick bats off a net? These three were either crazy or totally committed. And oddly, she yearned to be like them.

Johnny was now talking fluidly with Bill. Something he always did as the night wore on. Annie figured that doing what he thought was an onerous task was his strategy for keeping awake. Although she was chatting with Terri, she had been picking up fragments of her colleagues' conversation ever since she heard Mike McNeil's name mentioned. Evidently, Johnny had run into him at a Nature Conservancy event.

Now that she and Terri had grown quiet, she listened more intently to what Johnny was saying.

"McNeil was one of four guys on this panel. He made a pretty good case for prescribed burning."

The timer went off and Annie jumped up. This would be their last retrieval of the night before tearing down.

She reached the river and wasn't looking forward to another plunge. Almost all the way across the river, she spotted a bat near the top of the net. She hollered for Bill and the two of them brought the net far enough down for her to bag it.

Now, everyone back at the table, they gathered around as Annie pulled the bat out of the bag.

"This one's kinda cute," Terri said, admiringly.

Annie ran her gloved finger down the back of the mammals head.

"Yes. It is. The most beautiful bat in North Carolina."

"What kind is it?"

"An eastern red bat."

Annie held it so she could examine its belly, exposing four nipples.

"She must have just finished lactating," she said. "The juvenile has to be on its own by now."

After taking the bat's weight and measurements, they carefully tagged her foot. Annie ran her finger down the back of the bat's head once more, then released her into the air.

By the time the team had disassembled the nets, Annie's teeth were chattering. It had grown lighter, and she turned around and could see the sun beginning to rise beyond the mountains. Annie remembered Terri's comment that they were making history and it made her smile. Every living plant and animal had a place in the world, all a part of the fabric that held everything together. One at a time, thousands of species were disappearing from the planet, never to be seen again. It had been another rough night, but she felt fulfilled by it. Even proud. They *were* making history, the kind that would help build a safety net for the little creatures she had held in her hand that night.

MAE ELLEN SIMMS SAT staring out the window of the house her father left her twenty-one years ago. It was on the river across from the highway in Bat Cave. Although a rather humble abode, it did have three bedrooms, and the place was a big step up from the rundown shack on the mountain above the town where she had lived for the ten years after she married Buck. If it weren't for her father's gift, she'd probably still be up there eking out another miserable winter with a couple of propane heaters and a cookstove.

The house was built in the late 1800s to put up lumbermen hired to harvest the thousands of acres of chestnut trees that grew all over the Hickory Nut Gorge before a blight wiped them out. There was one big room filled with mismatched furniture, a kitchen at one end and a stone fireplace at the other. Back when it was one of her father's summer rentals it had a homey look, but old and worn furniture had since been replaced by a haphazard assortment of castoffs from Mae's clients.

The Rocky Broad River galloped by her window less than fifty feet away. A narrow gravel road separated the house from a treacherous drop ten feet to the river. Rumors still persisted that shortly after Annie was born Mae's husband either fell in, or was pushed. He was last seen by a neighbor in a drunken frenzy demanding money from her father who was getting the place ready for the season. Whichever way Buck Simms disappeared, he was never heard from again.

Mae rocked back and forth thinking about that tumble down shack and that terrible night her neighbor's house burned to the ground. Things got a lot better for Mae after that. She'd never been able to get off the mountain to find work until her father gave her an old Chevy pickup and she started cleaning houses and cabins in Chimney Rock and Lake Lure. She was sure all the rumors going around about Jack gave her father the fatal heart attack a short while later.

Mae rocked and stared blankly out the window in spite of the place looking like it could use a good straightening up. It was almost as if, after working most of the week cleaning other people's houses, she felt it was now her turn, and she was waiting for someone to walk in and clean hers.

ANNIE PULLED OFF ROUTE 64 and onto the bridge over the Reedy Creek just before it hit the Rocky Broad in Bat Cave. Then she took a sharp left onto a dead-end road running along the river and dotted with modest homes and summer cabins. As she often did, she felt grateful to her grandfather for leaving them the house. That and her mother's cleaning jobs marked the family's leap from being dirt-poor mountain folk to the usual middle-class type you'd run into in that speck of a town. She could barely remember the shack they'd left when she was six, and just hazy memories of her mother's face always being bruised.

Before going into the house, she strolled over to the river. The savage water still held an irresistible allure. Like a bevy of otters at play, it either sluiced its way between the massive boulders lying in its path or danced over them. Jack and she practically lived in it all summer and were familiar enough with the giant rocks to give them all names.

Whenever the water got high, they'd race to the river with their tubes, ride the rapids as far as Chimney Rock and walk back. Once they hit their late teens, they made the trip in their kayaks. She took a deep breath and sighed, then walked to the gate that led to the back of the house. She would enter by the kitchen door since her mother always left it unlocked.

An old rubber tire swayed from a rope tied to a limb of a giant oak in the backyard, and Jack's bike leaned forgotten and rusted against the side of their barn. She went to the shed sheathed in chicken wire at the back of the house, pulled a dead vine from a door that was hanging from one hinge, and went in.

Cages and glass terrariums covered with spider webs sat on musty shelves. She had coveted these treasures when she was a kid, spending every penny she could get her hands on to buy them or the feed for the critters they held. She smiled to herself, recalling all the newts, frogs, spiders and snakes she'd collected running barefoot with Jack all over that mountain. It always broke her heart to let them go when school started.

She studied her abandoned laboratory one more time and decided to get everything packed up and over to her cabin that winter. Some day she was going to have kids and teach them all about the species that roamed those mountains. She'd want them to be as familiar with them as if they were old friends, just like she had.

She reluctantly pulled herself away from all the sweet memories and ran up the steps to the kitchen door and went in.

"Hi, Mom," she said as she went over and gave Mae a kiss, pleased she didn't pick up on the scent of whisky. Good, it was already after three-thirty and her mother hadn't started drinking yet. Annie opened the fridge and looked around before taking out a carton and smelling it. She emptied it in the sink saying, "Mom, you're gonna need more milk."

She got out a plastic bag and strolled around the room emptying ashtrays and clearing plates of dried up, half-eaten food.

"When's the last time you talked to Jack?" Annie asked.

"This morning. Are you going to see him next?"

"Un-huh."

"I thought so. I made some cookies for you two. They're in plastic containers on the fridge."

Annie was now doing the dishes, concerned there weren't that many.

"Mom, I want you to cut back on your cleaning. Now that I'm paying for all your utilities, you really don't have that many expenses. And Jack's gonna take care of the property taxes."

"He doesn't need to do that."

Annie turned and looked at Mae. "He can afford it. With customers all over the South practically begging him to cane their chairs, he's got enough work lined up to keep him busy for the next six months."

The mother and daughter talked easily with each other even though they lived in different worlds. Annie knew this, and more than anything, always wanted to keep one foot in her mother's world. She believed her mother's love for her and Jack was the lifeline that had kept Mae from falling into total ruin.

As it stood, her mother slipped every once in a while, but the days of finding her dead drunk on the back steps after a night out, like often happened when Annie was a kid, were long gone.

Finished cleaning the kitchen and straightening up the house, Annie took up a broom and listened to Mae's chatter.

"I was cleaning over at your aunt Ella's this week. She wants you to come visit."

"Sure, Mom. I'll stop in and see her tomorrow."

"Oh, and another thing."

The way her mother emphasized "another" made Annie stop sweeping and look over to her.

"I'm gonna be cleaning the McNeil place again."

"During the winter?"

"Mike's staying there. As part of his divorce agreement, his Lake Lure house was sold."

"What about Susie?"

"She's moved to Raleigh to be closer to her parents."

Mae pulled a cigarette from her pocket and lit it. "For someone who keeps telling me she doesn't want to hear anything about the McNeils, you sure are askin' a lot of questions."

She took a deep drag, then blew it out with the casual ease of having done it a million times. "It was no surprise to anyone," she continued. "Miss Priss had no business marrying the likes of him. I guess, with all his family's money..."

"Stop it, Mom. It's not good to talk like that; and for the millionth time, I'm not interested in what Michael McNeil is doing."

"Well you sure were when you were little. You used to tell me you were gonna marry him when you grew up."

They were quiet for a moment, then Mae said, "Come over here, girl. I wanna give you a hug."

Annie went and bent down so her mother could reach her, and the two hugged. As Annie pulled away, Mae lovingly ran a hand down her face.

"You've always been such a good girl. Most of the time I was sure the hospital gave me the wrong baby."

"Don't say things like that, Mom."

Annie went to the kitchen and started making her mother a sandwich.

"It's true. You're more like my daddy than me," Mae continued. "He could move mountains, too. An overachiever, they called you. I was so proud when you got that big scholarship and all those swimming trophies. You were one sporty little thing."

Annie brought over a plate with a sandwich and placed it in her mother's lap.

"I'm going to sit here 'til you eat it."

Reluctantly, her mother picked it up and took a bite.

While her mother ate, Annie sat mulling over all of Terri's exploits.

"Mom, if you want to see a genuine wonder woman, you've got to meet my new roommate."

"Is she a bat girl, too?"

"No. More of a cat with nine lives. And I mean that literally."

Annie got up and meandered over to the kitchen window that looked out on the back yard.

"Mom, once things slow down a little, I'm gonna move all my terrariums and cages over to my house."

"Good. Every time I look at that mess out there, I get the shivers remembering all those varmints of yours. Remember that baby bat you found on the lawn? Girl, how you carried on until I took you all the way into Hendersonville to old Mr. Marley's pet store so you could get things to feed it with."

"I liked old man Marley. I was just a kid but we hit it off, especially when he bought all the garter snakes I took him."

"I'll never forget how you walked right over to him while he was talking with a group of children and their parents and whisked that bat right out and showed it around, almost in their faces. It took everyone a moment to recognize what you were holding, but once they did, they ran screaming."

Annie laughed. "It didn't help that it had opened its mouth and showed all its teeth." She took her mother's empty dish to the kitchen, remembering the bat. She had thought it was cute and was heartbroken when she showed it to all the kids on the street and they made the same ugly faces they did when they saw Jack. She loved both her brother and the bat more because of it.

She washed the dish, then pulled her chair closer to her mother in a way to signal it was time to get down to business.

Mae knew this was the prelude to one of Annie's talks. It was always the same. First she'd clean, then she'd make her something to eat, and then came the lecture. There'd never been a visit without one, and this time she was actually curious to hear what her daughter had to say.

"Mom, we gotta get Jack out of here."

"What are you talking about. You just said he was doing well."

"And he can do just as well somewhere else. His customers are from all over. It doesn't matter where he lives."

"All these fires in the mountains are scaring you, aren't they?"

"It's so unfair, Mom. Anyone can see Jack would never hurt anybody. He's the kindest person I know. Why can't they leave him alone? It was so long ago, and he hasn't done a single thing wrong since."

"I don't think you're gonna get him to leave that crazy place he lives in," said Mae.

Annie went over to the front window, pulled the lace curtain aside and looked out at the river.

"It's not crazy, Mom. But he does have to leave." She thought for a moment, then looked over at her mother. "Tell him you can't take these winters anymore and need to be in Florida, Mobile, anywhere else but here. He'll move for you."

"I'll lose all my clients."

Annie crossed her arms and strolled over to her mother. "Come on, Mom, nobody's got better job security than you.

We'll never see the day no one wants their house cleaned. Besides, once you sell this place, with the two of you living together, you'll do just fine." She gently squeezed one of her mother's thin, heavily veined hands. "Plus, you know you can always count on me."

Hovering in the back of Annie's mind was the fear that her mother might start drinking heavily again if she and Jack moved away. But that was a risk she was willing to take to make sure Jack was safe. Then Terri crept into her thoughts. If she couldn't get her mother to move south with Jack, maybe she could get Terri to move in with her mother.

With the rent, her mother wouldn't have to work at all. The two of them would be a good fit, and she could always find another roommate. The thought that if Terri were staying with her mom, they could still be friends crossed her mind—something she felt was inevitable.

She put her hands on her mother's shoulders and gently massaged them. "I swear I'm gonna get Jack out of here if it's the last thing I do. And he's got to go far enough away that his name won't pop up every time they need to round up the usual suspects."

Mae reached up and squeezed Annie's hand. "I love you, child."

"Mom, there's going to be a lot more of these fires. The climate's changing. Promise me you'll think about it."

"I promise."

She said goodbye, and as she drove to her brother's house, couldn't keep Mike out of her head. She remembered wanting to borrow one of the books in his bedroom and asking her mother if she would talk to him about it. Later that afternoon, she had bumped into him as she turned a corner with a basket of laundry, and he stopped her and said she could borrow any of his books and keep them for as long as she wanted.

It was the first time she had called up the nerve to look directly at him. He had the bluest eyes she'd ever seen. Deeply tan and with dark hair, his easy smile lit up his face. She was only twelve at the time, but she was in love.

After that friendly encounter, she felt like she had the right to take a few liberties, and would browse around his room whenever she was sent up there. Among all the books she borrowed, her favorite was the first one she took home. In fact, she loved *The Call of the Wild* so much, she still had it. She didn't know why she couldn't part with it, but suspected it was because it somehow connected her to the kindhearted boy who told her she could keep it for as long as she wanted. She wondered if he had any idea that his library had sparked her determination to learn everything she could about the animal world.

It wasn't until her senior year as a biology major that she decided to get her masters in mammalogy—back when white-nose syndrome was just becoming a major threat and on a lot of scientists' radar, along with what was happening to the bees.

She made a turn off Route 74A, a couple miles out of Bat Cave, and started up Burnshirt Mountain, taking a turn onto Jack's long driveway a quarter-mile up.

HERE COMES THE BATMOBILE, Jack said under his breath as he spotted her truck through the wall of glass at the front of his A -frame. With all the pipes roped to the roof rack, it had to be his sister. No one else would be driving a rig like that except a plumber.

Annie pulled up and jumped out, smiling and waving a plastic container. He put down the strand of natural rush he was caning a chair with and headed over to his makeshift kitchen to put on coffee to go with the cookies he was sure his mother had sent.

He had built his house from plans he purchased on the internet, and had lived in a small trailer next to it for a large part of the two years it took to get it finished enough to move into. Nestled on the side of the mountain, a stone chimney distinguished the house from the usual summer cottage and ran from the basement he used as a warehouse and workroom, then up through the roofline two stories above.

Annie rushed in, tossed the container on the counter, then came from behind and wrapped her arms around him, rocking him and making him spill some of the coffee grounds.

"Darlin,' I know I'm adorable, but let's not go overboard."

She rested her cheek on his back. "Oh, Jack, I love you so much."

Annie looked around. "Where's Anita?"

"Atlanta. With her folks."

Annie sensed something was wrong.

"Why?"

"Nothing much. She just ran into an old school chum of mine."

He went over to the counter, took the lid off the container and picked up a cookie. "He was kind enough to tell her the charming story of my boyhood."

"Oh, Jack. I told you to tell her a long time ago."

"You're right. It wasn't fair."

"Don't worry; she's going to be okay with it. She'd never believe you could do anything bad."

He leaned back against the counter and bit into the cookie. "I get a kick out of you, Sis. For a scientist, you sure are leaning a lot on blind faith."

"Not really. As a scientist, I've methodically assessed hundreds of facts about you and they all add up to your being a good guy."

"Well, not everybody uses the same math." He examined his cookie. "Take Anita, for instance. She named a hundred and one of my endless shortcomings as reasons she was breaking up with me; but let's face it, she didn't want to go to sleep after an argument, wondering if she would star in the female version of 'The Burning Bed.'"

He grinned sardonically at her and then munched on the treat. He was tall, blond and handsome, the male version of Annie, except he lacked her spirited glow, as if he'd been hollowed out.

"How's the old bag?" he asked, changing the subject. "Had she hit the bottle by the time you showed up?"

"Don't be so flippant. You know you love her."

The coffee was ready and he poured two cups and handed her one.

"Here. Let's go sit down and make nice."

He ushered her over to two cushy school-bus-yellow easy chairs with large red hibiscus blooms plastered all over them.

"Where in the heck did you get these?"

"Where else? The Mae Ellen Boutique. Mom pulled up with them piled in the back of that beat-up truck of hers. I wanted to tell her to take them back to where she got 'em, but... let me put it this way, Anita was crazy about them."

He gave her a wry look. "That kinda takes the sting out of the breakup." He took a sip of coffee. "Talk about breakups, how's your love life?"

"Jack, I didn't come here to talk about me. You gotta get out of these mountains. Believe me, with all the fuel that's lying on the ground and the drought we're in, there's going to be more fires."

He sank way back in his chair. The way he had clasped his hands behind his head, stretched out his legs and crossed his feet at his ankles, Annie could tell she was making progress.

"I hear ya, Sis."

This conversation was going better than Annie had hoped. "Have you thought about Florida?"

"It's funny you mentioned it. I'm beginning to like Florida. I've got business coming in from all over that state."

His forehead wrinkled and eyes narrowed as he thought. "Before I could sell this place, I'd have to find another one, maybe around Ocala where my money will go farther."

Annie's eyes shot up to the second floor that was open to the great room.

"Have you finished the upstairs yet?"

"It won't take much. The sheet rock's lying up there and the plumbing for the bathroom is in place. Putting up the railing and finishing the staircase is going to take some effort, though."

Jack sat rubbing his chin and thinking out loud. "I've got an order that I've got to deliver in Jacksonville in a couple of weeks. I think I'll take a few days and look at property, get the lay of the land."

Annie had jumped out of bed that morning inflamed with the

intention of getting her brother to think about going somewhere else, even if it meant putting her mother at risk. And now he was racing down that track like a runaway train. Jack didn't have to be coaxed and her mother didn't need to go. She felt the tension start to seep from her muscles as she sank back in the chair.

She'd been so intensely focused on getting her brother to consider a change, that his ease in getting on board with the concept suddenly thrust her into a giddy mood.

"Jack, don't beat yourself up about being dumped by Anita. Keep in mind she loved these chairs. Besides, the same thing happened to me, and look, I'm over it. Believe me, when George said goodbye, my heart was broken for all of fifteen minutes. I don't know what I saw in that guy to begin with."

"Let me see," said Jack. "He was rich, good looking, in a prestigious law firm...."

She grabbed a pillow from her chair and tossed it at him.

"George was so afraid I was going to give him rabies, that when I came home from a survey, he wouldn't touch me until I took a shower and washed my hair. Then he went around spraying disinfectant on my shoes and car keys."

She giggled. "I don't know what made me do it, but I was so sick of it that one evening I gave him a lot of big smoochy kisses, then I waited awhile and feigned a bunch of rabies symptoms. You should've seen me." She laid a hand on her forehead and let out a pathetic moan. "I think I've got a fever. When that bat bit me, I didn't think its teeth penetrated my skin."

They both laughed.

"He totally freaked out, and it took me all night to calm him down."

"That's it, sweetheart. No more rich, handsome lawyers for you. You've got to find yourself a bat man."

Annie stayed for a while longer and mentioned that when he got ready to sell, her roommate would probably be happy, for a price, to stage his house. She even offered to lend him some of her furniture. Pleased with herself for allowing Terri into her life, she smiled as she drove down the mountain to Bat Cave. Twice today her roommate fit in with her plans to keep her family safe.

ANNIE WAS FOLDING her laundry when the phone rang. "Hello," she answered, tossing a pair of socks into a laundry basket.

"Hi, Annie. It's Mike McNeil. How are you?"

Annie felt her heart rate quicken.

"Fine."

"Can you come to the lake house for dinner this Saturday?"

Annie wrinkled her brow. "Is there a special reason you want me to come?"

He laughed the easy laugh that she had always envied. "Just how special does it have to be to get you to go out with me?"

She rolled her eyes. Why did she say such a stupid thing? She could see he was in a playful mood and she didn't want him to think she couldn't handle it.

"If I don't have to clean your house while I'm there, it'll be special enough," she deadpanned.

"Hey, I was your knight in shining armor and always pitched in."

"Pitched in!? You left so many socks on your bedroom floor, it looked like a rug."

"I promise, if you come over, there won't be a sock in sight."

She listened to the silence on the other end for a moment, then took a deep breath, slowly let it out, and said, "All right, when do you want me to come over?"

"Come over? Chivalry is not dead, my dear. I'll pick you up around seven."

After Annie told him how to get to her house and said goodbye, she looked over at Terri, who was sitting on the couch, grinning.

"What's so funny?" Annie asked.

"It's about time you had a date with something other than a bat."

THE NEXT MORNING, Terri came downstairs in her pajamas and leaned against Annie's office doorway.

Annie looked up. "Aren't you working today?"

"No. Tomorrow I'm starting a three-day gig, so I'm taking the day off."

"What are you gonna be doing?" Annie said as she went back to working on her computer.

"One of my clients has some bigwigs coming from LA and she wants me to do all the cooking, cleaning and serving."

Annie gave her a peeved look. "Does she have a maid's outfit for you to wear, too?"

"I have my own."

"You're kidding."

"That's part of the deal. God knows she can cook better than me, and she already has a cleaning lady. She just wants someone who knows how to play the part of the dutiful, Southern servant so it looks like that's the way she lives on a regular basis."

Annie peered at her, saying nothing.

"I've gotten pretty good at the servant stuff. She taught me how."

Terri came into the office, slid down onto an easy chair and casually hung a leg over its arm.

"Besides, I only have to do breakfast and lunch. She's got a chef coming in to prepare dinners and a dude in a tux to bartend every night. That's another thing she doesn't need. Believe me, that lady knows how to mix a drink."

"Can I ask how much she's going to pay you for this?"

"The last time I did it, she pressed four hundred dollar bills in my hand as I was leaving."

Annie gave her an incredulous stare. "Do you think she could use another maid?"

"Oh, you wouldn't like it." In a detached lowcountry accent, Terri mimicked, "Yes, Ma'am. I'll get that right quick for you."

Annie was about to tell her that for four hundred dollars for two days work she'd be more than willing to fake a Southern accent, when her phone rang. Someone from The Nature Conservancy told her that yesterday one of their volunteers grooming the trail that led up to their bat cave found what she thought was a dead Appalachian spotted skunk. She had said it was on the trail halfway up the one-mile trek to the cave and the volunteer had covered it with a pail.

"Thanks for calling. I'll go get it and send it to the lab."

She looked out her window at a beautiful cloudless sky and then over to Terri.

"You want to take a hike with me this morning?"

"That depends. What are you sending to the lab?"

"Nothing but a little dead skunk that you won't have to touch. They think it's the kind we haven't seen up there for quite a while, and I need to check it out." She narrowed her eyes. "And I think you could use a dose of the real world."

An hour later, Annie's truck pulled into a parking space next to a rustic roadside stand in Bat Cave. A picnic area sat in a woodsy spot next to it, and up ahead, a narrow staircase led to a footbridge behind a locked wooden gate.

"Come on," Annie said to Terri as the two got out.

Annie put on her backpack, ran up the steps, and punched in a code to open the lockbox that held the key.

"Why 'No Trespassing?'" Terri asked.

"All the caves in the gorge are off limits due to the white-nose syndrome."

Annie locked the gate and they started across the footbridge. The Rocky Broad roaring below them brought memories back to Annie of the hundreds of times Jack and she had joyously floated underneath it on their tubes. She stopped for a moment and pointed up the river.

"My mother's house is just beyond that bend."

They reached the other side and proceeded up a narrow path through a dense woodland. After ten minutes of uphill climbing, Annie could see Terri needed a rest, so she found a rock for her to sit on.

The way Terri sat looking around, Annie could see she was taken with the beauty of the forest.

"You should see this place in the spring," she said. "It comes alive with wildflowers."

"After you get the skunk, can you show me that cave?" Terri asked.

"No. But if you want, I've got things we can put on our shoes so you can go up to the entrance and peek in; but that'll be all we can do."

They continued on the trek until Annie got a whiff of skunk. She looked around and spotted a large blue pail that had been flipped over. She took off her backpack, squatted down and got out her supplies, then put on a pair of latex gloves and carefully lifted the pail.

The small animal had a skunk's typical black color, except instead of two white stripes down its back, it had a large white spot on its face and zebra type white stripes along its sides.

"It's an Appalachian spotted skunk all right," said Annie as she held it in the air with disposable tongs and took a good look. "At one time it was widespread and hunted for its pelts, but its numbers are declining. These days, we're only finding it in remote places like this preserve." She dropped it in a plastic bag. "The lab will tell me what killed it, but I bet the poor little guy had a run-in with a fox or coyote."

She put the bag in the pail. "We'll leave it here and pick it up on the way down."

Annie put the tongs and then the gloves in a paper bag and dropped it in the pail before they continued up the trail. After a while, the climb grew more strenuous. Annie found herself having to lend Terri a hand to mount some of the rocks, fondly remembering her brother doing the same for her when she was a kid.

"It sure looks different up here," said Terri as she gazed at the steep rock-faced mountain above. "Some of those rocks are as big as a bus. The way they've broken away makes it look like the mountain's falling apart."

"It's exfoliating," said Annie. "Large chunks of rock get

pried apart when water gets into the cracks. When it freezes, it expands the size of the crack, and keeps repeating this over a long period of time. After that, you see more large slabs break off due to gravity.

"That's how we got all the caves here in the gorge. Some of these slabs break off, slide down to the base of the cliff, and then lean back against the mountain. They land just far enough away to form a tall, narrow opening, creating what they call a fissure cave."

As they reached the final turn, Terri stood in awe at the sight in front of her. Two slabs of rock that had to be seven stories high and weigh thousands of tons stood guarding the entrance like Roman centurions. A fifteen-foot-wide gap at the base stretched upward. Two boulders jammed in askew at the top connected them, making it resemble a church entrance.

"I've never seen anything so big in my whole life," said Terri.

Annie looked admiringly at it. "It really commands respect."

Terri pointed to the boulders stuck in the peak of the arch. "Can they fall out of there?"

"Oh, yeah. This mountain hasn't stopped moving yet."

"*Please,* can we go in?" pleaded Terri.

"No."

Annie dug two pairs of hazmat shoe covers out of her backpack. "Put these on and you can step up to the entrance and peek into the main cavern."

The two quickly put them on and started for the entrance.

"I can feel the moisture in the air. It's just rushing out of there," Terri exclaimed, then she looked quizzically at Annie.

"It comes from vents all along the side."

Annie took out a flashlight and directed the beam into the cave. The sound of water dripping on puddles echoed through the massive dark, dank chamber. The ceiling appeared to be at least eighty feet high and the length endless.

"Wow!" said Terri as her eyes followed the beam."

"You're looking at the largest granite fissure cave in North America."

"Where are the bats?"

"It's been such a warm fall, most of them haven't arrived to hibernate yet, but the ones that have, are hidden in another chamber farther down. Rattlesnakes are probably coming in for the winter by now, too."

Annie flashed the beam toward the ceiling. "You can see that this cave isn't the kind with picturesque stalagmites that you get when groundwater dissolves limestone. This one was formed by rock splits, boulder movements and other motions of the earth."

"Do you ever go in it?"

"Every January I do a bat survey with a partner. We wear hazmat suits and follow the recommended protocols so we won't spread the white-nose virus to the other caves we survey."

Annie turned off the flashlight. "We better start back. I've got a lot of work to do and have to send off that skunk."

Annie put the shoe covers in a plastic bag, then the two took a long, last look at the gorge. From that vantage point they could see all the way to Chimney Rock.

They worked their way down the mountain until the sound of boys laughing and shouting drifted from below. Annie stopped and put her finger to her mouth, signaling for Terri to be still. They focused on the trail that disappeared behind a huge rock, expecting someone to come from behind.

"Stay here," Annie whispered to Terri. She made her way to the moss-covered boulder, and as she came around it, spotted two boys who looked to be in their late teens or early twenties coming up the trail. Suddenly a boy appeared above her on top of the rock.

Annie shouted up to him. "Please come down from there, young man. And please try not to disturb the moss. It's a rare species."

Just then, the older of the two boys coming up the trail shouted at her. "Who do you think you are, a cop?"

"I'm afraid you fellas are trespassing in the Bat Cave Preserve. It's private property that belongs to The Nature Conservancy," said Annie as he approached her. "How did you get up here?"

"Wouldn't you like to know."

"That's tellin' her, Billy," said the younger boy as he came up next to him.

Billy nudged him and laughed.

"It looks like we have a little girl scout here."

"I want to ask you young men to please turn around and go back to where you came from."

"Who's gonna make us?" said Billy.

He looked her up and down and stepped menacingly close, then raised a hand toward her face and snatched her cap. He stood examining the embroidered words.

"North Carolina Wildlife Resource Commission," he read aloud. He turned and grinned at his friend. "Well, well, how do you like that? We got ourselves a genuine tree hugger." He shoved her shoulder enough to make her fall back a step, then put the cap on this head and let out a rebel yell.

The younger boy gathered his courage and sneered. "Ever since that rich old lady gave this land to that nature group you're talkin' about, things haven't been the same on this here mountain. My pa, his pa, and his pa before him all hunted this here land and all the land around these parts. Now it's all damned *protected.*"

"Who is your father?" Annie asked.

"Hank McNetter. That's who." He put his fists on his hips. "We're all McNetters."

Annie didn't know these boys, but she knew plenty about the McNetter clan, especially how they had tormented Jack so much when he was in school that he had to be transferred to another district.

The boy who'd been up on the rock suddenly appeared, shouting, "Let's go, I'm dying to get in that cave."

Annie eyed a slingshot stuck in his belt and stepped in front of him.

"I'm sorry, young man, but entrance to that cave is strictly prohibited."

He pushed her out of his way so hard she almost fell.

"Come on, you guys. She can't stop nobody."

As the boys proceeded up the trail, Annie quickly took off

her backpack, pulled out her phone, and started to dial the State Park Service. Billy glanced back, and seeing her with the phone, rushed down and grabbed it.

The other two boys came running after him, shouting, "Come on. Let's go!"

"I'm warning you. You boys are going to be in a lot of trouble if you go in that cave," said Annie.

Billy put his hand on her chest and shoved her to the ground.

"Now you just sit there and keep your mouth shut, and after we've had our fun with those bats, maybe you'll get your phone back. We're goin' into that cave and you're not gonna stop us."

"Oh, yes we are!"

All eyes shot up to the trail ahead. Terri had come from around the huge boulder and was waving her phone.

"I've got it all on this! And I've just texted it to our office!"

She came close and thrust the phone in their faces, showing the video of Billy shoving Annie to the ground.

"You boys are in big trouble," said Terri. "We're talking assault and battery."

"Let me see that," Billy said.

"You watch it from there," said Terri as she held the phone up again.

He studied the video with the other two, then looked up at Terri.

"You texted this?"

"Uh-huh."

The youngest of the three suddenly lost his bravado. "Pa's gonna kill us!"

Annie thrust her hand out to Billy. He reached in his pocket and put her phone in her palm. She put it in her pocket and reached her hand out again. He took her cap from his head, slapped it against his leg and gave it back.

"What are you going to do with that movie?" he asked Annie.

"It all depends," she said as she settled the cap back on her head. "Nothing right now if you go back where you came from and never step foot in here again. But, I'll warn you. We know who you are. We're going to keep this on record and won't hesitate to use it if we hear that any of you stepped foot on this or any other posted property."

The three of them promptly turned and skittered down the mountain, leaving Annie wondering how many bats over the generations that family had killed.

"Thank God that lady gave this land to those nature people to protect," said Terri. "Or bullies like those guys would kill every last bat in that cave."

Annie nodded, smiling to herself. Her little protégé was catching on. She slipped on her backpack, and looked over to her.

"By the way, who'd you text that to?"

"No one. I didn't have time."

M IKE PULLED ON A SWEATER and asked himself the same questions he'd been asking himself all day. Why had he invited Annie for dinner? She'd been stealing into his thoughts ever since he learned she'd broken off with her boyfriend.

He stood admitting to himself that he had yearned to get to know her ever since he met her, but they'd been like two planets orbiting the sun, both spinning in the same direction through the same universe but never connecting.

A spirited essence of her had run parallel with his life, as if she were a ghost sister, and he hoped he wasn't about to find out she wasn't at all like he had envisioned.

He'd never been one to hold himself back when he wanted something, and if it turned out that Annie was the same girl who had kept surfacing in so many of his lingering thoughts, he had a hunch he was going to do something about it. He'd already wasted too much time getting a life.

Other than the time at the fire academy, where he knew who she was the minute he set eyes on her, he hadn't seen her since she was fourteen and he was bound for college. He recalled his disappointment the following summer when she took a job as a lifeguard at a nearby camp and never came to the house to clean again.

His mother always kept him and his dad informed about all her goings-on, however. Once the summer was over, his mother would always mention Annie's various swimming awards when she read about them in the local paper mailed either to their apartment in DC or their house in Hendersonville. Then, when they moved back to the lake house for the summer, he could count on frequent updates from Annie's mother. Was the young woman about to join him for dinner anything like the legend the two women had lovingly crafted?

He put on jeans and slipped into a pair of loafers, smiling to himself remembering the first time he saw her. He was twelve when the clatter of a noisy exhaust drew him and his mother to the window. Annie's mother had pulled up to the house in her dilapidated pickup.

"You gotta come and see this, Roger," his mother called out to his father. "I don't know how I let the pastor over in Bat Cave talk me into hiring this woman. I deserve heaven for this. I could smell alcohol on her breath when she came for her interview. At nine in the morning!"

"Would it have made a difference if it were at five?" his father asked sarcastically.

Then the truck's passenger door opened and an energetic little girl of around seven jumped out and ran to the tailgate to help unload. While her mother hurried in the house with a mop, she grabbed a bucket loaded with supplies. She struggled to carry it and had to lean in the opposite direction and stretch out her free arm in an effort to balance the load. She'd stop and put it down every few steps, then pick it up again, slowly trudging toward the basement door.

"Roger, I said to come over here. You've got to see this spunky little thing. That pail is way too heavy for her, but she's hell bent on getting it in here."

His father finally came, and after taking a look, said "Son, go and help her."

Mike took that command as permission to help Annie and her mom whenever he could, and at the same time, Annie's five-minute display of bulldog tenacity stole his mother's heart.

He ran out the door and down the stairs to get the pail, but Annie shooed him away.

"It's my job," she insisted. "We're getting paid good for this and we need the money."

He looked up at his parents who watched from the window and shrugged, then followed her into the laundry room. She put the pail down, then ran back to the truck, got something off the front seat and hurried back in. He leaned against the wall with his arms folded, waiting to see what this tenacious little girl would do next, when her mother called for her. Annie looked around, put something on a shelf and ran off.

He went over and picked up the tattered cardboard harmonica box and opened it. A big, black beetle sat on a carefully folded bed of lettuce with a few breadcrumbs scattered around. Aware that she had returned, he quickly closed it.

She took the box from him and placed it back on the shelf. "That's my pet beetle."

"You can't have a beetle for a pet."

"Well, I do, and his name is Peewee."

Mike went over to the shelf that still held the books from his youth and smiled. His mother never had the heart to dismantle his old room. Or, had she been saving it for the grandchildren that never came along? Then he remembered how Annie would borrow books all summer long. She had returned them all except for one of his favorites. On one of the last days she came with her mother to clean, he ran into her in the basement and she got flustered.

"I haven't finished reading it yet," she blurted out.

Amused, even though he knew what book she was talking about, he asked, "Reading what?"

The Call of the Wild," she piped up.

He pulled out a book and slowly fanned the pages and pictured the feisty little girl curled up in bed reading, and he wondered if she still had the book.

Mike checked the time. Six. He'd better start setting up the dinner. He went downstairs to the kitchen and got out a few cheeses and a serving board. As he went about preparing the tray, a veil of guilt descended on him. The surge of anticipation for the coming evening with Annie kept dragging him back to melancholy thoughts of the first time he went out with his ex-wife. Until death do we part, he had pledged to Susie. Even though the State of North Carolina had dissolved their marriage and it was Susie who had wanted it done, he felt they both had failed to honor a sacred oath.

Mike put the food he was going to serve in bowls and put them out on the dining room sideboard, then took off to pick up Annie.

ANNIE TOOK A LONG LOOK at herself in the mirror. She wore a dress she had fallen in love with when she saw it in a catalog, but never had anywhere special enough to wear it. Terri had braided some of her hair and wrapped it into an uplift. She turned around, barely taking her eyes from the mirror. The close fitting top showed off her figure so much more than the baggy tee -shirts she always wore. The image in the mirror delighted her; it wasn't as if she had wanted to go all out for this dinner, some-how it had just happened.

The yelping of Terri's two dogs announced Mike's arrival and she started rummaging around her closet for the pair of heels she knew she had. Usually taller than her dates, she rarely wore them, but tonight she hardly had to worry about towering over Mike's six-foot-four frame.

She was putting them on when Terri suddenly erupted into the room, closed the door behind her and fell against it.

"Oh, my God. He's such a hunk!"

"Shush...do you want him to hear you?"

Terri eyed Annie. "Good Lord, it doesn't look like you."

Annie laughed as if pleased with herself.

Once downstairs, she showed Mike around the house, con-vinced he was impressed with the framed document that hung over the fireplace, when it was more likely that her stunningly feminine appearance was having that effect.

"I barely remember my grandfather, but I never forgot com-ing over here and always seeing that deed hanging there. It con-nected me to this house and all the people who came before me. When my mother told me my uncle was going to sell this place, I moved heaven and earth to get my hands on it."

They didn't talk on the way to the lake house until he finally broke the silence.

"Whatever happened to Peewee?"

"Don't tell me you remember Peewee?"

"Oh, who'd forget?"

"I took him with me on my first day at school. A couple of kids grabbed the box, and to tease me, played catch with it until Peewee fell out and someone accidently stepped on him."

"Oh, no. Not Peewee!"

"Yeah, good old Peewee. I cried so hard they took me to the principal's office. To quiet me down, she found a ladybug on one of her plants and put it in the box. When she tried to hand it to me, I kept screaming 'I want Peewee!' and my mom had to come and get me."

They pulled up to the house and Annie felt strange walking through the front door as a guest. The only time she'd gone out on the massive deck was to wash the windows. She'd never been in the house at night, and it looked more magical than monolithic all lit up. The lights cast soft shadows on all the lovely furnishings she'd never really noticed before, even though she had dusted them a hundred times.

He ushered her to the kitchen, poured two glasses of wine and promptly started slicing a baguette for the cheese tray.

"You bring the wine," he said as he took the tray into the dining room and led her to the sideboard.

"Welcome to *Café Michael,*" he said in a parody of a French accent. He swooped his hand along a surprising array of food, including three different kinds of fried chicken. He handed her a plate and motioned to some mixed raw vegetables. *"Les crudités."* Then to a salad. *"Salade de mesclun."* He gave her an exaggerated wink as he pointed out the potato salad. *"La pièce de résistance, pommes de terre au gratin."*

She rolled her eyes up to him.

"What'd you do? Buy out the whole deli?"

"Be nice. I'm living off this stuff." He took a plate and enthusiastically helped himself. "Actually, I'm thinking about writing a book: 'How to Eat Like a King on a Deli Diet.'"

She shook her head and let out a smug little laugh. "'How to End Up in the Hospital on a Deli Diet' sounds more like it." She filled her plate with salad and sat down. He was casually dressed and hadn't bothered with a tablecloth or candles, leaving her feeling a little overdressed for the occasion.

He said she looked nice in a way that she suspected he understood her discomfort. When he smiled at her, she recognized the same smile from when he was a boy. But he'd grown ruggedly handsome, and no longer had the build of a strapping young man, but a stature swathed in solid muscle gained from strenuous efforts to help save his little corner of the earth.

Annie looked out the picture window at the lights from across the lake. Reflections from the moon flickered on the waves with the liveliness of a flock of birds fluttering in the sky, just like her heart was doing. All week she'd racked her brain for a reason why he would ask her out, and she kept coming up with the same answer: he was interested.

She looked around the room and fought an impulse to make up an excuse to leave. She didn't fit in this elegant picture. An alcoholic mother, a brother labeled an arsonist, and a missing father they still gossiped about? It was never going to lead to marriage, the only outcome she could accept. And a bad ending would destroy the comforting fantasies she'd harbored about Mike all her life. If she got out of there now, at least she'd still have those.

Then her eyes landed on the boy who had grown into a man who was interested in her. All she had ever learned about biology told her why he had invited her there that night. The same primeval instincts harbored by every species that walked the earth, that same visceral reaction she felt the minute he gave her that broad, self-confident smile as she came down the stairs that night.

Suddenly, the old determination not to let her grim family background define her, took hold. On the face of her own accomplishments, there was no question in her mind that she could be the right life partner for Michael Samuel McNeil, whether he knew it yet or not. She took a deep breath, and a wave of calm rippled through her like it always did when she faced a challenge. Not only hadn't her family history ever stopped her from going after what she wanted, the effort it took to overcome it had made her that much stronger.

She finished her meal and casually said, "How'd you get into this field?"

He laughed as if he had noticed her sudden confidence, and started to pour her another glass. She quickly put her hand over it.

"Thanks. One's enough for me."

He poured some for himself saying, "Your mother told me you said you were going to marry me when you grew up." He looked at her with a raised eyebrow and a smile tugging at his lips.

She put her fork down and gave him a look, convinced he wanted to provoke her enough to break the ice. It might have worked if she hadn't been in love with him since she was a kid. Stay focused, she told herself, just like she had hundreds of times at the start of a race as she listened for the signal to jump in the pool.

"Keep in mind, Sir, I was only seven at the time and not yet wise to the ways of the world." She tapped her fingers on the table. "Now, for the second time, Mr. McNeil, please tell me why you go around starting fires."

"Okay, you win," he said as he placed some cheese on a piece of bread. "I started out with the Florida Forest Service, working mostly with land management and wildlife habitats. I wasn't into fire back then, but you could call Florida a highly pyrophoric state. It's just a place made to burn, and every couple of years most of their habitats do."

She liked listening to him talk as he casually ate, like she pictured he did a lot with his fellow firefighters.

"At the beginning, I worked on human/black bear conflicts. Then I got into species that are sort of fire dependent, like the red -cockaded woodpecker. It roosts in live pine trees, which is rare amongst woodpeckers. They eat insects, and more or less, the longer you go without fire, the more hardwoods and shrubs encroach, resulting in fewer insects.

"I was there for three years, then I took this job with The Nature Conservancy so I could concentrate on prescribed burning. Taking it pretty much ended my marriage."

He had tried to sound matter-of-fact, but Annie could see a flash of hurt in his eyes.

"Didn't Susie know what you wanted to do from the beginning?"

"She knew, but she and her father, the Honorable Theodore Richards, weren't going to let a little thing like that get in the way of their plans. The whole two years I studied at Florida State, I dreaded the day I would have to tell him I had accepted a field job with some state forestry division. He never quite forgave me for turning down the desk job he had wrangled for me in North Carolina's Forestry Division in Raleigh."

He spooned some of his salad onto a piece of bread and handed it to her.

"Here, try this. Greek kalamata olives with feta." He winked at her. "It's my favorite."

"You've had a little too much of this stuff if you've eaten enough to have a favorite," she said as she took a bite.

They lapsed into silence until Mike pushed his plate away. With his elbows on the table and his hands clenched under his chin, his tone turned more pensive.

"Controlled burning is going to save our forests and therefore our plants and wildlife, and as corny as it sounds, I feel it's my responsibility to protect as much of that as I can.

"That's why I took this job. The Nature Conservancy has been into controlled burning for over twenty-five years. All our efforts come from the point of protecting biodiversity. That's the core of it. Nothing else in the world has contributed to the decline of biodiversity more than fire suppression... not native invasive species, nothing.

"You go out into our forests and they're dark and dense, and you're not going to see a lot of flowers and things in the understory... bees, butterflies... that's just two examples. There's a myriad of species that depend on flowering plants that just won't grow there. In a nutshell, that's why I do what I do."

He reached for his glass and took a sip. "Now it's your turn."

"I feel pretty much the same," said Annie. "Especially when it comes to bats and all the other threatened mammals. Actually,

I'm kinda proud to be among the ranks of scientists in this worldwide movement to save the planet." She blushed. "All those books you let me read when I was a kid kinda got me started on the serious study of animals."

"That reminds me," he said, "I don't think I ever got *The Call of the Wild* back from you."

Noticing his playful grin, she said, "That's because I'm not finished reading it yet. Remember, you said I could have it for as long as I like."

"Something tells me there's only one way I'm ever going to get that book back," he said.

She blushed again, and decided to change the subject. She didn't think she should say it, but she couldn't stop herself. "It's hard for me to believe your wife didn't see your career the same way as you."

"Don't get her wrong, Annie. She saw it that way, too; she just didn't want me to be the one doing it. She's a great gal, and in my own way I'll probably always love her, but she's ambitious to the core. The life I had to offer was suffocating her.

"I wouldn't be surprised to someday turn on the TV and see her on some big network. But, from the minute we got married, she only saw what she wanted to see. And nothing was going to dash her dreams, no matter how much I kept telling her I didn't want to go into politics like both our dads."

There was kindness in his tone, although the pain was evident in his eyes. "I gotta hand it to her, though. For five straight years she tried her darndest to put the two of us on track to end up in DC. It's easy to see her as a hotshot TV anchorwoman, but not me doing what my dad does. Not now, anyway. Maybe when I get too old to do what I'm doing, I might take another look at it."

His eyes narrowed and the pained look returned. "The first time I got called to go out west to help in a wildfire on TNC lands and didn't come home for a month, she quit her job at WLOS in Asheville and took one at a Raleigh TV station. That pretty much ended it."

"It sounds like she couldn't stand you getting hurt."

"I'm sure that was part of it, but if you're going to intention-ally set fires to manage a forest, you've got to know what you're doing. There's no question setting them is an inherently danger-ous activity. But if you're going to light fire, you've got to know how to fight fire. That way, if you have a prescribed fire that gets out of containment, you'll know how to suppress it."

Annie looked into his dark blue eyes and could understand why Susie didn't want him risking his life. Then she thought of the dangers her job entailed, and those faced by the thousands upon thousands who battle every day in hundreds of ways to pre-serve this planet, and of the first responders who are always run-ning towards danger, not away from it. What in their character lets them put aside concern for themselves in order to attain a higher purpose? What drove her? As far back as she could re-member, everything about the earth and the things that grew and roamed in it were sacred to her, and somewhere along the line, just like Mike, she had decided to be their protector.

Mike leaned back in his chair, clenched his hands behind his head and threw her one of his easy smiles. "Now that I've spilled my guts about Susie, why don't you tell me about... what did your mother call him? George?"

"Yeah. George Harwood."

"Is he that lawyer in Hendersonville?"

"Yep."

"The Conservancy uses him sometimes. He's supposed to be a real up and comer."

Annie slowly ran a finger around the rim of her glass.

"You don't have to talk about him if you don't want to," said Mike.

"There's nothing to talk about. Suffice it to say that bats are the last thing he wants to have anything to do with."

Annie couldn't resist telling the story of her pretending to get bitten by one, and the two of them had a good laugh.

She rose, saying, "Let's get this stuff back in the fridge before it spoils. It's unhealthy enough when it's fresh."

They started taking the food into the kitchen, and on their way back, bumped into each other. He grasped her arm and said he was sorry, but held on to her longer than he needed to. Later, as they stood at the sink washing his mother's cherished Spode serving dishes, their arms touched and neither of them moved away.

As he wiped a tureen dry, Mike said, "I'm sorry if I embarrassed you about what your mother said."

"Well, you can't blame me. You were pretty cute back then." She turned to him, bit her lip and shook her head gravely as she studied his face. Then she ran her hand down his cheek. "You didn't have this rugged five o'clock shadow." She touched a scar on his forehead. "Or that."

"Don't you be making fun of that scar. It's my badge of honor," he said as he grasped her hand. "I won it in a tug-of-war with an overprotective mother raccoon."

They stood there saying nothing. He brought her hand to his lips and kissed it. He looked intensely at her, and his dark cornflower blue eyes almost took her breath away. She slowly pulled her hand away. She wasn't ready. This was too important. They had to get it right.

"I gotta be going," she said as she took off her apron. "I'm on duty tomorrow at the Lake Lure Fire Department. With the fire potential up so high, they've called a bunch of their volunteers in so they've got a crew ready to roll."

They were quiet on the drive back to her house. Nervous about how the evening was going to end, she kept tapping her fingers on her knees. His truck hit a big rock on her washed-out road, and in spite of her seat belt, he instinctively reached across to hold her back. Without thinking, she clasped his hand and felt his calluses. The knowledge of the backbreaking labor that went into creating them filled her with respect.

He pulled up to her house, and when she reached for the door he stopped her.

"You stay right there. I don't want you breaking your neck in those shoes."

He came around and opened her door, then put his arms under her, swung her from the seat, and carried her to the house. He slowly let her slide down. She stood leaning against the wall.

He was close enough for her to hear him breathe.

"I'm glad chivalry's not dead," she whispered.

He rested his forehead on hers. "How can you go out and save the mammals of the world with a broken leg?"

She put her hand on his chest and gently tried to push him back, but he wouldn't budge.

He looked into her eyes. "Well, are you gonna let me kiss you or not?"

"May...be once," she said teasingly.

The door opened and Terri's two dogs were suddenly all over them.

"Oops!" said Terri. "I didn't hear you drive up! I was just letting the dogs out. I'm *sooo* sorry!"

Annie giggled, then wriggled away from Mike and started inside. "Goodnight, Mike. I had a nice time." She hesitated for a moment and added, "I guess I'm just gonna have to owe you one."

PART TWO

The Dragon Wakes

Day One

Saturday, November 5. IT WAS THE SORT OF glorious day that makes one grateful to be alive, a stolen warm afternoon with a clear blue sky the late fall rarely calls its own. As usually happens in the fall season, leaf peepers were nonchalantly driving through the picturesque mountain town of Lake Lure, nestled on the eastern slope of the Blue Ridge Mountains twenty-five miles east of Asheville.

It wasn't at all like the summer weekends where traffic has to stop and let the colorful crowds cross in their bathing suits, toting kids, pushing strollers and pulling wagons filled with picnic supplies as they trudge to their cars or the ice cream stand across the road from the beach. And they had come in droves last summer, one of the hottest and driest on record.

Unless you're a tourist, there's not that much to do in the center of town, since the nearly five hundred households that populate Lake Lure are either scattered around the lake or hidden in the surrounding mountains and gated resort communities.

The town center sits on one tip of the sprawling alpine lake. Strung along the curved beach are the usual things one more or less would expect to find in a quasi-tourist town—an information center, town hall that also houses the police department and a community room, and then tennis courts and a rambling park. A neatly kept public beach with a water park sits next to a marina with popular boat tours featuring spectacular views of the massive cliff-faced Rumbling Bald Mountains hovering around the lake's twisting western rim.

Across the road from the beach, the historic 69-room Lake Lure Inn's *Jennifer Grey* and *Swayze* suites pay tribute to the cult-classic *Dirty Dancing* that was filmed on the lake. A lot of the old timers still glow as they tell about working with the camera crew in November after they painted all the fall leaves green to make it look like summer, and watching the freezing Patrick Swayze lifting the equally cold "Baby" from out of the frigid water.

Next to the Inn, a commercial building they call the Arcade houses a few small businesses, including one of the many real estate firms sprinkled all along Route 74A, the only way in and out of the town and the adjoining village of Chimney Rock, the gateway to the ten mile long Hickory Nut Gorge. Except for a quaint 2-bay gas station built in the 1930s, a liquor store, and the LaStrada restaurant perched on the side of the mountain with its million-dollar view, that's pretty much all there is.

The buildings on both sides of the road are in the Mediterranean style that, almost a hundred years ago, the town's founding fathers felt aptly reflected the ambience of the site. It was at that time that they dammed the Rocky Broad River spilling from out of the Hickory Nut Gorge and Chimney Rock. As the water filled the valley below, it twisted and turned around steep mountain contours forming a spiked cross with twenty-seven miles of shoreline.

No stone has been left unturned in the ceaseless effort to give the center of the town a picture-postcard look—manicured lawns, shade trees, and an inviting boardwalk lined with crepe myrtles that greet every Fourth of July with pink fluff. In recent years, this intrinsic pride of place motivated a grass-roots effort to transform a replaced bridge into a greatly beloved flowering bridge spanning the Rocky Broad River.

Other than operating a small store, restaurant or motel, it is the buying, selling and renting of vacation homes, condominiums and residences that are the town's main occupations. The majority of the populace are mostly retirees that either reside there full time, or who just come for the summer and are rarely drawn to the center of town.

However, an exception is made when the council holds its meetings. These vigorously attended sessions expose the underbelly of this affluent and well-educated community, many of whom own the two hundred or so upscale homes in the Rumbling Bald Resort sitting at the far end of one of the lake's four arms and hugging the Rumbling Bald Mountains.

The usual smooth western North Carolina mountain drawl is seldom heard in these often contentious meetings—the kind you'd expect from a group of people with inquiring minds and a lot of time on their hands. Instead, floating through the air is the crisp and assertive diction of what the few remaining locals call the "Yankees," or those they refer to as "halfbacks"—folks who left the north for Florida, and finding it too hot, came halfway back.

As is happening in a lot of formerly remote, yet beautiful sections of the mountains, as the natives drift away chasing jobs and opportunity, others with enough money to remediate the harsh but beautiful mountain features are filling the vacuum and streaming in.

IT WAS ALMOST FOUR THAT Saturday afternoon when Ron Morgan, the town's fire chief, was on his way to the station on Route 74A about a mile from the center of town. His truck weaved through the countryside that blazed with fall color, past folks giving their lawn the last mow of the season, past parents joyfully rollicking in the leaves with their kids, or people out walking their dog, all savoring what could be the last beautiful day of the season.

But to the driver of the red Chevy Silverado 1500, the picturesque leaf-covered mountains only represented one thing, a threat. They were in the middle of the worst conditions Morgan had seen in his twenty years as a firefighter.

It was his day off and he had already issued a fire ban the day before, but the severe drought and all the leaf litter on the ground put him so much on edge, he figured he might as well go in.

A medical call to carry out a patient from the Chimney Rock Park came over his radio, and he decided to back up the task crew that would be heading out any minute.

THE TWO TRUCKS responding to the park incident raced through Lake Lure with their sirens on, and then into Chimney

Rock where they turned onto the road that snakes for three miles up Chimney Rock Mountain. Annie, in a brush truck they also used for medical assistance, reached the parking lot at the foot of the famous monolith and jumped out. She grabbed a first-aid kit and started for a cluster of people tending a lady lying on the ground. Something in the distance that didn't make sense caught her eye, but she hurried to help one of the park rangers with the woman who appeared to have a broken ankle.

After they summoned an ambulance, Annie rushed over to the rim of the parking lot and looked out toward the Rumbling Bald Mountain range. A wisp of smoke rose from the far-off, two hundred foot tall cliffs that snaked around the mountains for nearly five miles. She suspected it was on the popular overlook a lot of the local teenagers hiked to that they called the Party Rock. This was not good.

Noticing a man nearby with a pair of binoculars strung on his neck, she asked to borrow them. She looked through them, and the image of rugged cliffs rolled across the lens until she finally zeroed in on the smoke, then she carefully adjusted the lens to sharpen the blurred image. The hair on the back of her neck rose as beyond the cross-hairs she saw a flaming log roll down a rock cliff and tumble off the mountain. She ran to the truck and radioed dispatch. "There's a fire on Party Rock."

MORGAN WAS JUST REACHING the town center when he heard the report on his radio. He looked across the lake and scanned the Rumbling Bald ridge. He spotted the column of smoke on the northern edge and knew they were in for a world of hurt. He knew what it took to fight fire on those cliffs. There was no way they could get to it with a normal vehicle. Even on an ATV it would take a lot of time and effort to reach the Party Rock. They would have to climb up there on foot and fight it by hand with whatever they could carry on their backs.

Morgan got on the radio and called dispatch.

"Call out all our trucks to the Party Rock Trail off Carsons Road. Requesting mutual aid from Chimney Rock, Fairfield Mountains, Bill's Creek, and Green Hill. Give them our frequency so they can dial up our channel and we can talk radio-to-radio." Then he diverted Annie's brush truck to the fire.

Morgan spun into strategy mode. The deeply rutted old logging road on the other side of the lake that the locals called the Party Rock Trail climbs west along the ridge, passes by the Party Rock, then finally goes up over to the Shumont Mountain plateau that rises above the Rumbling Bald Mountains.

He radioed dispatch. "Requesting mutual aid from Broad River."

In moments, Brent Hayner, Chief of the Broad River Fire Department, radioed Morgan. They were in the adjoining county and responsible for Shumont Mountain.

"What do you need and where do you need it?" Hayner asked.

"We've spotted a fire on Party Rock. Instead of my guys driving through Chimney Rock and Bat Cave and then north on Route 9 to get to the back side of the mountain, it's gonna be easier for you guys to come from the Shumont plateau down to the Party Rock and fight the fire from the top of the ridge down, while we fight it from the bottom up. That way, we can work this fire together. We haven't been up there yet, so we don't know how big it is. If you guys find it before we do, give a holler. And keep me posted as you come down."

Morgan sped through the town center, red lights flashing and siren blaring, past the beach and town hall and over the bridge into Chimney Rock, all the while picturing in his head an aerial view of the steep, heavily forested U-shaped bowl of wildlands containing the almost three thousand state-owned acres his men were about to tackle.

They had to kill this thing tonight, he told himself. If it spread north it would hit the Rumbling Bald Resort, west it would reach the Shumont plateau, and if it went south and over Round Top Mountain it would threaten the village of Chimney Rock.

Morgan hung a right past the bridge onto the narrow two-lane Boys Camp Road that twists, turns, climbs and dips for two miles along the foot of Rumbling Bald Mountain, dotted with homes and cabins, roughly running with one of the lake's four arms. He reached the end and made a sharp left onto Carson Road and climbed for less than a mile until he hit the dead-end. The logging trail used by hikers to get to the Party Rock, lay in a gaping forest opening.

Firefighters from Lake Lure and Chimney Rock began arriving on the scene. Morgan figured the fire probably covered a couple of acres by now and he worried about how much it might grow before the crew got up there. They faced a good mile and a half trek on a washed out trail littered with rocks and boulders, a grueling uphill climb all the way.

"It doesn't make sense to send a couple of guys rushing into the woods right now," Morgan told his assistant who had just arrived in one of the station's engines. "We're in for a long night. We better take the time to get our gear together."

As trucks pulled in, Morgan kept an eye out for the county ranger, Doug Thompson, and his assistant, James Bentley. Since the fire probability rating for that day was high, the two of them were on duty in their office at the Rutherford County Airport, all set to go when the call came in. He also looked out for Annie. She had to get everybody logged in.

Morgan pulled his gear from his truck. Somewhere in his early forties, with clean-cut good looks, he bore the image of a businessman more than a firefighter, but the well-worn and soot-smudged brush shirt and pants he yanked from his backpack testified to hours of rugged toil by a seasoned firefighter.

Trucks now lined both sides of the dead-end road with guys spilling out, yanking out their equipment, and gearing up. His team piled as much equipment as they could onto the station's UTV and ATV, knowing that the vehicles weren't going to make it to the top. But as far as the vehicles did make it, was that much less of a distance they would have to carry everything in on their backs.

With so many trucks now on the scene, Morgan barely saw Annie running up the road. He waved her over and handed her a legal pad.

"Log in everyone who goes in or comes out. I want to know

their names, division, when they go in and when they come out. We gotta make sure everyone's comin' back to us." He looked at her through narrowed eyes. "This is going to be a rough night."

"I can handle it," Annie said. She hadn't gotten her wildfire certification yet, so he couldn't let her go up, but she still felt his natural protective concern for a female teammate.

"Good. You know what to do. We should be ready to send the first crew up in another thirty minutes."

Annie went to work and he scanned the activity. The county ranger and his assistant had just pulled up in two engines. The state statute mandates that forest fires are the North Carolina Forest Service's responsibility, making Thompson the incident commander the instant he arrived on the scene. They'd brought two of their pick-up firefighters, men who either had full-time jobs or volunteered, and they began climbing out and suiting up.

Thompson was somewhere in his early thirties, but had a self-assured, no drama air about him that came from shouldering twelve years of responsibility for both the suppression of forest fires and the setting and managing of prescribed fires throughout Rutherford County.

He came over to Morgan rubbing his chin. "How long do you think it's gonna take to get up there?"

"An hour and a half. Maybe two."

Thompson gazed at the rutted dirt trail leading into the thick woods. "This is gonna be one heck of a job. The only thing they're gonna be able to use up there are fire rakes."

"We're sending up three backpack leaf blowers and two chain saws. That'll help some," said Morgan. "Somehow they're gonna have to get a fire line around it, but I'm afraid it's gonna be like hand-to-hand combat up there."

Just then, they heard helicopters overhead on their way to scoop water from the lake.

"I ordered two," said Thompson. "They should be able to get in a few dumps before dark. They're coming back in the morning."

Thompson decided to manage the fire in twelve-hour shifts and started making plans for the next morning's operational period. He got on his phone and ordered special bridge crews made up of prison inmates supervised by Forest Service personnel for early the next morning, while Morgan threw himself into the task of rounding up engine crews from the surrounding counties.

ANNIE NEEDED A MOMENT TO ADJUST, but only a moment. This might be the first time she'd been called out to a wildfire, but she knew how important it was that she get everything down right. Trained in the science of carefully cataloging bats that might be fading into extinction, she felt a chilling gravity charting men being sent on a dangerous mission who may not come back unharmed.

She followed behind Morgan's assistant, getting everyone's information as he cobbled together a mixed crew of twenty wildfire-certified firefighters from three companies and the Forest Service. She was impressed that everyone was so well trained there were no questions or confusion. Suited up in the heat-resistant green brush pants they called the "greens," yellow brush shirts they called the "yellows," and thermoplastic helmets, they knew what they were supposed to do.

She'd gone up to the Party Rock with Jack dozens of times when they were teens, and knew what a hard climb these men faced with their heavy low-slung back packs loaded with everything they'd need for a grueling wildfire. Large water bottles were stuffed in the side pockets, tools hung from loops, a fire shelter case was attached to their hip belts. Most of them had a radio harness strapped across their chest. A formidable force, heavily equipped and ready for action.

Within forty minutes of Annie's call, the first crew, led by the assistant forest ranger, James Bentley, started up the trail.

More men started arriving, and Thompson called Annie over.

"I'm gonna send eight Forest Service guys into the boulder fields to chase the fires the burning logs have got to be starting. Get all their info."

Annie looked confused. She'd been in there hiking and counting bats in the caves. "There's a lot of places fires can start in there and lock those guys in."

Thompson gave her a self-assured look. "We're an attack crew. This is what we do. We burn our way in, and if we have to, we burn our way out."

Annie logged them in, knowing where they were going and how tough it was going to be. She'd surveyed the fissure caves the rocks falling from the cliffs had created. Hopefully, the bats were deep inside and unaffected by the smoke, she thought as she watched the men get in their trucks and head to Boys Camp Road for the trail that would lead to the boulder fields.

Except for the chatter on the radio and the murmur of everyone on phones urgently gathering up resources, the base camp became quiet. She thought of the men trudging out to attack the fire in two dangerous places, and the urgency of the situation gripped her. Then she thought of the animals up on that mountain. By now, the bears had to be smelling the smoke and moving, as well as the deer and coyotes. She pictured newts and salamanders skittering across the rocks searching for a place to hide. She listened intently, but couldn't hear a bird or see a squirrel.

Morgan came over to her and handed her a list of their volunteers and paid firefighters.

"Call everyone who hasn't shown up so far, ask them to get here by seven in the morning, and keep a running list. And call around for food. We're gonna have to feed these people."

MORGAN LEFT ANNIE and listened to his radio as he called around for apparatus and personnel. A half hour had passed since Broad River radioed they had started down the trail. Bruce Cook, the assistant fire chief, finally reported in.

"We're having a hard time finding the smoke. With all the contours, we can't see it."

"The wind's not blowing, so it's going straight up," said Morgan.

"We can't even smell it."

"Just keep comin'."

An hour and a half had passed since the assistant ranger started the climb with his crew, when he radioed the base. Morgan listened intently to Bentley's report to Thompson.

"We're up here. It looks like the fire started right here on the Party Rock. It's pretty much a ground fire with a lot of smoke. Mostly burning leaves, but there's a lot of old dead logs from blowdowns that have caught fire. Everything's so bone dry they're just combusting. We're going to try to dig a line on either side of the fire. The cliff is at the front of it and the logging road winds around above it, so hopefully, if we keep it from jumping the road, and our lines tied to the cliffs hold, we'll be able to box it in up here. That's the plan anyway."

BENTLEY GOT OFF THE RADIO and decided that his first priority was to keep people away from the rock cliff. Once the sun set, it would be a fatality waiting to happen. The twenty-seven year old, six foot four bear of a man with a thick, dark, medium cropped beard quickly dug a fireline forty feet out from the cliff and flagged it off so nobody would go past it the rest of the night.

Twenty minutes later, Broad River's four-man crew arrived and joined the effort.

Bentley kept radioing reports that standing dead trees called "snags" were catching fire, cracking, then slamming to the ground, before rolling down the steep terrain and rumbling off the cliff, landing in the boulder field two hundred feet below.

As the sun was setting, Bentley radioed, "We've got the fire line in and we're trying to backburn, but can't make headway on the areas that are wet from the helicopter drops."

An hour later, his report was even less encouraging. "Every time we get a line established up here, the burning logs dropping off the cliff catch something on fire down in the boulder field. Then that fire creeps around and crawls back up somewhere on the other side of our line, and we have to fall back and dig another one."

They used that strategy all night. If they couldn't make a line stick in one place, they'd go to another.

The whole night, radio traffic went back and forth between Bentley at the top, and Thompson at the base camp. Bentley sent him GPS co-ordinates of where they were, and Thompson used the information to plot maps on his laptop so he could pass off the information to his replacement in the morning.

The din of leaf blowers, chainsaws and cracking trees was deafening. Even the men far back in the woods on top could hear the snags cracking and rumbling off the cliff. Once, a falling tree started a huge stone rolling down the steep mountain, and the rumbling and tumbling over the rocky cliff was hair-raising. The smoke and flying ash, the fires glowing in the dark, the snags burning like giant torches, and the eerie noises created an un-worldly scene.

Some of the terrain sloped as much as 45 degrees, and to keep from falling off, they had to dig their boots into the moun-tain and lean in. When a burning log came rolling down, they'd catch it with their fire rake and flip it to a burnt area they called "the black."

Two firefighters working side by side on the top were volun-teers from within the small tourist community of Chimney Rock, as were most of the members of that company. Bruce Godzik owned a coffee shop on Main Street and Bruce Button was a re-tiree who also served as a chaplain with the Billy Graham Rapid Response Team Ministry.

By nine, the crew was making progress, and when someone brought up a load of baloney sandwiches a volunteer put together on a truck tailgate at the base camp, they found a clearing and started in on them. Godzik sank down on the ground, suddenly aware of how tired his legs had gotten from the steep-mountain climbing. He took off the kerchief he'd been wearing across his face and shook it out. It didn't help with the smoke, but kept the hot ashes from singeing his face.

A lot of the equipment was turned off during the break, and it became quieter. As the men sat eating, they listened to the mu-sic floating up from a band playing on the balcony of the Lake Lure Inn below. Bruce nudged the guy next to him.

"Reminds me of the music everyone heard as they sat in their lifeboats and watched the Titanic sink."

His firefighter's dark humor got them laughing for the first time that night.

Around one o'clock, someone came up the trail balancing a carton on their shoulder. A shout rose. Everyone knew it had to be food. Someone else trailed behind with a case of water. Annie had called Larkins, a local restaurant, and they had sent over a load of hamburgers and French fries.

But Bentley's adrenalin had been pumping so strong for so long, he wasn't hungry. He was in a super focused state and so situationally aware he couldn't eat. For these same reasons he wasn't scared. He constantly asked himself, "Where are my guys? What are they doing? Are they all right?" leaving no room for fear.

Earlier, he had been looking forward to a change in the humidity. No matter how dry the conditions, typically in the night, the humidity comes back up. Fire behavior is controlled a great deal by the moisture in the air, and Bentley kept hoping it would increase and the fire would start to lay down enough for them to catch it that night. But it wasn't happening. This fire wasn't slowing down, and it wasn't acting the way it should.

Later that night, Bentley exclaimed over the radio, "A burning tree fell on the cliff right across our fire line and it's spreading out again! If we're gonna get ahead of this fire, we've got to cut another line farther back and somehow anchor it to the cliff!"

The base camp kept anxiously listening to them battle the fire at the top, until around two when Bentley radioed again.

"I think we've got it this time. We're just working to hold it."

Thompson sat in the ambulance stationed at the foot of the trail updating the fire's footprint on his laptop, when someone from the Bills Creek Women's Auxiliary handed him a cup of coffee. The engine was running, so there was light and a little heat. He'd been fighting the fire from base camp, making one strategic decision after another all night long, acutely aware that one critical error could get them in trouble.

Now, after battling it for ten hours, it looked like they were finally getting a handle on it, and he allowed himself a moment away from his attack mode to think about the guys up on the mountain and in the boulder fields below and thank God no one had been hurt.

No one in the sleepy little towns below knew what heroic efforts the men he'd sent in there were now exerting on that mountain. By now, the firefighters knew they weren't going to put the fire out that night, but they also knew it was their job to buy the team that would be taking it over in the morning, enough time to gather the force they'd need to kill it.

Like he frequently did in times like this, Thompson pulled out the Incident Response Pocket Guide from his shirt pocket, the firefighter's bible he was never without. It contained the Forest Service's rules of engagement, a collection of best practices that had evolved over time within the wildland fire service. If he stuck to them, he'd do his job safely.

And, as he also frequently did, he read the paragraphs on operational leadership.

"The most essential element of successful wildland firefighting is competent and confident leadership. Leadership means providing purpose, direction, and motivation for wildland firefighters working to accomplish difficult tasks under dangerous, stressful circumstances." Whoever wrote this, he said to himself, has been there and done that.

Then he read the bulleted items and asked himself if he had followed the directives. Satisfied that he had, he closed the notebook, put it in his pocket and went back to work.

EARLIER, WHEN THOMPSON gave Annie some forms and asked her to use them to log everyone in and out, she realized she now worked for the North Carolina Forest Service. Suddenly, the eerie sound of a cracking tree echoed through the forest and made her jump.

She checked her watch. Almost six. She gave The Legends Restaurant in the resort another try. This time someone answered and agreed to send fifty breakfast boxes with bacon, eggs and biscuits over by eight.

She hadn't had a moment to herself since she'd been dispatched to the scene, and finally took a few minutes to eat the baloney sandwich a volunteer had handed her hours earlier. Next, she'd better call Jack while she had the time.

She walked over to the trees where she wouldn't be over-heard and dialed. His phone kept ringing. Good, she said to herself, he's on the road and would have a cast iron alibi.

"Hello," a groggy voice answered.

"Jack, it's me, Annie."

"What time is it?"

"Jack, there's a fire on Party Rock. I've been here all night. It started around two yesterday afternoon. Where were you?"

"Here. I was working on my staircase. What time is it?"

"Almost seven. Was anyone with you?"

"Jeez, is this ever gonna end?"

"Okay. So, you don't have an alibi. It happened so long ago, I'm sure you'll be okay. I'm sorry I woke you."

"I'm glad you did. Thanks for the heads up, Sis."

Annie put her phone back in her pocket and began to worry about Jack. The land burning that night belonged to the state. Would they be the ones to investigate? What if the fire gets away from them? A mile to the north there were over two hundred houses in the Rumbling Bald Resort, over the mountain and at the western edge of the fire stood the Shumont Mountain ridge, covered in leaf litter ankle deep and mostly only accessible on a few narrow gravel roads. Then there was the historic village of Chimney Rock at the foot of Round Top Mountain on the south. If that place burned down, there was no replacing it—three distinctly different communities with their own unique challenges clustered in one horrible bull's-eye.

All night, she'd been hearing the same thing on the radio. The fire kept jumping their lines and they kept moving it back. If they were moving their lines farther and farther back, the fire had to be growing.

Morgan listened, too. He wanted to hear that a line had been established and they were backburning the fire and eating up all the fuel up there. That was the way they had to do it. Fight fire with fire. But, all that night, that wasn't what he was hearing. *Not on that mountain.* It was a beauty to look at, but a beast to fight fire on.

Day Two

*S*unday, *November 6.* THOMPSON KNEW THE fire wasn't contained when the crews came out of the woods at seven that morning, but it was confined, and he was pretty sure they weren't going to lose it. The helicopters were coming back, fresh crews were coming in, and there were a couple of places in front of the boulder field where they could gouge out a fire line with 'dozers.

The night before, he had ordered a replacement incident commander from the District 12 headquarters in Mt. Holly outside of Charlotte, and they were sending the assistant director, Ferrell Banks. The Forest Service adheres to a strict work/rest ratio of two to one. When they work sixteen hours, they have to take eight off. So, the minute he took over he knew he'd have to get someone to replace him in the morning. After sixteen hours of the kind of grueling firefighting they had experienced, they weren't only physically exhausted, but because of the constant demand to make decisions, they were mentally exhausted as well.

Besides, as the county ranger, he and his team are an initial attack force. The first 24 hours of a wildfire are theirs. Then an incident team takes over and they return to their "initial attack" mode and start fighting new fires.

ANNIE FINISHED logging out the last sooty, exhausted firefighter who trudged down the mountain and she was double-checking to make sure everyone who went up was accounted for, when Morgan tapped her on the shoulder.

"The guys have set up our operation trailer at the Rumbling Bald Trail. Get your truck over there."

Annie looked around. Fire engines, tanker trucks, pickups, and ambulances were revving up to move to the parking lot at the entrance to the state's hiking trails that the bottom crews had been using all night to access the boulder fields.

She gathered her materials, jumped in the brush truck that she had arrived with and drove it halfway down Boys Camp Road, then up to the state's parking lot. She got out and hurried over to the trailer. The back had been let down, creating a huge ramp. She jumped on and went in. Maps lay on the conference table with division leaders from the Forest Service pouring over them.

Spotting a coffee urn, she poured herself a cup, and left. She went over to a group of fire department volunteers stacking water in a mess tent.

"The Legends at the resort is sending up breakfast for everyone this morning," Annie told them. "And I called LaStrada last night and they're going to bring us pasta and pizza for lunch and dinner. Are you folks going to be around to help serve it?"

They told her they would, and she went over to help two officers from the Lake Lure police department put up cones to direct traffic to her log-in position.

She hadn't slept all night, but there was no one to take her place. It didn't matter. She was totally wired and 100% focused on keeping track of every firefighter and their apparatus. She looked down the driveway at the line of engines creeping toward her, took three deep breaths and slowly let them out, her old swim meet strategy. Then she tightened her grasp on her clipboard and stepped up to the first truck.

She didn't recognize the vehicle at first, but when she looked up at the ready smile, her heart thumped in her throat. Mike wore yellows and greens.

"You're here to help?"

"Morgan called me last night. He wants me to take the bridge crew up to the top once they get here. He knows I'm familiar with that mountain since The Nature Conservancy owned it before the state got it."

She felt his gaze as she logged him in.

"You've been here all night?" he asked.

She nodded and kept writing. As he pulled away, she didn't know whether it was because she was so wound up or just sleep deprived, but emotion flooded over her at the thought of him up on those cliffs, and she swiped away a tear while waiting for the next truck to pull up.

She went over and said, "Your name, sir."

"Ferrell Banks, District 12 headquarters."

She looked up from her clipboard. A muscular, thickset man in his early forties, with a blond stubble beard looked down at her. His well-worn baseball cap with the North Carolina Forest Service logo looked like it was molded to his head.

"Are you the new IC?"

"Uh-huh."

"I still gotta log you in."

He smiled. "You go right ahead and do your job."

FERRELL BANKS PARKED HIS TRUCK, and as he walked into the trailer with a roll of maps under his arm, Thompson greeted him with a recap of the night.

"This is a dirty fire. It's relatively small, but the location is as bad as it gets, and dangerous. We got a fire on top and one on the bottom. I had people on the bottom with trees falling down from the cliffs above and people at the top with the risk of falling off. We tried to tie them together all night, but were limited to what we could do to hold it—equipment equipment, people wise."

He opened his laptop and scrolled through several maps. "As the top grew, we had to keep widening the bottom because we knew things were going to keep chucking off the top, and we had to be there to catch it. We kept losing it and catching it all night."

As the two men talked, crew leaders started drifting in, until Ferrell opened his first meeting as the Incident Commander with a safety message. After a weather update and a review of the night before, the crew leaders got their assignments for the next twelve hours.

Ferrell ended the meeting with "Remember, our main goal

for the day is to hold onto that fireline and keep it from going after the Shumont ridge."

He looked over and saw the chief of the Broad River fire department, standing next to someone from Buncombe County's Emergency Management Division, and went over to them.

"Thanks for inviting us to your briefing meeting," said the chief.

"Well, if the fire's on the ridge a couple hundred yards from your doorstep, you can be pretty sure it's going to come see you."

They nodded. "And we intend to be ready when it does."

Ferrell went back to the trailer, dreading the possibility that the Forest Service might have to fight the fire on the Shumont Mountain range. Other than a plateau that was almost at the end of the treacherous winding and climbing Shumont Road that contained a scattering of houses and the Broad River Fire Department's substation, it possessed every attribute that would give them pause. Heavily forested, it had extremely steep valleys that intersected at all kinds of angles, mountain peaks that spiked from 1,200 to 3,200 feet with hollows, basins, gullies and ravines—with their overriding characteristic being "steep." There were a few paved roads, but most of the houses and cabins could only be reached on narrow gravel roads that were one step up from a logging trail. Fighting fire in there would be another kind of nightmare.

Once back in the trailer, Ferrell got busy ordering additional equipment. Because the Forest Service is responsible for all wildland fires in the state, they're prepared to get big fast. They keep bulldozers in all 100 counties loaded on a truck with an assigned operator, and they can mobilize as many as they need, when and where they need them.

In the western part of the state, they keep their helicopters in Hickory where they've also established a Single Engine Air Tanker Base they call a "load and go system." The base is capable of loading two single-engine planes, each of which can hold 800 gallons of fire retardant. The planes are "hot-loaded," meaning they put in the retardant while the engine is still running. The plane is directed along the runway, and a loader fills it with retardant, then sends the plane on its way like a NASCAR pit stop. One of the most unique features of the base is that, if the need arises, it can be packed up and relocated to another airport overnight.

In addition to the two planes at the Hickory base, they have planes stationed all over the state, including the Foothills Regional Airport in Morganton, fifty miles from Lake Lure.

BY NOON, ANNIE was still logging in crews, but it was down to a trickle. The wind had kicked up and the stray wisps of hair from her ponytail kept brushing across her face. She laid her papers on the ground, anchored them with a rock, and refastened her ponytail. That morning she could see a plume on the mountain, but now it was a lot wider and higher. She was beginning to get a bad feeling, a feeling of fear.

All afternoon, as the temperature rose, she could see the fire becoming more intense, and she kept turning up her radio and listening to the traffic. The fire was running and jumping and moving so fast, they couldn't keep up with it.

Someone hollered "There're so many rocks with vegetation in the crevices that there's no way we can scratch down to the dirt between them."

Annie recognized Mike's voice and her concern grew as she listened.

"The fire is creeping out, between, under and around them, destroying every line we put in. We can't get far enough in front of it to find a good place to set a backfire. We're just trying to keep it cut off at the top and at the bottom. That's the kind of fire we're fighting up here!"

Just then, someone pulled in with another load of sandwiches from the Legends Restaurant. Annie found someone to take over the logging-in process, and began organizing the tent housing the donations flowing in from all over. She knew who they had fighting the fire and where they were, and began sending sandwiches, drinks and snacks out to them by whatever means she could find.

By six, fresh crews started arriving and she took over logging them in again, and as the crews started coming out of the woods, logging them out.

BEFORE THEY STARTED the night briefing, Ferrell took the time to talk with the crew coming off the mountain; then he and Morgan had a quick planning session with Chase Payne, one of the district's rangers who was going to take over as the night shift Incident Commander. From all accounts, the fire was now spreading in two directions, south toward Boys Camp Road and north toward the Rumbling Bald Resort.

"The ideal place to have stopped it," said Morgan, "would've been on the top of the ridge last night where we had a good road bed. The men fought like the devil to get it to hold there, but it just wouldn't work." He pursed his lips and shook his head. "And between there and the Rumbling Bald Resort I don't see anywhere else that's a really good place to stop it."

Ferrell went over to a map and pointed to Boys Camp and Carsons roads. "We've got to use these roads as firebreaks if we want to keep it from the resort and the houses on Boys Camp. We've got to start backburning away from them and up that mountain tomorrow night when the humidity goes up." He looked questioningly up at Morgan.

"I think I can get four engine crews from Polk and three from McDowell to help."

"Good." Ferrell pointed to the Rumbling Bald Resort on the map. "I think it's time we face the fact that this fire might reach this community."

Morgan shook his head. "God help us if it does. There's two hundred houses in there. They're spread far and wide and covered in leaves. I'll get over there and come up with a structure protection plan."

Morgan left and Ferrell looked over at Chase. "Tonight, you've got to hold the line, top and bottom."

Just then, Dan Brandon, the head of District 12, walked in with more maps. He was Ferrell's boss and looked the part. Fifty-two years old and with twenty-nine years of fighting wildland fires with the North Carolina Forest Service under his belt, he was a burly, tough looking figure with a no-nonsense graying brush cut, a man's-man sort of guy. Yet, in spite of his rugged stature, he spoke in a relaxed, easygoing western North Carolina drawl. He was operating as the incident administrator for the fire and generating 36" x 36" maps using the GPS coordinates they sent him and printing them on their giant color copier in the district office in Mt. Holly, an hour and a half away.

Chase picked one up. "I'll tape this to the trailer and start the night briefing."

"Here's an infrared map you'll want to put up" said Brandon. "It's from last night, but it'll help."

WANTING TO GET IN on the night briefing, Annie relinquished her post to someone from the sheriff's office and hurried over to the trailer. The silhouette of the men in the eerily lit box poring over the maps, the ghostly way the temporary lighting uplit the smoke-veiled forest surrounding the parking lot, the chugging of the generators—all of it gave her the feeling of otherworldliness. She'd been up for thirty hours and was running on adrenaline and knew that was part of it.

The briefing ended with her thinking she might have to evacuate in the morning since her house was just off Boys Camp Road. Annie trudged over to the mess tent and started straightening up as the night crew stopped in for sandwiches, water and snacks to take up with them. She could hear the engines in the parking lot starting and men saying their goodbyes.

She pictured the three North Carolina Forest Service wildland firefighters who had the weight of a fire threatening three communities on their shoulders—the husky blond bearded Ferrell, with his firmly set cap; his boss, the burly but soft spoken Brandon, with his graying brush cut; and Chase, the lanky six-foot-six twenty-nine year old ranger with a long black beard whom they had pulled from their district for night duty. Then there was Morgan, the Lake Lure fire chief, who had to know that his turn was coming. If the fire reached the homes in the resort or Boys Camp Road, it would be his job to protect them.

She turned to leave and bumped into what felt like a wall. Mike smiled down on her. Covered in soot and reeking of smoke, he clutched a coffee cup like it was holding him together. She felt his exhaustion as if it were part of the atmosphere connecting them.

"You gotta go home and get some sleep," he said to her.

"I know. Morgan already told me."

She stood there, and for the first time since she saw the smoke plume, the enormity of the past twenty-four hours struck her. The suppressed fear of something happening to the brave men battling an obstinate fire on a treacherous mountain suddenly surfaced, and tears flowed freely down her cheeks.

He put an arm around her and pulled her close.

"Do you have a way home?"

"No. They want me to leave the brush truck. I'll get someone to give me a lift."

"That someone's gonna be me."

The drive to her house gave Annie an ethereal feeling. The smoke was so thick they could only see a few dozen yards ahead. Too tired to talk and ready to crash on the first flat surface they came across, neither of them spoke. He pulled off Boys Camp, drove up her road and stopped at her house. The lights were on and the dogs were yapping.

Mike tapped his fingers on the steering wheel for a moment, then turned to her. "How about that kiss you promised me?"

"Are you kidding? I barely have the strength to breathe."

He slumped back in his seat. "Me, too." Then he grinned at her. "But I'd still like one."

She groaned, gave his hand a squeeze, then opened her door and stumbled out.

"We're going to be backburning on Boys Camp tomorrow night," he hollered after her, "and you'll be evacuated. So when you get up in the morning, start packing."

THE SECOND NIGHT of what the North Carolina Forest Service officially named the Party Rock Fire was coming to a close with Chase and his crew fighting to hold their lines up on the mountain; Ferrell and Morgan trying to catch a couple of hours of sleep in their trucks; and the district head, Dan Brandon, back in Mt. Holly feverishly generating new maps for the morning. The firefighters lucky enough to live nearby went home to a hot shower and a warm bed, while the Forest Service rangers that had come from the district's nine counties snored in their trucks or lay curled up in sleeping bags on the side of the mountain.

Day Three

M onday, November 7, 4 a.m. ANNIE TURNED ON TERRI'S light and went over to her bed.

"Get up. We're leaving."

Terri sat up, looking incredulous. "What time is it?"

"Four. I'm taking you to my mother's. We're going to be evacuated sometime today."

"But my things?"

"I brought some boxes up. They're in the hall. Pack what you can."

"What about your stuff?"

"My office and all my equipment are already in your truck. I let you sleep as long as I could. I'm gonna go down and make you coffee and then we've got to go."

"What about the dogs?"

"I called my mother. The dogs are fine and so is Blackie. She's expecting us."

"But last night you told me everything was going to be all right."

Annie threw open Terri's covers. "I didn't want to worry you. Now get up! I've got to get you safely settled at my mother's, then I've got to get back to the command center before the crews start rolling in."

"Let me stay. This house has been here forever. Nothing's gonna happen."

Annie sank onto the bed and looked Terri sternly in the eye. "This fire is bad, Terri. It's acting funny and it's spreading. They're not saying anything, but I can tell they're worried. If it gets away from them and reaches into the gorge, all we'll need is one really big wind event and we can lose everything. I mean everything! All of Chimney Rock, Lake Lure. You haven't been here when we get what the Indians used to call the 'long winds.' But I've lived in this gorge my whole life and I've heard them howl for hours. And if it heads for the resort..."

"Did you get any sleep?" asked Terri.

"A couple hours. I had to get my office stuff packed and notify my supervisor. These guys are short-handed and I got permission to stay on for the duration of the fire."

Terri got up and went to the window. She pulled aside the curtains and looked out at the blazing mountain in the distance.

"Oh, my God!" she moaned.

"Hurry."

Annie rushed down the stairs to make another pot of coffee and her eyes landed on the deed over the fireplace. How could she have overlooked it!? She wrapped it in a towel and started to carry it to the truck. Then she thought of the book she had borrowed from Mike all those years ago. She rushed over and got it from the bookcase in the living room, and took both of them to the truck.

For the next half-hour, the two bustled in and out of the house with Terri's things, and just as Annie turned the key to the truck's ignition, Terri hollered out, "I forgot the dog food!"

"Go to the store and buy some. We've got to get outta here."

Annie raced Terri's truck down the road to Boys Camp and noticed the smoke had gotten even heavier. It wasn't five yet, but as she passed the entrance to the park's hiking trails and looked through the smoky haze, she saw a bulldozer being rolled off the ramp of a giant truck.

She swerved around a curve, exposing the orange blaze on the mountain above them, and for the umpteenth time, Terri moaned, *"Oh, my God."*

Annie reached 74A and turned into Chimney Rock. Someone had set up a huge portable digital sign that read "Dense Smoke Possible." As she passed the entrance to the Chimney Rock State Park on Main Street, she could see the cell tower on wheels Verizon had donated to temporarily boost the area's cell phone capability. Then, as she took the turn onto Route 64 in Bat

Cave, she was surprised to see the smoke was almost as dense three miles away. She pulled up to her mother's house and saw Jack's truck. Good; he could drive her to the fire station to get hers.

Annie jumped out, grabbed Blackie's carrier and raced to the front door her mother held open. Jack appeared, rumpled and half asleep.

"My office stuff has to come out. Put it in my old room," Annie told him.

Terri came through the doorway, and Jack gave her a big wink and tossed his head toward Annie. "I see she's in one of her devil-may-care moods."

Terri giggled. In spite of being awakened in the middle of the night, she seemed to be enjoying the excitement. As Annie and Jack scurried in and out with Annie's equipment, Mae made friends with Terri who was cuddling her dogs in her arms.

Mae cradled Terri's face in her hands. "You're just as darling as Annie said you were." She looked over at Jack who was toting a huge box. "Isn't she darling, Jack? And those two adorable dogs."

"They'll come in handy, Mom. You can have them dust the floors for you."

Mae tossed her hand at Terri. "He's always joking around like that."

Annie came in with a box of laptops and rushed to her room. She came out saying, "That's it, Jack. Now you've got to take me to Lake Lure to get my truck."

He grinned at Terri. "What else is there to do at five in the morning?"

As Jack drove down 74A, he asked, "Have you heard anything about who they think started the fire?"

"We're so overwhelmed fighting it, we're not even thinking about that yet."

"Maybe you're not, but you can bet the police are."

"That's something I want to talk to you about," said Annie. "Since it's on state property, the Forest Service's law enforcement division is going to take over the investigation."

"You're kidding."

"No, I'm not. I work for the state, remember? They'll definitely be called in to investigate it at some point."

"Damn!"

"Don't overreact, Jack. It may be a good thing. Maybe they'll find out who did this faster."

She reached over and squeezed his hand. "You'll get through this like you have in the past. They're gonna catch whoever did it, and you'll be in the clear."

Jack took the curve in Lake Lure, swung into a parking space facing the lake and the fire raging along the ridge, and slammed on the brakes.

"Jack, this is no time to sit and watch the fire. You've got to take me to my truck. You can watch it on your way back."

"Hold on, Sis. I have to tell you something."

"What?"

"It's about the fire."

"Have the police called you already?"

"No."

"Jack, I'm needed over there. So, whatever you have to say, please say it."

"It's nothing, really. It's just... forget it. It's nothing."

She hugged him. "Hang in there, Jack. I'm sure it's going to be okay."

He took her to her truck and as she drove back to the base, the thought of her brother facing another grilling made her shiver. She would never forget all the times someone had come to the door and taken him in for questioning. Every time there was a fire—anywhere or any kind—the whole family would brace themselves and wait for him to be hauled away.

She made the curve around the lake and just like her brother, abruptly pulled into a parking space facing the lake. She stared at the leaping orange swath writhing in the darkness of the night that a lot of the guys called a dragon and remembered how her mother, while telling her a fairytale, had said they never died. Is this one going to be like that? she wondered.

She should get going, but she couldn't take her mind off her brother. He was four years older than her, yet here she was, playing the role of the big sister. She'd escaped the hellish life the two of them had been trapped in as kids; it was so unfair that Jack hadn't. Why couldn't they forgive him? He was only ten. That was over twenty-five years ago. Was it the ghastly way old Sam Boswell met his end? No. They knew he was dead well before the fire hit him.

She rested her head on the window and thought back to all the times she had wrapped her arms around her brother and tried to comfort him as he quivered in fear. She was the only one he ever let see him that way, and it always stunned her when he would put on an air of swaggering *braggadocio* whenever he'd describe his interrogations to his mother. But even that didn't last long. It only took until he was in his late teens for the cloud of suspicion that always hung over him to break his spirit; and once it did, he was never the same.

She put her truck in reverse and thought that her brother's plight was probably why she latched onto fighting for bats—one of the most misunderstood underdogs of the animal world.

BY NOW, THE AIR QUALITY had gotten so bad that Ferrell decided to hold the Monday morning briefing in the trailer with the doors closed, since it had a filter system that would keep out the smoke. His boss walked in the door with new maps and plans, and Ferrell waited for him to get a cup of coffee from the mess tent before he got started. The trailer was packed with local officials, Forest Service folks, and a couple of rangers from the State Park who had a lot of knowledge of the terrain. Everyone studied the huge new topographic maps outlining the fire's perimeter as he taped them to the walls.

His boss walked in with his coffee, and Ferrell started the briefing.

"The fire grew to approximately sixty acres last night, so today we'll put everyone out to construct fire containment lines around its perimeter. At this time, no homes or structures are under threat, and although the fire is still actively burning, we anticipate minimal growth this shift.

"Weather permitting, we will be backburning along Boys Camp and Carsons Road tonight to stop its eastern and northern movement, using the two roads as firebreaks. This will increase the footprint of the fire to 300 acres and for the first time, extend beyond State-owned lands to private property. You're gonna see a lot of smoke as the interior of the fire keeps burning, and it's going to get even heavier tomorrow morning after the Boys Camp Road burnout. Remember, folks, our goal for the day is to hold our containment lines. Stay safe."

THROUGHOUT THE DAY, ANNIE kept one eye on her clipboard and one eye on the cliffs as she logged people in. Not only was she hearing that the fire was spreading out on both sides and crawling down to Boys Camp, she could actually see it. She was planning on working until the night crew was logged in, but around six, with the day crew off the mountain, she temporarily turned her post over to a volunteer who had been helping her, and dashed over to the trailer for the evening briefing. She could tell the situation had turned serious by the pattern of Ferrell's speech, direct and concise.

"This afternoon, we really put our backs to holding our containment lines, but the fire jumped it. As a result, it spread beyond the 60 acres and is moving north toward some areas of Rumbling Bald Resort. Between 45 and 50 houses in the areas of Quail Ridge and Huntington Road are now at risk of burning and residents in those areas are now being notified that they may have to evacuate in the next 24 to 48 hours. If evacuations take place, they'll be notified door to door and will need to leave immediately. Meanwhile, our helicopters are continuing to drop water on the fire.

"Lake Lure has declared a State of Emergency. This will initiate the town's emergency action plan and allow for evacuations and restriction of access to the area."

He went over to the briefing map and pointed to the area bordered by Boys Camp and Carsons roads. "As I mentioned this morning, tonight we will commence a wide-scale burnout of this area to secure our south line."

The evening briefing over, Annie studied the list taped to the side of the trailer naming the crews that would be doing the night's burnout on Boys Camp Road. Seeing Mike named as the burn boss, she hurried back to her check-in position, hoping she hadn't missed him.

As tired as she was, the sight of his truck pulling in excited her, and for the first time that day, she actually walked with a bounce.

"I logged you in," she said as she approached his window.

"Good. Thanks. Don't forget to add that I've brought three drip torches." He waved and took off across the lot.

Bruce Button, the retiree with the Billy Graham Response Team who had been helping her, must have read her mind.

"Don't be disappointed that he didn't stop to talk with you, sweetheart. He's preoccupied."

"That's not like me to forget to get his equipment listed."

"Don't beat yourself up over it. From what I understand, every girl in the county is setting their cap for that boy."

"Bruce, I hope you don't think I'm one of them."

"They're counting on him tonight. Fire burns faster uphill, so it's going to be a challenge. But don't you worry none about that boy. I've been in classes he's taught. He knows what he'd doing and he's gonna be fine."

Embarrassed, Annie threw her shoulders back and waited for the next truck to pull up.

Day Four

Tuesday, November 8, Presidential Election Day. THE RESI-
DENTS OF LAKE LURE and Chimney Rock had gone to bed
on edge the night before; not frightened, just on edge. The smoke
had been in the air for days and fire trucks had been zooming up
and down 74A. But other than for the folks who had been evacuated from Boys Camp Road, life in those two little towns had
been going on as usual. Tourists still streamed in and out of the
stores on Main Street in Chimney Rock, the staff at the Lake
Lure Inn was busy preparing for a Saturday wedding, and the
year-round residents in the resort were still teeing off at one of
their two golf courses.

But as the townspeople slept in their snug beds at 4:30 that
morning, Ferrell and Brandon trudged in the chilly night to the
mess tent to get another cup of coffee. They'd just finished talking with Mike and, confident his burnout crews had gotten rid of
enough fuel to keep the fire from jumping over Boys Camp
Road, they decided to have the evacuation lifted that day for residents only.

Portable light towers gave the densely smoky lot a bizarre
appearance with shadowy figures of firemen taking off their gear,
logging off and pulling out. The two commanders thanked a couple of firefighters who came in the tent to grab some water, then
they went back to the trailer to start making plans. They had to
project where the fire would go, how the weather would impact
it, what resources they had, what did they need, what was coming in, what was going out.

Suddenly, the urgency in Chase's voice over the radio made
them both stop and listen intently.

"A huge snag just fell off the cliff and landed across our fire line north of Carsons Road! The fire's moving fast! There's no point chasing it. We're not gonna catch it."

"This is it! This fire's going big!" exclaimed Ferrell. He grabbed a map and pointed to a zigzagged line on the western edge of the resort. "Carsons is our trigger point. If we're gonna get in front of it now, we're gonna have to fall back to this line Morgan came up with in the resort and set a backfire. We've got to connect all these roads in there and use them as a firebreak. I've started a 'dozer digging this checkline, but he hasn't reached the resort yet."

"Aren't there houses on the fire side of that line?" asked Brandon.

"Morgan said there's twenty-five. He plans to put engines in front of every house while we burn off everything around them."

"What are our chances of losing some?"

"I'm pretty sure we're gonna end up sacrificing a few. If we're battling strong winds, once they start on fire we're just going to have to let them burn and go on to the next one. We're not going to risk any firefighter's life."

Just then, Morgan walked in. He was rumpled and his face was flushed. He'd been sleeping in his truck when Chase's report woke him.

"We're falling back to your line at the resort," said Ferrell. "The fire's reaching around the side of the mountain and going right for it. The only way we're gonna stop it is if we burn out all the fuel in front of it before it gets there."

He pointed to the line on the map. "Our 'dozer has gotten up to here on that cockamamie plan you came up with. But darn, if it isn't gonna work! Once he's done connecting all the roads in there, we're gonna have our firebreak." He looked at Morgan. "This burnout's got to happen tonight."

"Those houses have to be prepped first," Brandon told Morgan. "If you want, we can bring back Thompson to show your guys how to do it."

"Tell Thompson I'll have my team ready for him this morning at nine," Morgan said as he started to leave. "Meanwhile, I'll go set up a command post in the resort and start lining up the engine crews for tonight."

Morgan left and Ferrell looked at his boss. "Even if we're lucky tonight and keep the fire from running through that resort, the way this fire is burning, it's gonna keep moving north and clawing its way around toward those two hundred houses. I've done all I can do, Dan. This fire is exceeding my Type 3 Incident Commander capacity. I don't have the authority to order what we're gonna need to combat this thing. You gotta call Raleigh and get a Type 2 team in here."

"You've been doing a good job wearing a lot of hats, Ferrell, but I agree with you. When it's impossible to change hats fast enough, that's when you gotta go to the next level."

One hour later, Ferrell, Brandon and Chase were about to leave the trailer for the morning briefing when Brandon got a call from the Raleigh office.

"Dan, we got your order for a Type 2 Team. Every IC team in the state is scattered to the winds. They've been broken up and dispatched to fires all over the western part of the state or to Hurricane Matthew. We're stretched so thin we're just going to have to throw one together.

"Since you're there, stay on as the Type 2 IC, Ferrell stays as the ops chief, and Chase as the night ops chief. We'll make up the rest of the team from here. If we have to, we'll bring people in from outside the state. We've made arrangements to use the town hall and dispatched a logistics guy. He should be over there this afternoon to start setting you up."

Brandon had put his phone on speaker, and when he hung up, Ferrell took off his cap, ran his fingers through his sandy colored hair, then reset his cap on his head. "I guess this means I'm sticking around."

The command team came out of the trailer, and Ferrell went over to the briefing map taped to its side and looked out at everyone. The crew leaders had been listening to the radio and knew they were headed for a new strategy, but the public officials and press sat unaware of the dramatic pivot the fire had just taken.

"We lost our north fire line early this morning and the houses in the Rumbling Bald Resort are now at risk," he said.

He pointed to the map. "We backburned all along Boys Camp and Carsons Road last night and are confident we've stopped its southeastern movement. With that burnout, the fire's footprint is now at 300 acres.

"Slope effect winds are contributing to the way this fire's moving and is pushing it north toward two of the resort's subdivisions.

"We'll be conducting burnouts there tonight while we fight to hold our other established lines. Ron Morgan, Lake Lure's fire chief, is now heading up this fire's structural protection division since houses are now threatened. He will be conducting fire protection in the resort tonight as the burnouts commence.

"We've called for a Type 2 Incident Management Team that can bring resources in from all over the country. They will be transitioning in tomorrow." He pointed to Brandon. "Dan Brandon, our District 12 head, will take over as the Incident Commander Wednesday morning and operate from the town hall's community room."

LATE THAT AFTERNOON, Thompson got a call from Brandon. He had crashed on his couch when he came back to his office at the Rutherford County Airport after showing Morgan's team how to pre-treat the houses, and after working a fire the night before.

"How did everything go at the resort?" Brandon asked.

"Morgan had his guys there and I showed them how to pre-treat the first house. We cut every bush and shrub to the ground, dropped every tree, cleaned the gutters, blew the leaves away from the house, the porches, out from under the porches, and dragged it all away. Then I told them to do the rest of them the same way."

"The fire's coming around that mountain pretty fast right now," said Brandon. "We figure it's grown another 50 acres since this morning. Evacuations in the resort are underway, and our bulldozer's been working on that firebreak all day."

"Do you think he can get it done by tonight?"

"Our 'dozer guy called me just a while ago and said there

were a couple of big boulders in the way. I told him to push them aside. Do what you have to do, I told him. We'll fix everything later. If we have to pay for anything, we'll pay for it, but you got to get that line in so we can burn tonight or we could lose the whole resort."

Brandon was quiet for a moment, then said, "I know you're worn out from fighting the Chestnut Ridge fire, Doug, but I'm gonna ask you to run the burnout tonight. You know that mountain better than anyone."

"Dan, you're setting me up to be either the hero or the goat. One or the other," said Doug. He thought for a moment. "You know, once we set that backfire tonight, the die is going to be pretty well cast. This fire's going to make a 90 degree turn, go up Rumbling Bald Mountain and over the top, then make a beeline for Shumont."

"We know. We've ordered hand crews and strike crews from all over the country. Hopefully, they'll be flying in here in the next couple of days. Doug, you're the best man for this job tonight. You drew up the pre-attack plan for that area, so you don't have to go through the process of thinking everything through. We're giving you a bridge crew and a burn boss. What do you say?"

"Okay, I'll grab a couple more hours of sleep here on the couch and get back over there by seven."

BY THE END OF THE day shift, the Boys Camp base was being dismantled and the command moved to the Lake Lure Town Hall. Starting that night, the wildland firefighters would be tracked by the new command, and the structure firefighters by Morgan's division.

Annie felt a little torn after bonding with the Forest Service team the way she had, especially Mike. On and off all day, she thought about him as she raced around in an ATV or a truck, handing out water, sandwiches and snacks to the wildland firefighters on the lines. When Morgan mentioned that Mike and his crew hadn't finished the Boys Camp burnout until 4:30 that morning, she made up her mind to make him dinner that night.

She had spent the previous night at her mother's, and the home-cooked dinner had gone a long way to ease her bone-deep tiredness.

Finished logging out the last firefighter to come down from the mountain, she rushed to the smoke-filled library to vote, then stopped by the grocery store. Since they were letting residents back on Boys Camp, she ran home, took a shower and changed before driving over to Mike's house.

His truck was parked at an angle in front of the basement door as if he didn't have the strength to walk an extra step. She gathered the food and went into the basement laundry room. His brush pants and shirt lay in a heap on the floor next to blackened boots, and the room reeked of smoke. She made her way into the hall and started up the wide carpeted staircase ahead.

"Mike, it's me, Annie," she called out.

She took the steps, listening for a response.

"It's me, Mike. I've come to make you dinner."

He suddenly appeared at the head of the stairs in a pair of jeans and a pullover, his hair mussed like he'd just gotten up.

She rose to the top step and started toward the kitchen. He blocked her way by leaning against the wall with an arm.

"Be nice. I'm here to make you a decent meal," she said.

"Not until I get that kiss you promised me."

She looked him in the eye and raised an eyebrow. "I'm saving that for dessert."

She put her hand on his chest, pushed him back and headed for the kitchen.

"You're a hard woman, Miss Annie."

She went over to the stove and turned on the gas grill. "I'd give my right arm for a stove like this," she said as she took the food out, "and I bet you haven't cooked on it once." She washed the squash and tomatoes and put them on the grill, then took out the salmon steaks, placed a sprig of rosemary on them and put them aside.

"Do you have any bread?" she asked as he uncorked a bottle of wine. He motioned toward the fridge with the bottle, then poured two glasses. She picked one up and took a gulp.

"I needed that."

By the time she put the salmon on the grill, she had drunk the entire glass. She finished setting the table in the kitchen, found two candles and struck a match.

"Please, don't," said Mike. "I'd rather eat with as little light as possible."

"I'm sorry. I wasn't thinking," she said as she blew out the flame. "Your eyes must be irritated after all that burning and smoke last night."

Once they sat down, Annie was pleased to see the way Mike was enjoying the meal, and she started to unwind.

"Tomorrow the Type 2 team's going to be setting up in the town hall," she said. "In fact, they're tearing down the Boys Camp base as we speak. I'll probably be assigned to the structural division tomorrow." She ran a finger around the rim of her glass. "I'm gonna miss working with those guys."

"Not as much as they're gonna miss working with you. They were telling us that every fire needs an Annie. Evidently, you've been a big help." He shook his head. "I don't know where they're going to get the crews they're gonna need to fight this thing. The whole Southeast is burning. The western fire season is over, so a lot of those people are laid off or doing something else."

"Then where are they going to get them from?"

He helped himself to another piece of bread. "Alaska... all over the country. That's the beauty of NIMS."

"NIMS?"

"Yeah. The National Incident Management System," he said as he spread on some butter. "After 9/11, FEMA took a look at our ability to handle a national crisis and absorbed the National Wildfire Coordinating Group that had been around for over fifty years and rolled it into NIMS. Now, everyone in the country gets the same training. That's the beauty of it. You can get a guy from Alaska and he comes with a red card that says he's qualified and certified for a specific job.

"He'll understand his place in the organization and what he's supposed to do. That way, there's no territorial type issue. They know what their space is and they stay in it. That way you don't have a lot of drama going on. Plus, they know everybody else's job, so if they need something, they know who to go to. They don't become needy. That's important in an emergency situation. You don't want a lot of needy people around."

The dinner finished, Annie felt groggy from a second glass of wine, so she cleared the table and put on some coffee.

She finished pouring Mike a cup, when he grasped her hand and looked up at her. "Is it time for dessert yet?"

She strolled over to the window and looked out. "I've reconsidered that."

"Oh, no, you don't. That's not fair."

She turned and fixed her eyes on him. "It may not be fair, but it's sensible. We're both in a very emotional state right now; or at least, I am." She let out a wry little laugh. "Today, in the grocery store I ran into the lady who lives at the foot of my road and we flew into each other's arms and broke down crying."

She folded her arms and leaned back against the wall. "When this is all over...."

"I know. Then I'm gonna get my kiss."

"Mike, this whole thing is strange to me. I keep telling myself it can't be happening. Things like this just happen out west. This fire's such an unbelievable force. And it's happening in such a dangerous place. I feel like I've been snatched up into another world and there's no way out. A world of fire."

"It'll end," he said as he came next to her. He gently brushed a wisp of hair from her face. "We always win. We either put it out, or nature does it for us."

She could tell by the way she had to keep battling back tears that she had to get out of there before she fell apart.

"I've got to get home and get some sleep," she said.

She pushed herself from the wall to leave, and had to hold onto him to steady herself.

He gripped her shoulders and said, "I don't think you're in any shape to drive. You've had way too much to drink." He brushed his lips across her forehead and whispered, "And I think we could both use that dessert."

"*O..kay,* you can have *one* kiss, and then I've got to get outta here."

He started to take her in his arms and saw a tear trickling down her cheek. He gently wiped it away. "You poor kid; you're exhausted."

She put her arms around him and pressed her cheek against his chest, then let the dam she'd been holding in for the past four days burst.

"When you were up on the mountain Monday night all I could think about was how much you mean to your parents." She wept like her heart would break, then drew in a long, pitiful breath. "If your mother only knew what you were up to. And all the other men. It's so dangerous." He could barely make out what she was saying. "I've loved you since forever... and now all the girls in Rutherford County are setting their caps for you."

He threw his head back and let out a little laugh, then caressed her head with his hand. "I doubt all of them are."

She hung onto him and quietly wept.

"You certainly can't hold your liquor, sweetheart," he said as he picked her up with a deep grunt. "And being severely sleep deprived isn't helping much, either." He carried her up the stairs and into his room, then gently lay her on his bed. She curled up sniffling and hugging a pillow. He found a quilt and tenderly covered her. He stood there and watched her fall asleep, thinking she was still the spunky little kid who insisted on carrying a pail that was too heavy for her.

THAT NIGHT, THOMPSON DROVE down Boys Camp Road with Roger Hollifield, the county emergency management head who'd he had worked with on dozens of fires, then he swung a left onto Carsons Road and drove up to the dead-end. To his left was the now torn up logging road that led up to the Party Rock, and ahead, the freshly gouged out firebreak that the bulldozer had made going toward the resort. He drove onto it and the truck bumped and thumped all the way to the resort's threatened subdivisions. The whole area looked like a war zone, especially where their 'dozer driver had gouged around the houses.

A fire engine sat next to each of the twenty-five houses that lay within the burn side of the line. They had come from near and far to save the resort—McDowell, Rutherford, Polk, Henderson, Broad River, Lake Lure, Chimney Rock—and tonight, they'd be in a caldron.

Seeing the 'dozer driver standing next to his huge machine, Thompson went over and said, "I drove the whole way. The checkline looks good."

The driver clutched the back of his neck and shook his head. "I had to do some crazy stuff to connect these roads together; things no one should ever do. But the boss man made it pretty clear I had to do whatever it took."

Then Thompson strolled over to Morgan. "I see you finished prepping the houses. They look pretty clean."

"The Rumbling Bald maintenance folks helped. We couldn't have done it without them."

"Good. Let's go. I want to talk to every company before we start."

They went over to an engine from Polk County. Morgan started with a safety message, then Thompson said, "There's going to be pretty strong winds tonight, so we're gonna take our time and be careful. Since fire moves uphill faster than it moves downhill, we're going to take the houses one at a time, starting at the top and working our way down. That means we're going to be skipping around, instead of just going door to door. My convict crew will be doing the burning at my direction. And don't worry about having enough water. The command's been working with the water system folks to make sure you'll have as much as you need."

After Thompson had met with the fire companies, they waited until dark when the humidity went up, then started on the highest house. The men on the convict crew were fully equipped with wildfire gear. Each one carried a shovel and a drip torch. The canister was filled with fuel and once the tip of the wand was set afire, as the canister was tipped, the wand spread fuel and ignited the ground. They burned around the house going fifty feet out, and started downhill to the next one, leaving the fire department to make sure the fire was out.

Around one a.m., the wind picked up and the situation suddenly became critical. The firefighters flew into a frantic non-stop scramble to keep the flames off the houses and burning them to the ground.

Spending twenty minutes or so at each house, by two in the morning, Thompson's crew had five houses to go when Morgan shouted over the radio, "Stop! We got one on fire!"

The wind had sent an ember up on a pile of leaves on the roof of the last house they had finished and set it on fire. While the firemen attacked it, Thompson got his first chance to take a look at Rumbling Bald Mountain. Just like he had predicted, their backfire had made a 90 degree turn and raced up the mountain and gone right over the top. Trees tumbled and rumbled off the rock cliffs. Huge standing dead snags blazed like giant candles, and flames leapt ten to twelve feet in the air along a 400-foot stretch of horizon. It was an incredible sight.

They put the roof fire out, and the bridge crew began burning around the houses again, finishing around four in the morning. The exhausted firemen were unhooking their water lines, putting away their gear and starting to leave when Brandon's truck pulled up. He and Ferrell jumped out and shook firemen's hands as they made their way toward Thompson and Morgan.

Reaching them, Brandon said, "Your men are to be congratulated on the job they did tonight."

Thompson looked over at Morgan. "When I did my pre-plan last year, I figured, to save the resort and do the greatest good for the greatest number of people, we'd have to do structural triage. It's a miracle we didn't lose one house tonight. There's no doubt we would have without the kind of effort your guys put out."

Morgan bent his head for a moment, filled with emotion. He finally looked up and said, "Once those winds kicked up, it was touch and go all the way."

The four men cut a solemn silhouette against the blazing orange mountain as they silently looked on, knowing it was just a matter of time before the fire ran down the backside of the Rumbling Bald Mountain and started up Shumont, towering above it.

Brandon finally spoke. "Those hotshot teams from the northwest can't get here soon enough."

Day Five

Wednesday, November 9. WHEN A TYPE 2 TEAM PULLS IN, it's not just an Incident Commander who takes over, it's an entire entourage of trained, highly qualified personnel pulled in by the North Carolina Forest Service from all over the state to manage the team's four divisions.

The operations division takes care of the management of the fire, the planning division figures out what resources are going to be needed for the next operational period, logistics gets these resources and takes care of them once they get there, and finance pays for everything.

That morning as the sun rose, the Type 2 Team started rolling in and installing their standard set-up in the town hall's community room. The logistics guy had already scoped it out and found the space wasn't big enough, so they took a couple of the town hall offices and set up two tents behind the building, one for briefings and the other for their public information team.

AFTER THE BURNOUT AT THE RESORT, Morgan grabbed a shower and a couple hours of sleep in the station house and was now on his way back in for an early morning meeting. As he pulled into the smoke-hazed town center, a fireman was asleep in a hammock strung from two crepe myrtles on the roadway, and three more slept on cots on the lawn. The sun had almost risen, and across the lake, threatening orange flames crouched on the cliffs, ready to devour everything in its path.

He hurried into the command center through the side door. Everything was in full swing inside and he was surprised by the swiftness of the Forest Service's move-in. He poured himself a coffee on his way to the conference room. The whole management team was in there, along with emergency management people from all three counties, listening to the Forest Service's fire behavior specialist soberly project the fire's path. The specialist pointed to the perimeter line on a map taped to the wall.

"The fire is now almost 400 acres and we expect it to spread northwest on Rumbling Bald Mountain in the next 24 hours."

The fire chief from Broad River interrupted him.

"The projections we've been getting from you guys have been way off. This fire's been moving a lot faster than what you've been telling us."

"We know. We had been putting the information that made sense to us into the computer model; the type of fuel we had, the weather conditions. But the fire was moving faster than the model projected, so we started playing with it yesterday afternoon. We kept changing the fuel type, and by the time we got the computer model and the actual fire to match up, we were using the fuel type they have in southwestern California. That's the way this fire is burning, just like in Montecito."

Morgan listened to the fire behavior specialist's report feeling more alert and keyed up than he thought possible. At the start, with all the crews, helicopters and 'dozers they had attacking the fire, he had actually thought they would catch it. He knew they'd be going at it for days, but he was thinking for a few days.

As the fire chief of a town surrounded by mountains and forests, he couldn't help but have the specter of a devastating fire that would wipe everything out steal into his thoughts every time the fire season rolled around, and after listening to the Forest Service's predictions, he began to ask himself, 'Is this it?'

He quickly decided he couldn't keep gathering up extra crews day after day, night after night, and county after county to protect the houses in his district if this thing was going to get as big as they were predicting. He had to ask the North Carolina Fire Marshal's office for help. All the fire companies in the state were registered with them and they knew what fire departments had already been deployed to the fires raging all over the mountains, and therefore knew what emergency management people they could ask for more engine companies and brush trucks. They could also send field personnel to help manage these resources as crew and strike team leaders.

The meeting over, he left the command center with Roger Hollifield, the Rutherford County Emergency Management director who had been helping him pull in crews.

Morgan turned to him in the parking lot and said, "What do you think? Should we call the Fire Marshal and ask for fifty engines?"

Roger tossed up a hand. "Hey, we gotta start somewhere."

"Okay," said Morgan. "Make the call and get us fifty Type 1 engines with four-person crews." Morgan shook his head and thought for a moment. "You know," he said to the director, "I never in my entire career thought that I would be ordering fifty engine companies at one time."

"There's very few fire chiefs in the country that have ordered that many," said Roger, "except probably in California. By the way, you better find somewhere for these guys to stay. It's gonna get cold and they can't keep sleeping on the ground or on cots in the open like they've been doing. Call State Emergency Management and the Charlotte Emergency Task Force. They've got big commercial Western Shelter tents that can house your people."

Morgan said goodbye and hurried over to the station house to put in the calls. By now, everyone knew that the Party Rock Fire was the biggest in the state and they readily promised him tents by Saturday.

ANNIE SUDDENLY SAT UP in bed, panting. The nightmare was still fresh in her mind. She could see herself running along the ridge, tripping on rocks and slashing her knees with a fire-breathing dragon clawing at her heels. She looked around the darkened room and it took her a moment to get her aching head wrapped around where she was. Spotting the clock on Mike's bedside table telling her it was almost four, she got up and slipped quietly out of the house. Driving home, she recalled firefighters referring to fires as dragons, and she began fearing this one would become a North Carolina legend.

Once home, she listened to the message Morgan had left on

her phone and smiled to herself. He had officially loaned her to the Forest Service command to help secure local resources, and she was to report to them that morning.

She put on a Wildlife Resources Commission shirt and grabbed a cap with their logo. For some odd reason, she wanted the state's Wildlife Resources Commission represented as aiding in this struggle, even if it were only for one day.

The Lake Lure Fire Department's trailer was now parked near the entrance to the town hall, and several firefighters stood studying the maps taped to its side. Annie walked into the town hall's community room that was buzzing with activity when the logistics guy noticed her and waved her over.

"Are you the go-to girl for getting local resources they've been telling me about?" he asked.

She nodded.

"We need you to lock in as many rooms as you can and we need to know how many beds they've got. We're working with twelve-hour operational periods and planning on two people for the same bed, rotating them out every shift."

Someone needing help came over and asked him a question. As he started off, he gave Annie a quick glance over his shoulder. "Once you line them up, shoot the information over to me and I'll take it from there."

She found a chair at one of the tables lining both sides of the room and started making calls on her cell. A guy taped a big hand-written sign reading "Check In" onto the edge of a table next to the door as people scurried in with computers and office equipment, seeming to know exactly where they needed to go.

The Lake Lure Inn was the first place Annie thought of for rooms, but the manager wasn't going to be in for another hour.

She grabbed a phone book and began calling every motel in the area, then every vacation rental place she knew of. She dialed the first one. They had four cabins on the lake.

"Hello, I'm Annie Simms and I'm calling for the Forest Ser-vice..."

"Yes! You can have everything I've got."

Annie took down the information and mentioned that the

Forest Service paid standard rates, and someone would contact them. As she continued to call, she kept getting the same emotional response. She couldn't get the request out of her mouth before they offered to provide rooms. It touched her to her core. These people didn't know any of the folks that would be using their cherished, pampered vacation cabins, but there were no questions asked. They just jumped at a chance to help.

A woman plopped a laptop and a briefcase down on the other end of the table. Annie finished a call and looked over at her. The woman smiled, saying she was heading up the finance division and had flown in from Florida the night before.

Annie made another call to Patrick Bryant, the general manager of the Lake Lure Inn, and was put on hold. While she waited, she watched two men at the next table set up a big computer screen.

Behind them, a printer that had to be four feet wide sat on its own coffin-like box.

Noticing Annie's interest, the woman from finance said, "The one with the beard is our G.I.S. guy, a Global Information Systems specialist. He makes up any kind of map you could possibly think of—progression maps, fire, weather, zoom-ins on structures from Google Earth, you name it." She pointed to the huge printer. "And he prints them out on that thing."

The hotel's general manager finally picked up.

"How many rooms can you give us?" Annie asked.

"We've got a lot of evacuees staying with us, but I'm pretty sure I can come up with fifty."

"Good. Let us know how many beds."

THEY'D BEEN SMELLING smoke at the Full Moon Farm Wolfdog Sanctuary up in the Shumont Mountains for five days now, and the woman who ran it was beginning to get nervous. And that was saying a lot, for Nancy Brown had conquered a plethora of professional and personal challenges in her sixty-two years; plus anyone who would take on building a wolfdog rescue from scratch in what a lot of people would consider the wilderness isn't easily frightened.

She called down to the Broad River Fire Station from her home a short distance from the sanctuary, and they assured her they would give her plenty of time if it looked like the sanctuary was in danger. Nonetheless, with seventy-five wolfdogs currently at the preserve, she'd better start getting the place staged for an evacuation in the event things did go bad.

She pulled onto the gravel road that led to the sanctuary's 17-acre chunk of mountain. Large fenced enclosures were tucked into the rolling terrain, mostly underneath huge poplar and ash trees. Others were sprinkled along a maze of grassy paths. As she pulled in, the wolfdogs recognized her truck and let out long, mournful howls, setting off a welcoming chorus. She got out of her truck and took a minute to gaze at the cemetery adjacent to the grassy field they used for parking and camping. Over one hundred small mounds had rocks carefully piled on top with lovingly painted names on the grave markers.

As usual, volunteers raced around doing their morning chores, filling the buckets in every enclosure with fresh water and more feed, and scooping up poop.

Nancy knew every wolfdog by name and temperament. Most of them came into her hands through the efforts of wolfdog rescues, animal control or wildlife agencies, either seized because of abuse or neglect, confiscated as illegal, or picked up running at large. A few had been given up by owners who could no longer care for them.

Her heart went out to these creatures bred by man for their "woofy" characteristics. Their wolf content ran the gamut from 95% to less than 10. Mostly wolf mixed with German Shepherd, Alaskan Malamute or Siberian Husky, the majority of them only had memories of bewildering human expectations, emotions, and cruelty. Many of them, who were products of home breeders looking to make easy money from "wolf puppies," ended up spending their lives in abusive situations, or in squalor without adequate food, or as failed guard dogs, forgotten in the back yard or locked in a shed.

She waved to the volunteers as she hurried down the winding lane to the house she used to live in and now functioned as an office. She had to find a place to take the wolfdogs if they had to evacuate, and then enough crates to get them there.

AFTER LISTENING TO the command team's predictions all day, Morgan was convinced that the fire was about to explode, and as the third planning meeting of the day wrapped up, he faced the fact that he wouldn't be able to go the distance with a couple hours of sleep in his truck or at the station every night and decided to get on the same twelve hour duty shift as the wildfire guys. He would take the day shift and his assistant the night shift.

He came out of the planning meeting, met up with his assistant, and the two of them headed to the tent for the evening briefing. Local officials and some press sat on folding chairs placed on grass. Brandon walked in and kicked off the briefing with a grim set of facts. "The fire has been spreading northwest on Rumbling Bald Mountain all day and is now around 435 acres. We are keeping existing evacuations in the resort in place and notifying an additional 20 residences they might have to leave within the next 24 hours. The fire is 30 percent contained. That containment is on the fire's south side at Boys Camp Road. Today and tonight we'll be working with increased winds with gusts up to 30 miles per hour, and we're concerned that leaves falling off trees may reignite this contained section."

He looked over at Ferrell. "I'll let our ops chief fill you in on our fire strategy."

Ferrell went up to the briefing map. "Our 'dozers have been extending our check-line farther north all day to secure the upper section of the Rumbling Bald Resort. Plus, we're continuing to put 'dozer lines around more of the remote residences in there. Again tonight, we will conduct burnout operations to create safe 'black' around these additional properties, and the Lake Lure fire chief will have 20 fire engines with four-man crews standing by to protect them."

LATER THAT NIGHT, two of Morgan's volunteers pulled up to the entrance to the resort and a deputy came up to them, poked his head in the window and addressed the man behind the wheel and the woman next to him.

"We're here to report to the fire command for tonight's duty," the driver told him.

"I figured that. But can you do me a favor?" He looked over to an elderly woman who couldn't have weighed over 90 pounds standing next to her Honda CRV on the side of the entrance. She threw them a wave with a hopeful smile.

"She's been evacuated and her cat's still up there."

"You don't expect us to go find it, do you?"

"No. She just wants someone to drop off some food."

"Sure. We can do that. What's the address?"

"Forty-one Bluebird Lane."

The deputy motioned for the woman to come over, and the driver respectfully got out of the truck as she approached.

"They're gonna take the food up there for you," the deputy told her, then he rushed off to attend to another vehicle that just pulled up.

"It's so kind of you to do this," she said in a frail voice.

"No problem, ma'am."

She handed him a plastic bag. "Here's her favorite food and a bowl. Put it on the back porch. That's where I feed her every night."

He took the bag and started to get back in the truck.

"Wait!" she cried out. "I'll be right back."

She scurried away and returned with a carrier that he was surprised she could lift.

"If you see her, please bring her back in this."

"Okay. What's her name?"

"Fluffy."

"What does she look like?"

"She's a long-haired gray tiger."

He chucked the carrier in the back and continued on to the command post next to the resort's swimming pool complex. Fire trucks and emergency vehicles sat at the ready in the parking lot. He pulled up and got logged in. Then the guy handed him a map and pointed to a location.

"We're going to be backburning over here tonight once it

gets dark, and we want you to go up and down these roads that have already been burned out and check for spot fires all night. Embers are going to be flying and we could get reburns in there. If you see anything, radio and we'll send up an engine."

The driver studied the map, handed it to his partner, and pulled out of the lot where he took a right.

"You should've gone left," exclaimed his partner after examining the map.

"I want to go up Bluebird, drop off the food for the cat and get that behind us. Once they start that backburn, we're not going to have time for it."

They found a mailbox with 41on it at the bottom of a long asphalt driveway. Painted green with colorful flowers, it looked strangely ethereal sitting in a sea of black. They turned onto the driveway and drove up to a stately brick house sitting in a deeply rutted field. A bulldozer had gouged wide swaths around it and pushed what looked like a ton of landscaping into a huge pile, now ghostly black. The two got out.

"Wow, is this a mess," said the driver as he grabbed the bag of cat food.

"I guess that's what it took to save the place," said his partner.

"Let's go. She told us to put the food on the back porch."

They climbed over tall ruts and tangled roots as they made their way to the rear of the house. The driver opened the cat food can, spilled the contents in a dish and set it on the porch. His partner nudged him.

"Is that a cat over there?"

He looked in the distance and saw what appeared to be some kind of animal peering out from the charred woods. "It's either a cat or a raccoon."

His partner slowly walked toward the woods, gently whispering, "Here, Fluffy." As she neared, it ran up to her and leaped into her arms, making her laugh. She petted its thick ash speckled coat and listened to it purr all the way back to the truck, then they put it in the carrier along with the food the driver had thought to retrieve.

"Let's swing back to the gate and give them the cat in case that lady's still there," said the driver.

He pulled up to the deputy. "We got the cat. The carrier's there in the back." He looked around. "I see she's gone."

"She's staying at the Lake Lure Inn. We'll take it over to her the next time someone's going to town." The deputy reached in the truck bed and pulled out the carrier, then peered in the window. "You two did a good deed. She told me her husband died a couple months back and the cat's all she's got left."

Day Six

*T*hursday, November 10. "I'M WORRIED," SAID Dustin Way-caster, the structure division's night ops chief, at five that morning as he handed Morgan his plan for the day. "The crystal ball folks over in command are predicting this thing is going to be on the move again tonight and it's going to spread in every direction." Like Morgan's, his eyes were bloodshot and his face etched with the strain of not knowing what would happen next.

"How did it go last night?" asked Morgan as he studied the plan.

"We evacuated 18 more houses in the resort and set engines around as many of them as we could." He pointed to a map on one of the sheets he had handed Morgan. "You've got nine crews coming in this morning to prep these houses over here."

The noise level suddenly rose at the far end of the tent and made them look over. A bunch of firefighters were logging in at the resource table.

Waycaster looked over at the gray-haired man signing everyone in. "I don't know where you got him from, but he's one heck of a logistics guy."

"State Emergency Management sent him to us," said Morgan. "He's a retired fire chief from Shelby. I've known him for years. The guy teaches this stuff. At any given moment you can go up to him and say that you need to get in touch with a crew or firefighter, and he can tell you where they are and give you their contact numbers. He's an expert at managing everything operating on this fire: men, equipment, trucks—anything that belongs to us or doesn't belong to us. When he walked in the door yesterday, I wanted to hug him."

Just then, one of the Lake Lure paid firefighters and the

shift's group supervisor showed up, and they went over the day's plan with him.

"Let's go grab a cup of coffee before we head out to the tennis courts," said Morgan.

They walked to a small mess tent someone had set up.

"The fire shot up to 885 acres last night and is burning like crazy on both sides of Rumbling Bald," Morgan's assistant told the supervisor.

"I hope the Forest Service hurries up and gets more wildfire fighters in here," the man shot back. "Once it hits the Shumont Mountain range, they're in for one tough slog. I just heard on the radio coming over here that we've got twenty forest fires blazing in the mountains right now and the governor just declared a state of emergency and closed every state park in the mountains so they can use their personnel to help fight them."

They got their coffee, Morgan's assistant went home, and the two walked over to the tennis courts where the structure firefighters they had drummed up from local stations were assembling.

Morgan addressed the thirty or so men. "I want to thank all of you for getting here. This fire is on the move and we have 200 houses in the resort that it's going after. Our goal for the day is to pre-treat as many on the fire's front as we can, so we can get the fuel around them burned out tonight. I'm gonna start with the first crew. When I call your name, you're to go over to Roger over there. He'll make sure you know what to do, where to do it, and how to do it."

With everyone assigned, the teams got their instructions and left. Before Morgan went to the morning briefing, he went back to the structure command tent to talk with the firefighters just coming in from the night shift

Finished getting first-hand reports of what had gone on overnight, he headed out to the tent for the morning briefing now attended by media from Hendersonville and Asheville, along with regional emergency management officials. Throughout the presentations, Morgan couldn't keep from worrying about how long it was going to take for the 50 companies he'd ordered to start rolling in. His local resources were plumb worn out.

With the dire predictions of how fast the fire would spread that night, he had to get back to the structure tent, gather his thoughts and make sure he'd be asking for what his assistant would need for the coming night's shift. Operating under the protocol of the National Incident Management System, the day shift would attend all the meetings, then come up with a strategy for fighting the fire for the next 12 hours, and give a hand-written plan to the logistics folks who would scare up the resources needed to meet the goal. The night shift did the same for the incoming day shift. With every resource working on the fire using this system, they were able to create organization out of what could be a chaotic clash of resources.

The briefing ended with Brandon delivering the kind of confidence-instilling summary the tired, worried audience needed.

"The Party Rock Fire is now the number one priority in the state. We've got contract wildland firefighters on their way here from all over the US, engine crews are coming from fire departments all over North Carolina, and the Charlotte Fire Department is sending us Western Shelter tents to house these guys."

Once the briefing ended, Morgan left the tent and decided to hurry over to the resort and see for himself how things were going, to actually put his hands and eyes on the operation before he went into the meeting with the planning and logistics people the county Emergency Management had sent him.

He reached his vehicle parked next to a truck Duke Energy had on standby to take care of fallen power lines blocking road access. He started to open his door, then stopped. He looked across the lake at the smoke billowing from the mountain. This fire was a big, hungry monster looking for prey, and they had plenty of it for the taking.

A surge of pride rippled over him. The monster didn't know what it was up against. At that very moment, people were going to work, going to school, going about their business, totally unaware of the vast interconnected web of emergency management entities spread across the state always on the ready to respond to any and every kind of disaster. That's what they are there for. They train, gather up resources, connect with each other in a brotherhood dedicated to aiding their fellow man. A smile tugged at Morgan's lips. Today, that dauntless force was sending him everything they had.

He got in his truck and took off for the resort. He'd taken their now torn, smudged site plan with him and drove around making notations on it. Spotting the crew supervisor, he stopped to talk.

"What do you think? Can you get every house circled on that plan they gave you cleaned up today?"

"I think so. This is a fresh crew. We should move right along."

The minute Morgan got back to the base, he went over to his planning and logistic guys. "It looks like they'll finish those houses. We're gonna need 22 engines if we want to put black around them tonight."

"I'll do my best," the logistics guy said. Then he shook his head. "Those fire companies from the east better get here soon. Our resources are getting thin. Those guys from Polk and McDowell have been at it now for six days. They need a break."

"See if you can get a fresh convict crew to do the burnout," said Morgan.

"I'll do what I can," said the logistics guy.

IN FAIRBANKS, ALASKA, Mac Willard was anxious to get over to the station and see what kind of assignment he was being sent on. As a hotshot contract wildland firefighter he could be working 8, 16 or 24 hour shifts on the callout, so he tossed an extra jar of instant espresso and a tin of Vitamin B12 powder in his duffle bag. He'd already stuffed in his sleeping bag, along with two weeks' worth of clothes.

In the past six months, the US Forest Service had sent him to fight fires all over the lower forty-eight, including Texas and Montana, putting in over 2,000 hours; but he expected to be laid off any day, now that winter had arrived and the western fire season was over.

He pulled into the station, and could see everyone scurrying around. A resource order had come in for a twenty-man strike team for a fire in North Carolina, and they were readying to head for the airport.

The Forest Service had wrangled enough seats in two planes for the crew, and they assigned him to the first one out of Fairbanks. The flight would take twelve hours, with stops in Seattle and Atlanta.

The warm feeling of camaraderie surged as he found his seat in the plane next to two other firefighters. Seated all in a row, with their muscular builds and heavy beards, they looked like they'd said goodbye to being six feet tall by the time they hit fourteen. In their late twenties or early thirties, they looked forward to seeing another part of the country.

"They're calling it the Party Rock Fire," said one of the men.

"I love parties!" piped up Mac.

"Me, too!" said the guy next to him.

The three of them let out a whoop, high fives all around.

ANNIE NEVER KNEW THERE were so many places to put people. She'd locked up every room in the Lake Lure area and then reached out to motels in Hendersonville and even the nearby Equestrian Center.

She was sitting in the command center when the wildland logistics guy came up to her.

"You've done a great job with the rooms! Now I need you to find us a caterer that can provide three meals a day for at least three hundred firefighters. Now that we're ramping up, we can't keep expecting the community to come up with all the food."

"You're right," said Annie. "The Old Rock Café in Chimney Rock had to donate a hundred dinners tonight so we could feed everyone."

He shook his head. "I can't get over the outpouring of support we're getting."

She smiled. "The officers on road patrol at the barricades told me that every day the folks from LaStrada send someone down on the street with a menu to find out what they want to eat."

The logistics guy slapped his leg. "We've got a lot of people coming, and we have to feed 'em, so let's get this up and running within the next 48 hours. Again, once you line it up, shoot the information over to me and I'll take it from there."

He left, and Annie sat there, relieved. The fire had grown too big for the local restaurants and the army of volunteers who had been conjuring up meals and bag lunches on a meal-to-meal basis from food donated by people, churches, auxiliaries and food distributors. It would take an operation with resources like the Lake Lure Inn to feed all the people they had coming in.

In moments, she was on the phone with their manager. "How fast can you get set up to feed three hundred firemen three meals a day?" asked Annie.

"You're kidding."

"And they want this happening within the next 48 hours," said Annie.

"How about two meals? Ingles Grocery Store is set up to do breakfasts."

Annie eyed the logistics guy nearby, motioned him over and asked the hotel manager to hold on for a moment.

"The hotel across the street can do lunch and dinner," she told the logistics guy.

"Good. Tell him to come over and talk to me about tents."

Annie got back on the phone. "Did you hear that?"

"I'll be right over."

Annie finished the call and dialed the grocery store.

"Sure, we can do 300! We can even do more," said the manager. "Coffee might be a problem. Can you ask the inn if they can help out with that?"

Annie collected her paperwork and noticed a flurry of activity around one of the tables. Brandon was looking over the fire behavior specialist's shoulder, studying his computer screen. The concerned look on his face told her something was up, and she decided to get in on the evening briefing that would be getting underway soon.

"WE EXPECT THE FIRE to reach Chimney Rock and Shumont within the next 48 hours," the command's fire behavior

129

specialist solemnly announced. A stunned murmur rose from the fifteen or so in the briefing tent. Everyone knew that sooner or later it would get to Shumont, but this was the first time the historic little town of Chimney Rock appeared on the command's radar.

"The fire is now at 977 acres," he said, pointing to one of the large maps. "In the next 12 hours we expect it to continue to spread northwest, west, and southwest at a rapid pace."

Brandon felt forced to step up and comment. "Due to all the fires in the Southeast, we've been having difficulty getting the folks we need in here fast enough. As I told you this morning, crews will start arriving in the next few days, but until they do, we're not going to be able to fight this fire with the force we'd like to, and that means it's gonna gain on us."

People whispered to each other while the fire behavior specialist went on. "The fire continues to burn actively at night due to low humidity and the extremely dry fuel conditions in its path. Nighttime fire growth is also being enhanced as it climbs upslope as fuels are preheated by the approaching flame front."

Ferrell went over to the map and pointed to the Shumont plateau. "Yesterday, we put in a 'dozer line from Shumont Road to Bald Mountain Road up on top here. We're prepared to start burnout operations from this line if the fire starts to approach the houses up there.

"As far as the sprawling Rumbling Bald Resort is concerned, it's still at risk and we are continuing to conduct structure protection and burnout operations for the houses in there."

After the briefing, Brandon ran a hand over his brush cut as he went over to talk with the Lake Lure mayor. "Can you get hold of the Chimney Rock mayor and get him in here for tomorrow's briefing? We've got to talk with him about evacuation procedures." He ran his hand over his hair again. "You better get the folks from Bat Cave and Henderson County in here, too."

IT SEEMED LIKE it would be a night they'd enjoy, thought Peter O'Leary as he put on a fresh shirt. The whole community would be at the Lake Lure Inn's Roosevelt Room for the showing of *Come Hell or High Water,* a locally produced movie about the devastating flood of 1916 that barreled down the Hickory Nut Gorge and tore up everything in its wake.

He listened to a message on his machine. Bob Keith, the Lake Lure mayor, was inviting him as the mayor of Chimney Rock to a morning briefing over in the park complex.

"I guess it's some kind of informational meeting," he said to his wife, Ann, as they got ready to leave for the movie. "They probably want to keep me in the loop. It should be interesting to see what they're doing about their fire."

Watching the movie, there was something morbidly fascinating about seeing graphic pictures of a disaster's remnants, especially one that happened in your own backyard one hundred years before—whole houses swept downstream, piles of broken lumber lying like pickup sticks on the banks of the river, forlorn folks raking through scraps where their houses once stood.

Ann and Peter came out of the movie, grateful nothing like that had ever happened to them. After all, everything they owned was in the gorge. Their business, Bubba's General Store, and their home above another store they owned sat on Main Street smack-dab in the middle of Chimney Rock.

The latest fascination in town was to park along Lake Lure's beach at night and watch the fire burn on the mountain, so after the movie, Peter decided to drive up to LaStrada's parking lot where they'd get the best view.

"What a show," Peter said as they watched the dramatic scene of a blazing orange fire crawling along the crest of Rumbling Bald Mountain in the dark of night.

"I wish the kids were here to see this," said Ann.

Day Seven

F riday, November 11, 2 a.m. NO ONE WAS MORE ANXIOUS for the out-of-state wildland hotshot crews to arrive than the Forest Service night ops chief. For the past six nights Chase Payne had been running here and there with a crew of five or six, holding down everything they had accomplished during the day. They'd walk the lines and make sure it wasn't spreading, and corral it in if it were. Typically, fires lay down at night, but this fire, Chase decided, had one burning period, from midnight to midnight.

The 6 p.m. briefing over, he lined up his resources and headed for the resort. Tonight, he had three people helping him hold the line on the back side of Rumbling Bald, but he wished he had more.

The crew had to make their way to the creek alongside a checkline their dozers had put in to stop the fire from running up into Shumont, and the only way to get to it was through the resort. The convoy drove up a winding resort road past remote homes and estates tucked in the mountainside until they hit the logging trail that led to the creek.

They parked the trucks, unloaded their four-man UTV and took off, stopping at a spot where they could partially dam the creek for water. They took out their gas-operated pump, then stacked some rocks to make a pool, put plastic down, and threw in a suction line.

Chase squinted as he looked up ahead and spotted a faint glow. He quickly took off along the 'dozer trail on the UTV. A huge snag had caught fire. It was a matter of time before it would start tossing embers across their line and start climbing up Shumont Mountain. There had been a bit of a breeze down there in the gully next to the creek where they had set up, but he'd heard someone on the radio mention that the wind was howling and running 50 to 60 miles per hour in near freezing temperatures on top of the Shumont ridge.

After holding this line for so many nights, he wasn't going to let the fire get up there now. He raced back for help, but by the time they returned, embers from the blazing snag had started a spot fire.

They jumped off and began to stomp it out with their shovels, when it suddenly exploded into a firestorm, leaping from the size of a car hood to three acres in seconds. One of his crew standing in front of it ran for his life and jumped off a ledge to escape the flames, tumbling down a 30-foot embankment.

The race was on! Chase got on the radio to warn the folks in Shumont that the fire was headed their way, then he joined the search for the guy who went over. The fallen fireman's radio had come loose from his chest harness, so they hollered into the darkness and searched for him with flashlights. Somehow, they found him unharmed and got him back up to the line. The way the fire raged, there was no way they could battle it, so they hightailed it back to their vehicles.

Chase jumped in his truck and tore out for Shumont. All he could think of was what their fire behavior specialist had been telling everyone for the past two days, including the Broad River fire chief, that it would be three or four days before the fire showed up at Shumont. How many people up there were sound asleep in their beds?

He wasn't getting a response from Shumont on his radio, so he had to get over to the other side of the mountain fast. But first he had to get out of the resort, then to 74A, race through Lake Lure, Chimney Rock and Bat Cave, then head north up Route 9 and climb up Shumont Road with all its hairpin turns.

MEANWHILE, NO ONE UP ON SHUMONT was sleeping sounder than Jeanette Stender. The day before, she had finally finished making the last of forty Amish Friendship Cakes and a ton of barbeque for her niece's wedding reception. The phone rang, waking her husband, Bruce. As he reached over and picked it up, a big red 3:45 on the digital clock on the bedside table caught his eye.

"Bruce! The fire's crested on Shumont! I'm looking right at it!"

It was their closest neighbor. His house stood on the ridge above them, facing Lake Lure. With five little girls, he had been nervous about the fire and knew Bruce was a volunteer fireman. Bruce quickly dressed and jumped in his car. He raced to the department's substation on the Shumont plateau while making a report to Chief Hayner on the radio.

"Shift all traffic to the Broad River frequency," the chief told him, "and go to the station and stand by."

Bruce switched from the county-wide radio frequency and listened to Hayner talk to dispatch.

"Send the word out to all the Broad River firemen to get over to the substation as soon as possible."

That order to dispatch was followed by a lot of calls back and forth with men he was sending to various sections of the mountain.

Bruce, the first one to reach the substation, jumped out of his car and gasped. A mile-long line of flames blazed on the ridge. Scores of 100-foot hemlocks, long dead from the wooly adelgid blight, were flaming up and glowing like giant gas lanterns. The sight sent chills down his spine.

Chief Hayner arrived, quickly established an incident command post, and before leaving to put his eyes on the fire, hollered at Bruce to call the Full Moon Farm Wolfdog Sanctuary and alert them. Meanwhile, the fire department's only other paid employee got things rolling at the station. He and the chief issued assignments and constantly communicated with each other while Bruce documented everything on a huge wall board so they knew where everyone was.

Even though, days earlier, they'd evaluated the houses in their district and told people the fire would be coming and what they had to do to clean up around their homes, men were sent out with rakes, leaf blowers, drip torches and chainsaws to prep the houses in the immediate path of the fire, and by 7 a.m., Buncombe County Emergency Management was on the scene.

BRANDON AND FERRELL knew better than to trust this fire that was constantly going against whatever their experts told them it would do. Since wind gusts had been predicted for that night, they feared the fire could pull another nasty trick on them, and they forsook their beds at the inn and slept in their trucks parked outside the command center door.

Chase's report that all hell had broken lose on Rumbling Bald and the fire had jumped their Shumont line blared on Ferrell's radio and woke him. He jumped out of the truck, gave Brandon's door a thump and ran into the town hall.

A fireman stationed to watch for spot fires on Boys Camp Road radioed in. "The fire's burning back down the mountain and spreading on the back side of Round Top!"

Brandon heard it as he came in. He looked at Ferrell and said, "You better take a look."

Ferrell ran out, and Brandon began pacing and listening to the radio.

Another urgent call came in. "It's Chuck! I'm up here on the far north end of the resort. The fire's comin' this way!"

What had to be the voice of Morgan's assistant shot back, "We've got engines on the way!"

Minutes later, Ferrell reported in. "The fire's running up the bowl on the back side of Round Top. The flames are leaping the highest yet. At the rate it's moving, it's gonna be over the ridge and knocking on Chimney Rock's door tomorrow."

For the first time since the fire started, a strange feeling of otherworldliness washed over Brandon, but he quickly shook it off. The only force other than God that the three communities of Chimney Rock, Shumont and Rumbling Bald could count on right now was the North Carolina Forest Service and all the divisions now operating under it, and he was in charge. He quickly ran through his options.

The Broad River folks had been attending their briefings and had already started surveying and prepping the houses up there, and Brandon knew, if necessary, Buncombe County Emergency Management would pull in every fire company in the county to protect them. Morgan had fire trucks stationed at almost every house in the resort with fresh crews on the way, and his wildland firefighters were beginning to trickle in.

Chimney Rock, however, was another story. All they needed was just one of those little stores on Main Street to ignite and it was all over. Memories of the times he had been there as a kid flashed through Brandon's brain. They had to come up with a strategy to save that town, and they had to come up with it fast!

On his way over to the coffee urn to pour himself a cup, Brandon acknowledged with a nod the G.I.S. guy who was printing out maps for the morning. Their eyes met.

"I'm running off an infrared map for you," the guy soberly announced. He had obviously been listening to the radio.

Brandon passed by the finance table where a woman looked up at him.

"The bills just keep coming in," she said as she shook her head. "These folks are small business people and need to be paid right away." She said it almost as if embarrassed about staying up half the night to make sure no one had to wait for their money.

If only it would rain one of those deluges that swelled every river and every stream and made everyone fear a flood would wash the mountains straight away, thought Brandon. But that wasn't going to happen. The only prediction they were getting from their meteorologist was that a big wind event was right around the corner.

Just then, Ferrell came barging through the door.

"Dan, you gotta get on that SAC conference call this morning! I need four of their heavy air tankers to drop retardant to slow this fire down!" He went over to the G.I.S. guy's table and leaned over a map. "We've got to build a retardant line from the top of Bald Mountain all the way around that ridge to Boys Camp. We gotta slow the fire down enough so it comes down Round Top nice and easy and lets us catch it just before it hits Chimney Rock." He pointed to the fire's northeast flank. "It'll help slow it from running across the resort and across Shumont, too." He looked at Brandon. "I hope those companies Morgan's ordered show up soon. We need them!"

Every day, SAC, the Southern Area Command of the US Forest Service out of Atlanta, coordinates a conference call with all the incident commanders with fires in their district, and every incident commander gets a chance to plead for the resources they need.

"Don't worry, I'll ask for the tankers," said Brandon, "but remember, they've got all kinds of fires going on in western North Carolina, Tennessee, South Carolina, Virginia... all begging for stuff. I'll do my darndest, but they're gonna prioritize."

AT 8:10 THAT MORNING, Brandon got off the phone with SAC, then joined Ferrell in the briefing tent where their fire behavior specialist was making his report.

"Well?" Ferrell whispered.

Brandon grinned. "You're getting your tankers."

Ferrell closed his eyes and sighed.

"Believe it or not," said Brandon, "the Party Rock Fire is not only the number one priority in the state, it's number one in the nation... and they're gonna give us whatever we need. In fact, if we need something that someone else is using, they're gonna take it away from them and give it to us." He ran his hand over his brush cut. "I've never commanded a fire that was the number one priority in the country before. Heck, I've never been the number one priority in the region."

"When are they going to get here?"

"As long as it takes to load up and fly from Chattanooga."

THAT MORNING, as Peter O'Leary drove to the town center for his first meeting with the fire command, fire trucks sped up and down 74A, making him realize something was up. Already late, and with fire engines and emergency vehicles all over the place, it was taking him forever to find a parking space. He finally pulled into the Lake Lure Salon & Spa's lot across the street and hustled over.

The grounds bustled with activity, and someone directed him to the briefing tent. He walked in, and it stunned him to see representatives from every emergency agency in Rutherford, Buncombe and Henderson County, along with a bevy of press.

Then, when Brandon announced that the fire's footprint had grown another 1,525 acres overnight, nearly doubling in size, and that the Shumont Community and the Village of Chimney Rock were now threatened, Peter was shocked. The Party Rock Fire was no longer just a Lake Lure nighttime spectacle.

The discussion quickly centered on evacuation plans for the two threatened communities. When the Rutherford County Emergency Management director told him he needed to officially order a Chimney Rock evacuation for six o'clock that night so that the Sheriff's deputies could get started notifying residents door to door, the situation became dire.

As Peter drove back to the village and saw all the sheriff's cars racing around, it didn't seem possible this was really happening, and he was still convinced the fire would never get to Chimney Rock. His staff had already opened his store and waited anxiously to hear what was going on. As he told them all he knew, and as everyone began processing what it meant, someone burst through the door shouting, "There's smoke on top of Round Top!"

They ran out and stood in awe of the gray smoke billowing from behind the mountain in front of them. In minutes it started turning black, and then leaping flames suddenly appeared along the ridge. The deputies, seeing the flames at the same time, made an on-site decision and began telling everyone to evacuate immediately.

Peter ushered everyone out of the store, quickly locked up and ran up to his house across the street.

"Ann! We gotta get outta here! The fire's right above us."

Ann feverishly rummaged through a desk. "We have to get our papers! Our pictures!"

He grasped her hand. "Honey, there's no time. We've got to save our lives."

Their daughter had been in an accident and was immobile,

so he ran to her room, swooped her up and carried her to the car as Ann threw some clothes together.

He locked their front door and looked up at flames licking the top of Round Top, thinking that this kind of thing only happens in the movies. On the way to the Lake Lure Inn, several town residents zoomed past him. Nobody said, "We're gonna stick this thing out." They saw the flames and understood it was time to leave. As a battery of patrol cars and fire engines raced past him toward Chimney Rock, Peter glanced in the rearview mirror, haunted by the possibility that he might never come back to his home and business again.

AT NOON, WHEN THE tactical supervisor in the air attack plane radioed he was ten minutes away, Ferrell got his first inkling that this scheme of his just might work. He grabbed his radio, went outside and watched the plane come over the mountain and circle overhead. As the four jet tankers radioed their approach, the tactical supervisor sent them off to the side. Next, the pilot of the lead plane took a run in to study the terrain, then circled around for another run.

Ferrell kept an eye on the sky over Round Top and listened.

"Send in tanker one," said the tactical supervisor.

As the lead plane came over the mountain, someone on the ground radioed when it got on target, and it put out smoke to indicate where the tanker should drop the retardant. The tanker followed behind and shot out jagged spears of bright red crystals, creating an air show the Blue Angels would be proud of.

Ferrell watched as the jet flew across the lake. A ridge on the other side was completely obscured by smoke, and Ferrell held his breath until the pilot pulled out and cleared it. No sooner was the jet on its way back to Chattanooga to reload when the air attack plane radioed, "Send in tanker two."

Ferrell marveled at the way the air tactical supervisor moved planes around like figures on a chess board. Not only was he operating as the air traffic controller for the four heavy air tankers, he was also managing the two helicopters and a small single-engine air tanker out of Morganton working the eastern end of the fire with water. When a tanker came in, he cleared everything to the side, and as the tanker left, he sent everything back in, always making sure everyone was talking to each other and on the same page.

THE MOOD IN THE PLANNING meeting early that afternoon was somber as the whole team listened intently to the weather forecast from the meteorologist that the National Weather Service had sent them. After he outlined the major wind event that was coming, their fire behavior specialist depicted the ways it could grow the fire. They kicked everything around for a while, before Brandon summed up what he believed to be the only long-range strategic objective they now had open to them.

He grabbed a marker, drew a line on one of their latest briefing maps and spoke in the easy, confident tone that had reassured his team through all kinds of crises through the years, and what exactly was required at that very moment.

"We all agree that this fire is going to keep running past Chimney Rock and down 74A, and we're not going to get a chance to stop it until it hits Highway 9 in Bat Cave." Brandon looked at the faces around the table. "God help us if it jumps the highway and takes a run up Chimney Rock Mountain on its way."

Then he drew a line going north up Highway 9. "We've got to confine the fire to the east side of this highway. If it jumps that road and gets away from us there and we get that strong wind they're predicting, it'll run all the way down the gorge." He drew another line shooting from Highway 9 up across the wildlands to the northeast corner of Shumont Mountain. "Hopefully, we can stop it here." He looked around at them again. "I can't believe we're operating almost strictly on a few logging roads up there. We're gonna need every hotshot and smoke jumper we can get our hands on to fight this fire in there." Then he drew the line along the zig-zagging checkline separating the resort from the fire's perimeter. A bunch of their 'dozers had been extending the line north every day since the white-knuckle night Thompson and Morgan saved the resort. He looked over at Morgan. "If we lose it here, it could burn out the resort and run up and over Youngs Mountain." He tied the line into Boys Camp Road, then casually tossed the marker onto the map. "This, gentleman, is our new and expanded containment box."

THROUGHOUT THE DAY, the air tankers flew across Round Top, dropping retardant and putting on an air show that drew spectators from all around. Across the lake, people photographed the spectacular bright pinkish-red retardant shooting across the smoky fire. Mid-afternoon, the whole team assembled in the conference room for another planning meeting.

As the meteorologist gave his forty-eight hour weather prediction, Ferrell watched the faces of the folks from Henderson and Buncombe counties, now in the same kettle of fish he'd been in for the past six days. The night the snag fell across their line at Carsons Road he knew the fire was going to go big, but he never thought this big.

When he got the call the first night of the fire to go to Lake Lure to relieve Thompson, he never imagined he would end up as the operations chief of the forest service's number one priority in the country. He'd been running on adrenaline for so many days since, it felt natural.

He wasn't worried about the long-term damage to the wildlands now burning in those mountains. They would grow back, and the newfound sunlight would regenerate the forest with seedlings and plants. But the little village of Chimney Rock was a North Carolina icon that would never grow back. There'd be no way of replacing the two-block-long jumble of shops that had been cobbled together over the past hundred years to tap into people's underlying yearning to escape into an earlier time. The place might not be anything more than a hodgepodge of mom-and-pop operations with rustic facades, yet it represented a big chunk of the state's heritage. The last thing he wanted on his record was to be listed as the guy in charge of operations when it burned to the ground. As far as he was concerned, if he lost Chimney Rock, the fire had won.

With the wind prediction finished, it was his turn. He took

off his cap and ran his hand through his blond, tightly cropped hair, then firmly reseated it.

"The retardant is slowing the fire down and buying us time like I hoped," he said. "We're gonna keep laying retardant once the fire's over the top of Round Top and moving downhill, but we're gonna need a heck of a lot of fire trucks to welcome it when it hits the town."

"When do you expect that will be?" asked Brandon.

"It'll be crawling down that mountain all day, then probably all night and all day Saturday. I'd guess in the middle of the night Sunday morning, so we need to start cleaning up the fuel around those stores and cabins. And we'd better get as many engines as we can in there tonight. All we need is one bad spark and the whole town could go up."

Brandon looked at Morgan, "How many engines can you spare?"

"Everything I've got is committed to either the resort, or I've got them up on Boys Camp Road," said Morgan. "That includes two engines from Chimney Rock. They've got their third engine defending the station."

"When are those crews the fire marshal's sending you supposed to get here?"

"Not 'til either late tonight or in the morning," said Morgan.

The Emergency Management head from Henderson County spoke up. "Henderson County will defend Chimney Rock tonight."

"Thank God," said Ferrell.

"How soon can you get everybody here?" Brandon asked.

"We've got three trucks working down there now, and should be able to get seven fresh companies here by six tonight."

Richard Barnwell, the Bat Cave fire chief, walked in and Ferrell acknowledged him with a nod, then continued. "When those companies start showing up from all over the state tomorrow, we've got to put them out on 74A. They've got to go house to house to house to house prepping them all the way from Chimney Rock to Bat Cave. And we've got to be right behind them putting down 'black' before this wind event shows up. I don't know if this plan is going to work, but it's the only one we've got."

He looked at the Bat Cave chief. "As far as the prepping along 74A, Route 9, and the Henderson County section of Shumont Road is concerned, most of the crews we'll be sending down there are city people coming from Chapel Hill, Greensboro, Winston-Salem... and they don't usually deal with this kind of operation. And the ones from the east coast who do fight wildland fires are used to just plowing around it with a 'dozer. So, we've got to show them how to prep one house, and then tell them to go to the next one and make it look the same. These guys don't have forestry gear, so our resource guy is scrounging up some they can borrow.

"As for the burnouts along 74A, we're gonna have to combine our wildfire guys with firefighters. The Forest Service will be doing the burning and the firemen will have to be ready with their hoses in case something goes bad."

The meeting over, Brandon and Ferrell walked over to the huge banquet tent that the Lake Lure Inn had ordered and workers had just finished filling with tables and chairs. A few volunteers the inn had mustered from the community, many who were evacuees staying with them, were already manning it with snacks and coffee.

"Every once in a while, I get a weird feeling about this fire," said Ferrell as he poured himself a coffee. "Like we all went out and got married to our complete opposite. We're wildland firefighters. We find a fire, dig in a firebreak and start a backfire. When the two fires meet, they extinguish each other because there's nothing left to burn. But the structural protection component of this fire isn't letting us do that."

He let out a little laugh. "Those fire chiefs and the county emergency management guys don't care if they have to bring in every fire company in the state that's never met a mountain before to protect those houses on those mountains. If that's what they gotta do, that's what they're gonna do. The way those firemen have doggedly stood by those houses, day after day, night after night... it's really something."

Ferrell was right, Brandon said to himself. He'd never seen a fire this complex and that demanded this level of cooperation between wildland and structural firefighters in all his years. They finished their coffee, and once Ferrell left, Brandon decided to gather his thoughts for a few moments before going to a meeting with their G.I.S. guy. He sat assessing his situation. They'd been at it for seven days now, and the fire was still spreading out in every direction, and all the communities around it were now under threat of burning to the ground. He looked around. Several volunteers were laying out sandwiches and food, and a few firefighters drifted into the tent—people who believed in serving their community for a cause bigger than themselves.

He picked up his coffee and walked outside and past the tent filled with donations. Firefighters getting ready for the nightshift sifted through carton upon carton of eye drops, lip balms, shoelaces, cases of water, Gatorade, and all kinds of soft drinks and snacks that had been pouring in from all over the state.

Everyone was plugging for them, he thought, from the little family he saw pull up to the checkpoint and run out with a case of water, to every emergency management entity in the state and nation they had asked for help. It was a twist of fate that he happened to be the guy who had to make it all work. Of all the fires he had fought, he couldn't help thinking that this was the one he had spent the last twenty-nine years preparing for.

ROBERT GRIFFIN, THE FIRE CHIEF from Edneyville, was in his office on Route 64 between Bat Cave and Hendersonville when he got the call from the Henderson County Emergency Management chief.

"I just left a strategy session here at the Party Rock fire command. I think they're getting ready to lose Chimney Rock. The winds are picking up and it's beginning to be a wind-driven deal, which means pretty soon it's gonna be burning in Henderson County."

"What can I do to help?" Griffin asked.

"Last night, the fire blew up in every direction and the Lake Lure fire chief's got his hands full protecting the houses in the resort and along Boys Camp Road; he can't turn his crews loose to do Chimney Rock. They've reached out to every emergency management asset in the state for assistance, but they won't be getting here 'til tomorrow, maybe some tonight. I told them we could send six or seven companies up there by six to defend Chimney Rock tonight, and I want you to supervise it."

"No problem," said Griffin. "I'll start making the calls."

WHEN MORGAN REACHED the command center for the six o'clock briefing, he couldn't help but notice the tension on the faces of the town's officials. The fire coming down Round Top Mountain the night before had been seen on high ground for miles, and watching it had turned into a spectator sport. When the command ran through the litany of evacuations in three counties, several people gasped.

Meanwhile, the Edneyville fire chief showed up in Chimney Rock with two fire trucks. Now turning dark, when he saw the flames on Round Top leaping ten feet into the air, the hair on the back of his neck stood up. If one of those buildings in that town caught on fire, they'd all go up in flames and there'd be no way they could keep up with it. And being so dry, with the heat from those burning buildings and the flying embers, the fire would jump the river, climb up Chimney Rock Mountain and keep going all the way to the top of Sugarloaf Mountain in Henderson County.

By six-thirty, all seven Henderson County companies had arrived. They were familiar with the little village, but not with the narrow twisting road behind the stores dotted with summer cottages and a few homes. Although it was dark and heavy with smoke, they could see the structures were knee deep in leaves.

The sound of leaf blowers and chain saws began to roar up and down the mile long lane as they cleared leaves away from the buildings and cut off hanging limbs. A truck followed behind foaming the buildings. This assault continued into the night, ending around 3 a.m. As exhausted as they were, the Henderson County firefighters stood by at their engines until they were relieved the next morning.

Day Eight

Saturday, November 12. MORGAN WAS SO KEYED UP over getting the extra engines in time, he'd only been able to get a couple hours of sleep at the Lake Lure fire station after spending half the night at their resort command post. Now, just past 4 a.m., he raced down 74A to the command center.

As he took the curve and drove into the town center, he didn't know if he would laugh or cry. Fire engines lined the road for as far as the eye could see, waiting to be checked in. As he passed them, he couldn't resist reading the emblems on their sides: Winston-Salem, Cypress Point, Blounts Creek, Wake Forest, Puppy Creek, Zebulon, some towns he'd never heard of. The next time he laid eyes on anyone from the fire marshal's office, he was going to give them a hug they'd never forget.

The scene at the park complex was rife with frenzied activity. Dozens of fire engines that had been checked in lined the outer fringes waiting to be assigned. Someone directed a tractor trailer loaded with two huge generators onto a section of the formerly pristine lawn. UTVs, equipment trailers, and loaders were parked helter-skelter, and huge message boards and light towers were scattered all over the rambling, once meticulously maintained property.

He drove past the check point, pulled up next to his tent compound and ran in. A handful of firefighters crowded around the logistics table to report in. One of the firefighters who had just pulled in with his engine came up to him and offered his hand.

"Remember me?" he asked.

Morgan shook the man's hand and thought for a moment. "Wilmington! Hurricane Floyd!"

"You got it. You guys have been helping us out with hurricanes and floods for years, and we figured it was time we got up here and helped you out for once."

"Thanks," said Morgan. "By the way, you didn't get here a moment too soon."

He patted Morgan on the back. "We're glad for an opportunity to pay back. I heard the Fire Marshal put out a statewide request for as many as 150 plus engines and brush trucks."

Morgan nodded. "He told me he believed this was North Carolina's largest mutual aid request in decades, and maybe in the state's history."

Another firefighter stepped up to them. "Driving a Type 1 engine around those mountain curves on those narrow roads in the dark was something I wouldn't want to do every night, though."

Morgan finished talking to the guy when someone tapped him on the shoulder.

"A tractor trailer just pulled in with the State Emergency Management tents," the man said.

Morgan checked his watch. He had to go to a morning meeting, but not until he took the time to thank them first.

He went out, and when he saw a huge white tent go up, he was filled with emotion. These were going to be the only warm shelters for the hundreds of firefighters now arriving from the coast, the piedmont, and scores of towns, big and small, scattered around the state that had committed to provide mutual aid to his little mountain fire department.

Morgan went up to the captain of the set-up team. A surge of gratitude rolled over him, and as he shook the guy's hand, no words were necessary. The camaraderie was clear. The man patted Morgan on the shoulder and said, "We know what you're going through, buddy."

On his way to the briefing tent, Morgan could see them erecting a second tent and lining up a dozen porta-potties next to it. A State Trooper stopped him and motioned toward a stainless steel trailer.

"The Greensboro Fire Department has brought some kind of a mobile shower unit. Where should I tell them to put it?"

"Check with command logistics in the Town Hall," he replied. He smiled to himself. The county's emergency management folks had thought of everything.

THERE'S SOMETHING GRATIFYING about feeding people, for there's no more fundamental need than food. It doesn't matter if the food is for a beloved family member, a guest you want to honor, a pet, or even for someone who's walked into your restaurant for a meal, because for that one fleeting moment you're the indispensible provider of essential sustenance. And to meet this fundamental need for men and women who have answered your call for aid and traveled to your doorsteps from far and wide on planes, fire trucks and every kind of emergency vehicle to help you, is more than gratifying; it's an honor.

At five-thirty that morning, the folks from Ingles Grocery Store in Lake Lure rolled into Morse Park with their hot boxes and started serving scrambled eggs, biscuits, and sausages to the firefighters pouring in from fire companies all over the state or who had flown in from around the country and were about to set out for a twelve-hour shift. It was Ingles' first breakfast and it took the help of employees and managers from their other stores to make it happen.

The Lake Lure Inn manager, now an evacuee himself, shouted over his shoulder, "Get those lunch sacks in the van," as he and one of his staff struggled with a twelve gallon urn of coffee the inn had promised to provide. "And don't forget the orange juice!"

With the van loaded, he drove across the road onto

what was left of the park lawn. His staff rushed into the catering tent with the boxes of lunch sacks while the hefty urn was being toted. The lunch sacks had been assembled the day before by a crew of volunteers from the community, many of whom were now spreading the sacks out on a table for the firefighters to help themselves to as they left for their assignments. They contained two calorie-heavy, double-size ham and turkey sandwiches, along with a 600-calorie peanut butter and jelly sandwich, as well as candy bars, snack packs, nutri-bars, and crackers.

Once the operation was running smoothly, the inn manger left the tent and glanced at the rising sun. The unnatural way the dense smoke filtered the reddish sunrise made him feel as if he were on another planet. He shook the feeling off. He had no time to get dragged into a jittery mood. He had to get back to the inn and get the volunteers started packing the lunches for the next day and then help his staff get ready to serve their first dinner that night.

MEANWHILE, UP ON SHUMONT, the women's auxiliary had been bringing in food from their houses to feed everyone. This morning, Jeanette Stender drove up and ran into the substation where they had pulled out all their apparatus and set up tables for eating. She asked a couple of volunteers to help her get several cartons of food she was donating from the trunk of her car.

Not seeing her husband, she went into the community room. The massive operation underway at 5:30 in the morning stunned her.

Flocks of firefighters studied Forest Service maps sprawled all over the walls. Printers and laptops hummed on every table top. Extension cords and wires crisscrossed the floor, while modems stood along the windowsills searching for a signal. She spotted Bruce and motioned him over.

"Honey," she whispered to him. "I called your niece and told her we couldn't make it to the wedding or the reception."

"What about all those Friendship cakes you made?"

"They just took them out of my car. I brought the barbeque, too."

IN SPITE OF THE MASSIVE fire fighting maneuvers going on all around it, the historic Lake Lure Inn still stood at the foot of the lake with its Baccarat crystal chandelier at the entrance and the huge, ornately carved antique music boxes from the 1880s sprinkled around the tastefully decorated lobby. Usually the perfect place for an elegant wedding, relaxing conference, or festive banquet, on this November day, the whole charming ambience of this antique historic inn was tipped upside down and in crisis mode.

Every one of their 69 rooms and three cabins was booked. Evacuees milled around the lobby, as did the dogs and cats they had brought along with them. Fifty rooms were being used by Forest Service personnel and firefighters, with the beds rotating out in twelve-hour shifts. When a firefighter got up, they'd put their sheets in a box with their name on it, and when the next guy came in, he'd take his sheets out of his box, make the bed and go to sleep. Their housekeeping staff even washed and pressed their clothes.

In addition, their restaurant division was hectically preparing its first dense, calorie-rich dinner with a double portion entrée to serve the firefighters that night. When they drove their van to the mess tent across the street and saw the hungry men and women lined up by the hundreds down the field, they couldn't get their commercial hot boxes out and set up fast enough.

That night as the inn's manager helped the volunteers clean up the catering tent, he thought of the back-breaking effort it had taken to transition in a span of only forty-eight hours from the laid-back routine of a quiet, easy November in the off-season to a full-service catering operation putting out 300 meals a day, but somehow they had gotten it done.

Finished, he meandered outside the tent and looked up at the fire and wondered how many of the people he'd served that night were now up there battling it. He smiled to himself. He could still hear the brave men and women they had served that night laughing and talking in that noisy, crowded tent as they ate a hearty meal. He suddenly felt a part of something larger than the inn, stronger and more enduring than the pain of overworking or the stress of not knowing what was going to happen next. The inn was just like all the volunteers, all the firefighters, the first responders, people and businesses from within the area and without, who out of duty, or a feeling of community, or just plain old common decency rolled up their sleeves and committed to doing whatever they could to save this place and all that was in it.

ANNIE WAS GLAD SHE had insisted that Terri stay with her mom for the duration of the fire as she started for Bat Cave. Exhausted, she had wanted to crash on a cot in one of the Western Shelters, but she had some serious catching up to do with Jack. She decided to stop at her mother's first and make sure everything was okay.

With Route 74A closed, it would take her at least an hour to get there. She pulled out of what the locals now called "Tent City" and drove south until she reached Highway 26, then went west to Hendersonville. She got off at the Route 64 exit, and headed north again to Bat Cave.

She made the final curve down the mountain and neared the turnoff to her mother's house. Up ahead, rotating red lights from emergency vehicles at the roadblock to Chimney Rock revealed a crowd of onlookers. She pulled onto her mother's road, drove up to the house, went in through the kitchen door and was struck by the incongruity of *Jeopardy* playing on the TV, while across the river, strobe lights flashed from a bank of fire trucks and flames danced up on Round Top.

"Have you had dinner yet, sweetheart?" her mother asked.

"No, I'm okay. I already had something to eat."

Annie looked around, pleased to see dinner dishes stacked by the sink. Having Terri stay with her mother was a good idea.

"I can't stay long. I'm on my way to see Jack."

"Oh, can I go with you?" Terri asked.

"Not this time, Terri.. We've got things to talk about. Next time for sure."

"It's okay. I was over there once already today."

Annie shot a quick glance over to her mother who was staring back at her. Blackie jumped out of Mae's lap and came up and rubbed against Annie. She picked him up and brushed her face across his fur as she strolled over to the couch Terri lay on. Terri drew her feet up to make room for her.

"So you went to visit Jack?" Annie asked, stroking her cat.

"Uh-huh. He's taking me with him to Florida next week."

Seeing the puzzlement on Annie's face, Terri prattled on. "While he's going up and down looking for property, it'll be a good chance for me to do some picking and get away from this smoke."

"Picking?"

"Oh, yeah. I make out good at it. Buy stuff cheap and sell them to a lot of the designers in Asheville."

Something on the TV attracted Terri's attention.

"Who is Mister Magoo?" she shouted in response to one of Alex Trebec's questions.

Annie nuzzled Blackie before putting him down, then she slapped her knees and stood up. "I gotta get going."

Her mother rose and followed her out onto the back porch.

"What's the matter?" she whispered to Annie.

"Nothing."

"You seem so uptight, honey. It's not like you."

"I know, Mom. This fire has really got me wound up. It's like an angry dragon's loose on the mountains. Sometimes I feel like I've died and gone to fire hell and I'm going to be there forever. No matter what those guys do, it won't quit. I wake up dreading to hear how much it's grown overnight. Sometimes I just want to walk away from it, but I can't. They're so short-handed that one day I actually started calling people at random from the telephone book to come help."

"Do you think we'll be evacuated?"

"You should be safe on this side of the river." She thought for a moment. "But you never know. If you are, get out right away and go to Jack's."

"What about down at your end?"

"They've got a fire truck stationed in front of my house, but yesterday morning, I heard one of the county's emergency management guys talking on the phone with someone in Raleigh. He told them that they thought they were going to lose Chimney Rock."

Mae gasped and put her hand to her mouth.

"Don't worry, Mom. With all the retardant they've been laying across that mountain all yesterday and all day today, it's slowing down. But it's so sinister, Mom, watching it slither down like lava."

"Where are you going to sleep tonight?" asked Mae.

"I don't know. I might come back here." Annie turned to go down the stairs and then hesitated. "What's with Terri and Jack?"

Mae raised her eyebrows and shrugged her shoulders. "Who knows?"

Annie gave her mother a quick hug and hollered out a goodbye to Terri, then left for her brother's house. Good, his lights are on, she said to herself as she came around a bend. She got out of her truck and saw him through the window working on a chair.

"Hello," she yelled as she let herself in.

He didn't lift his eyes from his work. "I knew it was you. Nobody comes up here at night except you and the bears."

She strolled over to him with her arms crossed. "Jack, I was just over at Mom's. Terri told me you're planning on going to Florida next week. I don't think it's a good idea under the circumstances."

He looked up. "What circumstances?"

She pulled up a chair and sat down across from him. "The state is sending a couple hotshot fire investigators from the Forest Service to look at the evidence up on Party Rock. I was in the command center when I heard the ops chief talking to one of them on the phone. With all the fires burning in the state, they didn't know when they would be getting here, but they asked us to cordon off the site."

She stood up and thought out loud as she paced. "It's highly possible they won't want to talk to you since it's been so many years. Let's not get all torn up over nothing." She stopped and turned to him, "But if they do, you're just going to have to ride it out until they catch whoever did it."

The look of fear she saw in her brother's eyes brought back painful memories she had thought were long forgotten. "We can get through this, Jack. You just have to buck up." She went over and put an arm around him. "You're gonna be all right, aren't you?"

He went back to his caning. "I lied to you when I said I was here working on my staircase."

"Lied? About what?"

"I was on Party Rock that Saturday."

She waved an exasperated arm in the air. "What in the world were you doing there!?"

"It was a beautiful morning... and... I don't know. I missed Anita and decided to go for an early morning hike down the trail like you and I used to do."

"I don't believe this is happening," Annie said, angrily stomping her foot.

Jack looked up at her. "Just like I usually did, I called Mom and told her I would need a ride back to my car, and I'd call her to come pick me up once I got down to Carsons Road. Then I drove up to Shumont, parked my car at the trailhead and started down."

"Oh, Jack. Of all the friggin' days you had to pick!"

"Stop. I've beat myself up over it a hundred times."

She started to pace again, this time more erratically. "We've got to think this through carefully, Jack. Maybe you should just wait and see if they come to question you. It's highly possible they won't." She stopped pacing and wrinkled her brow. "But then, if they do, how will it look when you tell them you were on the trail hiking at the very same time someone else was setting the fire?" She thought for a moment. "Now that I think of it, you're better off taking a chance that they're not going to come after you."

"It's not that simple, Sis."

She turned and looked at him. "What do you mean?"

"When I got near the bottom of the mountain, instead of going out on Carsons Road, I cut down on that old trail that leads to the boulder field and ends up at the new hiking trail parking lot. I called Mom, and as usual, had to wait almost an hour for her to drag her ass over there. Five minutes before she showed up—a lousy five minutes—a park ranger pulled up and posted a notice on their information board. I was sitting right there, so naturally I chatted with him. I know he's going to remember me."

"You haven't done a single thing wrong in the past twenty-five years," said Annie. "They have to believe you. And if they don't, you've got to demand a lie detector test. That's it! A lie detector test! That ought to prove your innocence." She thought again. "What time was it?"

"One-thirty. I remember that time because I was really getting ticked off that Mom was taking so long."

"That's good. The fire started up there just around then. You couldn't be in two places at one time. While you waited there, did you see anyone go in the woods or come out?"

"Just a few couples; but when I was up on the Party Rock, three kids were coming up the trail."

"How old were they?"

"Sixteen, seventeen."

"Do you remember what they looked like?"

"Not really. Just that one of the kids had a sort of punk rock look."

"Boy, Jack, you've got the worst luck in the world. You've really got no choice now. The police need to know about those kids. It can help with the search. And the sooner you take a lie detector test and get eliminated, the better."

She went over, bent down and looked him in the eye. "Jack, think everything over so it's clear in your head, and try to remember every detail about those kids. What they wore, the color of their hair, if anyone was wearing glasses, any detail. We'll go together to the Lake Lure police station tomorrow. Okay?"

"Sure, Sis."

"I want you to meet me there at ten sharp. The road's closed from Bat Cave to Lake Lure, so you're gonna have to go all the way around. You gotta plan for at least an hour. Also, you might have trouble getting to the town hall. If they stop you, just call me and I'll come get you."

He suddenly looked so forlorn she worried she would start crying, and if she did, she wasn't going to be able to stop. What kind of message would that be sending? She gave him a quick hug. "I've got to go now. Be sure to get a good night's sleep." She started for the door. "Remember, ten sharp. Jack, no matter what, it's going to be rough on all of us until they catch whoever did it. But trust me, they *will* catch them."

Annie knew exactly where she was headed when she pulled out of her brother's driveway and headed back toward the barrier on 74A in Bat Cave. She didn't have the strength to drive all the way around again. She had her Lake Lure Fire Department shirt on, and if she were lucky, whoever was there would know her and let her through. She recognized the officer at the barrier. He was one of the town's policemen. She waved, and to her relief, he signaled for her to go on through. She pulled down her window.

"Thanks for recognizing me."

"I'd know that rig you're driving anywhere," he said, chuckling.

Her headlights barely penetrated the smoke as she made her way around the curves that ran with the twisting river, first into Chimney Rock, packed with dozens of fire trucks, and then to Lake Lure. Halos around the banks of light towers all over the command center reminded her of van Gogh's *Starry Night*. A few firefighters stood studying the maps on the side of the fire department's trailer in front of the town hall, and a couple of deputies from the sheriff's office chatted in the lot with a group of State Troopers. She found a place to park in the back field, and the now familiar drone of generators and the smell of smoke greeted her as she got out.

The structure command's tents were lit up, but that wasn't where she was headed. She had run into Bruce Button in the mess tent that morning, and he had told her that the Billy Graham Rapid Response Team's mobile ministry unit had arrived the day before and he was now pulling chaplain duty.

With so many trucks, tents and tractor-trailers she couldn't find it right away, mainly because she hadn't been looking for anything that big. She expected a glorified camper trailer, not something 50 feet long with bumped out sides. She neared, then quickly veered in another direction as someone came out holding a cup of coffee. She didn't want anyone to know she was having a problem. In the fire service, it's "suck it up and get over it." If your teammates knew you were having emotional problems, how could they trust you to hold up your end? She walked past the mess tent, circled it, and went back. Good. No one was around this time.

She grabbed the door handle, took a deep breath and went in. The interior was surprisingly spacious and set up as a conference room with a cozy kitchenette and a few comfortable chairs. Recognizing Bruce at a desk in an office at the rear with his back to her, she went over and leaned against the door jamb and mindlessly twirled her ponytail. He swung around in the swivel chair and looked up at her.

"Well, hello," he said. "Can I get you a cup of coffee?"

"No thanks, I'm okay."

He shepherded her in, pulled a chair over for her, then closed the door.

He waited a moment in case she was ready to tell him why she was there, and when she didn't, he started with his standard opening remark. "I know you're working twelve hours shifts, how are you holding up?"

"I'm getting the work done, but it's embarrassing. I, I keep bursting into tears."

"You're having a normal reaction to an abnormal event," he said as he slowly rocked back and forth in his chair. "What happens to first responders in a prolonged crisis like this, is you get hyper vigilant when you're on duty. Your senses become really keen and you're so focused on the fire you get this adrenaline rush. If you don't do something to get rid of the stress, you keep on that adrenaline—you live on it—and it starts affecting your emotions. That's when you get to weeping."

"That's me, all right. We were desperate for more volunteers to run around handing out water and snacks to the firefighters on the lines. I called the Rutherford town hall to see if any of their employees would help, and when they called back and told me a bunch of their staff would do it all weekend, I sat down and bawled."

He rocked, mulling over what she had said. "Another thing is that a lot of times an event like this will stir up something you've buried or that's bothering you. *Is* something bothering you?"

She bit her lower lip and looked away.

He hunched forward as if he could tell he'd struck a vein. "Sometimes people push a problem to the back of their mind and hold it in, but it keeps building... and then some traumatic thing like this fire triggers it and they're flooded with emotion."

Annie wiped a tear. "It's my brother. He's in trouble. I think they might accuse him of starting this fire..." She looked up at him with an earnest expression, "...but I know he didn't do it."

Suddenly, Annie poured out her heart and told him the whole story. "Bruce, I've always been the strong one, and tomorrow when I go with Jack to the police I've got to hold up. I know the hate everyone feels for the person who started this fire. No matter how professional the police are going to be, we're both going to feel it. I hope I can handle it."

"Let me see what I can do. I've got a friend who was a Marine with me in 'Nam. He's retired from thirty years with the FBI and he's now in our ministry. He's in Charlotte. I'll give him a call tonight and see if he can come and talk to you, strictly on a confidential basis."

Annie's eyes shot up. "That'll help."

"You might have to get a lawyer, too."

"I know."

She rose, wringing her hands. "You'll let me know?"

"Yes. As soon as I can," he said as he got up.

He put a hand on her shoulder. "You've got to do something to relieve this stress. Are you eating well?"

She nodded.

"You've got to get at least six to eight hours of sleep every 24 hours. Are you doing that?"

She nodded.

"Anything else you can do to take your mind off this fire and your brother will help."

Annie thanked him and made her way back to her truck. There was only one thing that could take her mind off those two problems, and she was going to head straight for it. She drove down 74A and pulled onto a road that led to the lake, then pulled into the driveway at the end of the lane. His truck was there, but the house was cloaked in darkness. She got out, went in through the unlocked basement door and made her way up the staircase to the main floor. The house was silent except for the ticking of the grandfather clock in the hall. She crept up the stairs to his room. Moonlight streamed across the figure in the four-poster bed. She slowly disrobed, gently lifted the covers and slipped into bed.

Day Nine

*S*unday, November 13. AT 2 O'CLOCK THAT MORNING, Peter O'Leary, who was a volunteer fireman as well as Chimney Rock's mayor, was asleep in a fire truck in the parking lot of the town's fire station when his partner woke him up.

"Get up! It's almost here!"

He looked up at the flames crawling down the granite mountain sprinkled with trees and jutting almost straight up behind the station. It sat on the edge of town a couple hundred feet from the back of the buildings lining Main Street. Peter and his partner had witnessed the fire creep down from the top of Round Top throughout the day Friday and Saturday while the tankers dropped the retardant. The winds had abated, a big relief after hearing the horror stories of what it took for the firemen to keep flames off the houses in the resort Tuesday night.

The fire had been licking the ground with one or two-foot-high spikes all day, but it suddenly hit a dry patch of deep fodder and shot to five feet. Peter jumped from the truck, grabbed a hose and helped his partner put it out.

Up on Terrace Lane behind the stores, a line of fire trucks stood at the ready while a supervisor from the Forest Service gave instructions to the firefighters gathered around a truck.

"We're lucky," he said. "We've got so much retardant on this thing it's not going crazy on us right now. I know you guys are structure firefighters, but we're telling you when you see that fire coming down that mountain, you're not to attack it. You're not to do anything to that fire until it comes right into the back yard. Lay your hoses and wait for it to reach the wood's edge before extinguishing it with water. This way we're gonna burn up all available fuel so we won't have to worry about it burning on that mountain again. When we kill it, we want it to stay killed."

These were structural firemen trained to run into burning buildings to put out a fire if they had to. Waiting for it to reach them was new and unnerving, but that's what they did all night, and by daybreak the Forest Service was able to declare that Chimney Rock was saved.

FERRELL FINISHED DRAWING on the briefing map the G.I.S. guy had just produced, and tossed the marker down.

"This ain't gonna work," he said to the guy. He took off the cap he was never without, ran a hand through his blond hair and reset the cap tight on his head. He scratched his now scruffy beard contemplating the daunting situation. "It has to work! It's the only option we've got. If it doesn't work, where are we gonna go? Give me aerials of everything on 74A all the way to Bat Cave as soon as you can."

Ferrell looked up. It was five in the morning and four of his supervisors, including Mike, just appeared for an operations meeting. Ferrell gathered up a few of the maps and they headed to the conference room.

No one took a chair. They stood leaning against a wall or standing with their arms folded, as if they were afraid if they sat down they wouldn't be able to get up again. Brandon walked in wearing a clean uniform the Lake Lure Inn had washed and pressed for him, but he hadn't shaved and his brush-cut needed a trim. He dropped a stack of papers needing his signature on the table and took a seat while Ferrell spread out his maps. One of them showed the footprint of the fire with every day's growth in a different color. The men could see that the fire had split into two fronts reaching out in different directions, north toward Shumont and the resort, and west toward Bat Cave; and in the past 48 hours it had swallowed up another 1,100 acres.

"At this point, fellas, the fire's not our priority," said Ferrell. "Prepping the houses so we're ready for it as it heads for Bat Cave, *that's* our priority. With all the retardant and the downright heroic efforts of everyone, we've kept the fire from taking out Chimney Rock, but we're not stopping this thing 'til it gets to

Route 9. Hopefully, that retardant has bought us enough time to keep the fire off our backs 'til we finish prepping every structure on that road; then we've got to ease it down 74A and stop it cold at Bat Cave.

"It's possible we won't make it, but I'm betting the farm that we will. There are over a hundred houses scattered along the three miles between Chimney Rock and Bat Cave. Thankfully, it's nothing but woodland north of the highway. Up on the Shumont plateau, it'll be running on flatter ground, and they'll be able to fight it up there. They can widen those roads and do something with it. But down here in the gorge, the only place we can stop it is at the northeast corner of 74A and Highway 9 in Bat Cave. And, I don't need to tell y'all, it's your job to make sure this thing comes off like we know what we're doing."

His remark drew a cynical laugh from the men as they shuffled out, exhausted but bolstered by Ferrell's confidence.

ANNIE HAD BARELY FELT MIKE'S arm slide from under her head that morning before he left for the command center. The distant sound of a shower, then a gentle kiss on her forehead was all she had been conscious of before sinking back into dreamless oblivion.

The piercing caw of a raven flying past the bedroom deck roused her. It was daylight! She sat up and looked around until she spotted the clock on the night table. She had to meet Jack at ten. Seeing it was only eight-thirty, she fell back down and stared dreamily at the ceiling remembering the night, until the shadow of the fire fell over her and took control.

She quickly showered, put on one of Mike's T-shirts, and was running out to get her duffle bag from the truck when she saw a note on the dresser with her name on it. She unfolded it and read.

"I'm on the burnout on 74A today. I love you, Annie. Please be here tonight when I get home, Mike."

She picked up the framed picture of his parents that had been sitting next to the note. His father wore the same kind smile as the time he invited her to come to Mike's birthday party.

"It's going to be quite a bash," he had told her. "Our boy's only going to be sixteen once and his mother wants it to be really special." He winked. "And it will make her happy if you come."

She could still feel the thrill of being invited and blurting out, "Can Jack come, too?" and then recalled seeing his smile fade.

"No, darling, I don't think that would be a good idea, with his problem and all the kids being here. You understand what a difficult position that would put us in, don't you?"

She remembered Ruth McNeil later smiling at her after she handed her mother her check, and saying, "My husband told me you were coming to Mike's party next week. I'm delighted."

"Oh, I'm so sorry Mrs. McNeil. I don't think I can make it. I promised my aunt I'd go somewhere with her."

As they left the house, her mother said, "What was that about? Your aunt's not going anywhere next week, or any week after that."

"Nothing, Mom. It was all about nothing."

Annie folded Mike's note and wished he hadn't written it. Once she and Jack got finished at the police station, he'd hear about it and regret he ever wrote it.

Coming here last night was a mistake. What was she thinking? Then she pictured his easy smile and had to keep from getting weepy again. Everything had been going so well. If only she had gotten Jack out of there sooner. Then she remembered how pitifully defeated her brother looked last night.

She got her duffel bag, pulled out some clean clothes and got dressed, all the while facing the fact that whatever she had going on with Mike was pretty much doomed. It is what it is, she finally told herself. She had to "suck up and get over it" and focus on taking care of her number one responsibility, Jack.

She pulled into Tent City, parked in a back lot, and went over to the trailer in front of the town hall. She pretended she was studying the maps taped to its side as she waited for Jack to show up. Every once in a while, she'd look toward the entrance to the police department at the end of the building. Squad cars from every branch of law enforcement in the state were lined up in front of it.

The enormity of the force made her ask herself if sending her brother to face them in the state he was in was the right thing to do. Maybe they should go see a lawyer first. She remembered her old boyfriend telling her that one of his clients had him go with their son to turn himself in for a hit-and-run incident to protect his rights.

Get your head screwed on, she told herself. The hit-and-run kid was guilty. Jack isn't. Plus, they're probably going to come and get him for questioning anyway. She had to keep her eye on the ball, and not overthink this. She checked her phone for the time. Ten. Where in the heck is Jack? She phoned him, but he didn't pick up.

"Jack, please call me. It's important."

She waited another half-hour, and when he didn't show up or phone, she called her mother.

"Mom, have you heard from Jack today?"

"No. Why?"

"He was supposed to meet me at ten, and he hasn't shown up and isn't answering his phone."

"That's strange. He's good about answering his phone. It could always be a client."

Annie's mind was spinning. "Mom, you've got to do something for me."

"Sure, Baby,"

"Go over to Jack's place, and if he's not there, go in and call me. This is important, Mom. I'd do it myself, but they're back-burning all along 74 and I'll never get through. It'll take me forever to drive around."

"I'll go over right now." Her mother was silent for a moment, then she said, "There's trouble, isn't there?"

"Mom, just do as I say. We're gonna be all right. I'm handling it."

Annie hung up and dialed her brother again.

"Damn you, Jack. You gotta call me. I mean it."

Annie went over to the mess tent. Breakfast was over and the volunteers were cleaning up, but one of them spotted her and called her over.

"I think I can scrape together a breakfast for you, dear. We appreciate what all you firefighters are doing and we love you for it," she said as she took some foil from a large chafing dish and scooped up some eggs and bacon and put it on a plate. She rummaged around a stack of containers they were getting ready to take back to the inn, got out some biscuits, put them on the plate and handed it to Annie.

"Thanks," said Annie.

After she finished eating, Annie left the tent, and on the way to her truck, ran into Morgan.

"I wanted you to take the day off," he said, concerned.

She nodded. "I know. I was just going."

"I want you to get some rest. Tomorrow's gonna be tough."

By the time she got back to her truck, her mother was on the phone.

"I'm here, and Jack's gone."

"Okay, Mom. What does it look like?"

"What do you mean?" Mae asked.

"Go into his back closet. He's got a duffle bag in there. See if you can find it."

She drummed her fingers on the steering wheel and waited.

"It's not here."

"How about his sleeping bag. He always hangs it in there."

"No. It's not here either."

"Okay. He's got two big coolers. They're red."

She waited until she heard, "No coolers."

"Check the fridge."

"There's nothing in it. It's been cleaned out."

"Go on home, Mom. Promise me, you'll let me know if he calls."

Annie turned on the ignition, looked up at the burning mountain range, and whispered, "Run, Jack, run," then pulled onto 74A and headed straight for Mike's house. She would be there when he came home like he asked, and she would sleep with him again tonight, because like Morgan said, "tomorrow was gonna be tough."

AROUND NOON, THEY GOT A REPORT up at the Shumont substation that fire was licking around the bowl below the plateau and climbing up. The fire chief dispatched an engine and decided to take a look himself. He could get a good view of the whole area from the back deck of a house that hovered on the edge of the plateau.

He pulled in the driveway, jumped out and ran around to the back deck. Smoke billowed from the deep valley below. The fire was on its way up, and moving fast. He quickly got on the radio to central command in Lake Lure and called for helicopter dumps to knock the fire down. They were unable to break any loose, so he called the substation and told them to send over two tankers and five more engines.

They would need plenty of water to stop this fire, so once the engines arrived, they pulled two drop tanks from their trucks and popped open the portable folding frames. The tankers filled each of them with 1,400 gallons of water, then went back to the substation for more. They cleared away the fuel from around the house for a couple hours but knew they had to pound the fire down with helicopter drops or it would overrun them once it climbed to the top. They put in another urgent request for water dumps, and this time the command center was able to send them.

The copter's efforts slowed the advancing flames, but by dark, a wall of fire that looked a mile wide clawed its way up the mountain and roared like a dragon. They'd done as much backburning in advance of the fire as they could on that steep mountain and had poured on thousands of gallons of water, but watching the wall of forty-foot flames devour the dark mountain was terrifying.

Someone from the Forest Service recommended they sacrifice the house and fall back to Bald Mountain Road. The supervising structural fireman with forty years' experience under his belt, responded, "We've got a neighbor's house here, we're equipped to fight this fire and trained to defend it. It's not in our DNA to let it burn to the ground, so we're gonna stay as long as we can."

Finally, as the fire got close, the supervisor gathered every-one around. "Okay, guys," he said, "here's how it is. We don't want to abandon this house, but if we think for one moment that this thing's gonna overrun us, we're gonna pull the airhorn on one of these engines and we're gonna get out of here. We're not gonna let anyone get cut off in here. When you hear that horn, everybody who has hoses out, get your axe and chop them ...don't unscrew them ...we're gonna cut them and get gone. We're not gonna get anybody hurt."

It took five engines, two tankers, two drop tanks, thousands of gallons of water, and a dozen firefighters with a lot of grit to slay the roaring beast coming up the mountain and to save that house, but by midnight they had done just that.

Day Ten

M onday, November 14. THE NIGHT BEFORE, Annie had been told to report to the guy in the structure tent who ran logistics, and now, five in the morning, she went over to him and introduced herself.

He looked her up and down and said, "I understand you're with the Wildlife Resources Commission."

She nodded.

"Good. We're gonna start getting a lot more firefighters either coming in or being demobilized out. That means tons of paperwork all day long, and I need someone who I can trust to dot every 'i' and cross every 't.'

"Every incoming fire company has to check in with us, and your job is to find out where they're from, how many guys they have, and what vehicles they brought; then send them over to me and I'll assign them out."

The man's organizational ability amazed Annie. Everything ran like clockwork. She'd send somebody over to him and he'd tell them, "You check in over here. Check your people in over there. Go to that table and get information. In the morning you're going to meet up with so and so. This is where you're gonna sleep and this is where you're gonna eat."

Before teams could be released to go home, the gear they borrowed had to be accounted for and turned back in. But the command still had to keep them on their rolls, because a firefighter assigned to the Party Rock Fire, belonged to the Party Rock Fire until they got back to where they came from and called the State Emergency Operations Center and reported that they and their equipment were safely back home and they didn't have to worry about them anymore.

The structural division complex consisted of an office made up of two connected Western Shelter tents with a dirt floor. It had phones, and because the Forest Service had set everything up to be wireless so all the divisions could network, they had rented a wireless copier. With the fire now in three counties, there was a table for each with a county representative manning it 24/7, putting all the resources in three counties at their fingertips.

Mid-morning, Morgan radioed the Buncombe County official on duty from his command post in the resort. "We could use a couple of your engines over here. Do you have any you can spare right now?"

"We've got five of them in the lot right here at the command center waiting to be assigned. How many do you need?"

Morgan requested three, then got on the radio with the logistics guy. "Can you cut Annie loose to run water up here and along 74A? She knows where everybody is."

"Sure. Things will be slow here for the next couple of hours."

Annie hopped in the fire station's pickup and drove over to the stacks of water cases at the supply tent that looked more like a warehouse. Two of the dozen or so volunteers stacking and organizing the truckloads of donations looked up.

"Going for another water run?" the one asked.

"Yeah. Can two of you guys help me? We can do it twice as fast."

They quickly loaded the bed with water and sports drinks, and the two volunteers hopped on. Annie, about to pull out, noticed cases of bananas and figured the guys on the line could use some potassium.

"Throw in a couple cartons of those," she yelled, then took off hoping to catch site of Mike on 74A. The nights they'd spent together came rushing back to her. She couldn't wait until this monster was finally caught and extinguished. Then she would get her brother out of North Carolina so they wouldn't have to live with this nightmare ever again, and Mike and she could get to know each other in a normal setting.

She pulled off 74A and drove up Boys Camp Road, stopping at a group of engines. As the two volunteers unloaded a couple cases of water, she felt in her pocket for the note Mike had left her that first night. She pulled it out and read it. He had said he loved her a dozen times since, but she would always cherish this little piece of paper where he expressed it for the first time.

The guys thumped on the top of the cab and she took off down the road again. They finished running the water on Boys Camp and she drove down 74A and stopped at the Geneva Motel that had a couple dozen fire trucks parked in front.

"Drop some water off here," she yelled to the guys in the back. "Some of those bananas, too."

As the guys ran in the office with cases of water, Annie got out and started reading the insignias on the fire trucks: Etowah Horse Shoe, Valley Hill, Golden Valley, Charlotte. Tears trickled down her cheeks as she continued to read: Ashboro, Moyock, Lower Currituck. When she got to the Summit Fire Department from Flagstaff, Arizona, she broke down.

The guys came running back, and seeing her sobbing out loud, gave her a quick hug and said, "Come on, let's go!" as if an emotional outburst like this by a first responder was no longer cause for concern. They had a job to do.

She got back in the truck, wiped her nose with the back of her hand, then her face with the sleeves of her shirt and continued to Terrace Lane behind the Chimney Rock stores where they had a couple of crews mopping up the brush. The dragon could be slumbering in the thick peat underneath and they wanted to make sure it couldn't breathe fire on the town again.

They continued down 74A, dropping water off to crews as they passed. Smoke and ash from the backburning operation saturated the air, and she could barely see ahead. On a steep slope, rangers were spreading fire with drip torches. Mike had to be with them. A team of firefighters stood by their engine, hoses in hand, waiting for the forest litter to burn before putting out the flames with water. Mike was going to be tired tonight. She would make him a good dinner.

ANNIE CAME OUT OF THE SHOWER, put on a clean pair of jeans and a T-shirt and meandered around Mike's house. She'd been in it a hundred times as a kid, but this was the first time she saw it as an actual place to live. A place where she might live. She shook her head vigorously. Don't get ahead of yourself, girl. He'd said he loved her, but what did that actually mean? They hardly knew each other.

She smiled to herself, filled with joy. She might not know everything about his character yet, but she had discovered what his body needed and she would offer it to him again tonight.

Her phone rang. It was her mother.

"Have you heard from Jack?" Annie asked.

"They came to see me today."

"Who?"

"Someone from the Lake Lure police."

"What did they say?"

"The usual. When did I see him last? Where do I think he went?"

"What did you tell them?"

"I said that he was probably in Florida. That he goes there a lot to deliver the chairs he's fixed. I kinda suggested that he'd been gone for a couple weeks."

"Hopefully that'll throw them off for a while. But we gotta find him, Mom. Do you think Terri might know where he went?"

"Maybe."

Annie thought she heard Mike's truck pull in and perked up her ears.

"Just a minute, Mom." She went to the stairway and could hear him taking a shower in the basement. She got back on the phone. "Talk to her, Mom, and let me know."

"The smoke's bad here. They're saying the fire's coming to Bat Cave," said Mae.

"You might want to pack up some things and take them over to Jack's," Annie said as she walked to the kitchen. "If I can get there tomorrow, I'll help you load them and take my stuff over there, too."

"Thank you, dear."

"Mom, it's important you talk to Terri and find out if she

knows where Jack is."

Finished with the call, she opened the fridge and took out some leftovers from the night before. Sensing Mike near, she turned to find him wearing nothing but a towel and a tan. The rippling abs made her forget about Jack as he carried her into the bedroom.

Later, the two of them lay in bed in each other's arms.

"I heard you mention your brother on the phone when I came in. Is there a problem?" asked Mike.

"No. Why would there be?"

"Well... you know."

She sat up and looked at him. "What are you trying to say?"

He grabbed her and pulled her down again.

"Let's just snuggle up and go to sleep."

She got out of bed and went over to the window. She hugged herself and looked out. "Do you think my brother had something to do with this fire?"

"I didn't say that."

"I know you didn't say it, but are you thinking it?"

He propped himself up on an elbow. "Honey, I'm so tired, I'm not thinking anything. I just don't want you to get hurt."

"Hurt!? When it comes to my brother, I'm so hurt I don't feel anything anymore... and neither does he."

"Do you know where he was when the fire started?" asked Mike.

"It doesn't matter where he was. He would never start this fire. He's a really good guy who hasn't done a thing wrong in twenty-five years."

Mike sat up. "You still haven't answered my question. Where was he when it started?"

"As a matter of fact, he was there on the trail."

"You're kidding."

"No. But it's just an unfortunate coincidence."

"Darlin', I'm afraid it's a tad more than unfortunate, and a lot of people would debate whether it's a coincidence."

"I know. I'm worried," she said. "I tried to get him to go to the police on Sunday but he never showed up."

"Where is he now?"

"I don't know. He's disappeared."

"I know he's your brother and you love him, but how do you think this is going to look to the police?"

"What are you getting at?"

"You have to consider the possibility that he did it."

"No. That's out of the question. Trust me on this."

"It's not a matter of trust, Annie. I don't want you to get hurt. If he did do it, maybe it's not his fault. Pyromania is a sickness. It's distinctly different from arson. They start fires to induce euphoria. A type of impulse control disorder. A lot of times it's when they're under stress or suffering from depression."

"I know what pyromania is," said Annie, "and it has nothing to do with my brother!"

"Maybe not. But you need to keep an open mind."

"And so do you," she said, pointedly.

Annie paced around the room, then sat on the bed next to Mike. She put her hand in his. "Mike, my brother and I are very close. And it's kind of tied into this whole fire business. He's had a tough time of it. And when someone has the kind of history my brother has, it affects everyone in the family. The hurt, the shame, the suspicion. I'm telling you from the bottom of my heart that my brother would never, ever do anything like starting this fire. Believe me, he's not sick. He's a nice guy."

"Annie, all I'm asking you to do is to look at this from an outsider's perspective. We know your brother started a fire before, and now you're telling me he was in this remote, unpopulated location on the very day the Party Rock Fire started. Ask yourself, what kind of conclusion would anyone with half a brain draw from these facts?"

"It's obvious to me what kind of conclusion you've drawn," said Annie.

She got up, clearly annoyed, and started putting on her clothes.

"What are you doing?" asked Mike.

"Going home."

She pulled her T-shirt on and went over to the bed and

looked down at the face she loved.

"I can't believe I'm actually saying this," she said. "I've loved you since forever. But this isn't gonna work."

Mike reached for her hand, but she stepped back.

"Jack would never have lit that fire, Mike. I'd stake my life on it." She wiped a tear from her cheek. "If things go the way I'm worried they might, you and I will be forced to make a choice, and it's unfair to put you in that position. I'm not going to let that happen, because if I have to choose between you and Jack, I'm not going to turn my back on my brother."

"Aw, come on, Annie. We can work this out."

"You don't understand, Mike. This can end up as a big, nasty mess. You're a nice guy and you don't deserve to be dragged into it. You don't know my brother, and you barely know me. It's best we put an end to this before that happens."

It struck her as being unfair, but she couldn't help thinking of him as siding with all the hateful folks that couldn't forgive Jack for a foolish mistake he had made as a ten year old. She knew the hurt it had caused her brother and she hated them for it. She grabbed her duffel bag and started to leave.

"Don't go, Annie. I love you," said Mike.

Annie stopped and looked over at him. The thought of not seeing him again almost broke her heart. "Maybe after all this is over..." She shook her head as if dashing any hope, and then closed the door behind her.

Tears streamed down her cheeks as she thought about Mike on the drive to her house. Tomorrow, he would get up, suit up, and go back and fight the dragon. It was what he did. And tonight, in spite of their breakup he would sleep with the kind of peace that comes from a belief that everything will come out all right in the end. "We always win," he had confidently told her when he talked about the fire. "We either put it out, or nature does it for us." How uncomplicated, she thought, not to be filled with the kind of anxiety that was ripping her apart.

More than anything, she wanted to turn the truck around and go back and lay in his arms, but now was not the time for love. The police were looking for Jack.

Day Eleven

T uesday, November 15. THE LOCAL OFFICIALS who had been attending the briefing sessions believed they were already keyed up as much as a body could be and still function, but on this morning the meteorologist managed to ratchet up the stress level another notch.

"For the past couple of days, we've lucked out since the weather wasn't conducive for large fire growth, but these conditions will change later this week. We're expecting the passage of a strong cold front this Saturday that will bring strong gusty winds from the southwest starting on Thursday. This wind event has the potential to push the fire to the north and northeast, with the wind sending flames towards the evacuated communities of Rumbling Bald Resort.

"In addition to the wind, the temperature is expected to rise into the low 70s with the humidity dropping below 30%— weather conditions that stimulate rapid fire growth."

With that prediction causing a stir in the tent, Brandon didn't want to leave, but he had to take off for the communications tent. His PR folks had set up two radio interviews with national news syndicates, after which an NBC affiliate was going to do a TV spot.

His 12-person PR staff put out 2 press releases daily and answered at least 250 calls a day from the general public, with 40-60 calls from media alone, but he was occasionally called upon to give a personal interview. This morning, he had to be sure to hit the right tempo about the coming winds. He wanted everyone to be concerned enough to pay close attention to the fire advisories, yet he didn't want to panic them, either.

ONCE THE FIRE STARTED CLAWING its way into Shumont, things turned hectic up at the Full Moon Farm. The wolfdogs were now sitting smack in the middle of the north sector of the fire's containment box. The mountain was overrun with tractors gouging out firebreaks, and strike teams from all over the country were putting in hand lines where the tractors couldn't go. Dozens of crews were backburning the forest ahead of the fire now stalking them.

Nancy was unloading some crates borrowed from the Brother Wolf Animal Rescue in Asheville, when Dr. Beverly Hargus from Animals R Us in Flat Rock phoned her.

"How close is the fire to you guys?" she asked.

"Close enough that I've got to get some animals out of here so I can move the ones way out in the woods into their enclosures. There are no roads to get back there, so we're trying to get one in with a tractor I just bought. They're backburning the adjacent property, so ash is raining down on us and we're running around with face masks or bandanas."

"Bring as many animals here as you can. I've got a small barn in my boarding kennel with stalls you can put them in so they don't have to stay in their crates. You'll just have to come and feed and walk them."

What a godsend, thought Nancy. She got off the phone and assembled her volunteers in the front parking area. "Okay, everyone. We're going to crate up some of these animals and take them over to Flat Rock. Once we get them over there, we're going to have to get the wild ones out of the woods and move them up here and into the vacated enclosures."

"Are we going to tranquilize those guys in the woods?" someone asked.

"Not if we can help it," she answered. "Just the two crazies, Ronnie and Tony. They both have serious bite histories."

"Who are we taking to Flat Rock?" someone shouted out.

"Let's try to get the seniors and the biters. That way, if we have to evacuate everyone in a hurry, we won't have to deal with that as much."

Just as Nancy finished making a hurried list of the animals

she wanted crated, the Buncombe County Fire Marshal pulled in. She handed the list to a volunteer, told everyone to get started and went over and introduced herself. He stood there rubbing his jaw and listening to the dogs howl.

"You sure got a lot of wolves in here. They told me about you down at the Broad River fire house, but I wanted to see it for myself."

"We're getting ready to move sixteen out today and hope we don't have to evacuate the fifty-four we have left," said Nancy. "Some of them hate each other and some of them you can't touch. It'll take a lot of tranquilizer darts if we have to get them out of here."

"You know the fire's getting close, don't you?" he said.

"Oh, yeah. We can actually see it on the next property when we're in the back."

"I'll send the Forest Service guys over here to see what they can do," he said, then he got in his truck and left.

By noon, they had eight animals crated and on their way to Flat Rock, with Nancy, the only one licensed to tranquilize an animal, staying behind to make sure everything went well with the other eight.

A howl from one of the wolfdogs made her look up. The tall, burly guy from the Forest Service that had talked to her about the backburning on the neighboring property the day before, came out of his truck covered in red retardant from head to toe. She smiled to herself as he neared, remembering a volunteer calling him Grizzly Adams.

"We're knocking down the fire as it moves this way," he said, "but I'm afraid it's going to be at your back door any time now. I'm gonna be perfectly honest with you. We don't want those animals loose, so we're gonna do whatever we can to keep you safe. We're sending you two brush trucks and an engine company with eight firefighters. They'll be here in two shifts 24 hours a day for the duration."

He looked around. "When we were doing the backburn be-hind you, we heard the wolves howl." He chuckled. "I was with a Navajo strike team from New Mexico. When they heard them, they howled and broke out into what they said was a wolf dance. It was kinda cool."

Nancy was touched by the Forest Service's concern and respect for her life's work as she watched him stroll through the compound, sizing it up.

"You've got to move all the animals into a cluster so we can get to them with a fire truck. Our hoses have to reach every one of their enclosures. Do you have anything to get all these leaves out of here?"

"Yes, two backpack blowers."

"Get people busy right away blowing them as far away as possible. How about water?" he asked.

"We've got a gravity fed spring, and I didn't think we'd have enough water if this thing got close, so I bought a 1,500 gallon water tank. We ran a hose to a pond in back and we're pumping it in."

"That's good," Grizzly said.

He looked up as an engine pulled in, followed by two brush trucks. "These guys are from Arizona. You'll be getting a different crew for every shift, sometimes hotshots from out west, sometimes from right here in North Carolina. "We'll send food, but they'd appreciate coffee if you can come up with it."

"How about a 30-cup urn?"

"That ought to do it," he said, and left to give the crew their briefing.

MEANWHILE, IN Davidson County just outside Lexington in the Piedmont section of the state, thirty-seven-year-old Doug Leary, a lieutenant with the A-RC-H Fire and Rescue Company, was paying close attention to the Party Rock Fire. For a week now, he and his wife had been letting out a pained gasp every time the mountains where they had taken their two kids on vacation flashed across the TV screen in flames.

He sat in the station breakroom reading a newspaper someone had left behind. Fiery mountain photos made him feel sorry for the folks who might lose their homes, and at the same time, concerned for the firefighters, when he got the call from the chief.

"I just promised the county emergency management folks two crews for the Party Rock Fire. I'm sending you and two of our other guys up there with our brush truck and pickup. I'm getting a fourth guy from another station. That way we can serve 24 hours each day, two men on each shift, swapping out the brush truck. That's what they need and that's what they're gonna get. And, Doug, I wouldn't plan on getting back before Thanksgiving."

The A-RC-H Fire and Rescue Company serves the three rural communities of Arcadia, Reedy Creek and Hampton. Formerly solely an agricultural area, it now functions as a bucolic bedroom community for both Winston-Salem and Statesville, with its gently rolling country roads spooling by as many subdivisions as they do farms.

Doug ran home, packed enough clothes for eight days and hurried back to the station. Two of their firemen had already left for Lake Lure with the brush truck, and by five, he and his new partner, a twenty-one year old volunteer fireman from another company, took off in the station's pickup.

They pulled into Lake Lure around eight, and after checking in, were told to report to the tennis courts at five the next morning. They checked out the huge Western Shelters, and, seeing how crowded they were, decided to camp out in their own tents in a field next to the beauty salon across the road. Besides, with all the generators going, it was so noisy they didn't know how anyone could sleep.

THE LAKE LURE INN had been serving the evening meals and providing sack lunches for four days now, and Tara and Andy Normington had watched the number of firefighters they were feeding escalate daily. As insurance adjusters who covered disasters all over the country, they'd just gotten back home to Bat Cave from Hurricane Matthew when the fire broke.

Grateful for an opportunity to finally get a chance to help in their own back yard, they threw in with the band of volunteers the Lake Lure Inn had cobbled together to help serve food and make enough sandwiches to meet the ever-increasing demand.

Since the road between Bat Cave and Lake Lure was closed, they decided to haul the Airstream travel trailer that they took with them to disasters to a friend's house in Lake Lure. After a long detour, they had parked it in the driveway and had been sleeping in it for the past four days.

Tara and Andy had kicked off another smoky day at five-thirty that morning, helping to dispense the breakfast Ingles brought in, along with a good deal of appreciative smiles for the men and women about to go into harm's way to protect their mountain community.

No sooner had the last firefighter been served, and the mess tent cleaned, when the bevy of volunteers rushed over to a vacant store in the Arcade building across from the beach, where they pitched in making sandwiches and packing sack lunches in an assembly line fashion to be distributed at breakfast the next morning.

The hours between preparing the lunch sacks and helping the inn serve the evening meal were put to good use in the building attached to the inn's Motor Court used for weddings and special events. For the past week, the special event had been the Party Rock Fire. Located on the highway across from the beach, it was convenient for dispensing the massive amounts of homemade food coming in: hams, cakes, cookies, casseroles, and all kinds of lovingly prepared covered dishes. Firefighters, evacuees, volunteers, first responders, and anyone wanting something to eat when the mess tent was closed were heartily welcomed.

When six o'clock rolled around, Tara and Andy joined a dozen or so volunteers in the mess tent. Tara, dishing out beans, saw she was running low and mentioned it to the helper next to her. The woman took out the walkie-talkie the inn had supplied and asked for more. She checked the other chafing dishes and then peeked out of the tent at the line that spooled down the field, and added, "You better send more corn, too. By the way, is that chicken coming? They're going for it big time and we're almost out."

Just then, the inn's manager and his assistant rolled in a hot box, and she quickly added, "Never mind. It just showed up."

It was after nine by the time Tara and Andy and several other volunteers finished cleaning up the mess tent, a good fifteen hours after most of them greeted the morning at the command post.

"How many did we serve tonight?" asked the inn's manager, who was on hand every night to help clean up.

"Just over seven hundred," a volunteer wearily answered.

Andy whispered in Tara's ear, "They need somebody tonight to man the events room over at the motor lodge. Do you have the strength to work a couple more hours? They're expecting some hotshots working a sixteen hour shift up on the Shumont wilderness to be coming off the mountain around ten, and they're gonna be lookin' for somethin' to eat."

She smiled. "Sure, honey. We can't let those guys go hungry."

After saying good night to the cluster of volunteers with hugs all around, someone gave them a lift to the motor lodge. The inn's manager came right behind them with the van, and the three of them took the leftover chicken, ham and vegetables in. The inn's manager looked around. There had to be two hams, a dozen or so cakes and pies, and dozens of covered dishes.

A big half-sheet cake the bakery crew at Ingles had elaborately decorated with a fire truck and written "We love you!" across it caught his eye.

"You almost don't want to cut into it," said Tara.

"Folks can't show their appreciation enough," he said. Fatigued, he buried his face in his hands and slowly ran them down its contours as if he realized he was finally done for the night. He cast a pair of bloodshot eyes at the two and said, "I'm going back to the inn. I've got to get some sleep. I've been up since four. If you need anything, give a holler. Someone will bring it over."

The inn's manager left and Tara put on a fresh pot of coffee, while Andy heated up the chafing dishes. They barely finished putting out an appetizing array of fresh food when a string of dirty, sooty, bone-tired hotshots stumbled in and brought the harsh smell of charred wood with them. Tara could feel their pain.

The twenty firefighters from Taos Pueblo, New Mexico, helped themselves while Tara and Andy scurried back and forth with coffee and drinks. The team had been backburning around the fire line the 'dozers had dug up on Shumont, and been at it since six that morning. As Tara watched them polish off their loaded plates, she was so filled with love and gratitude that she had to blink back tears. But when she put Ingles' decorated cake on the table and they broke into high fives, she buried her face in Andy's shoulder and wept.

Day Twelve

Wednesday, November 16. BAT CAVE HAD BEEN A bustling little village before the Great Flood of 1916 barreled down the gorge and cleared away the town's post office and twelve of its commercial structures. Unfortunately, the town was never able to catch a second breath after that disaster, and slowly receded into the sort of place that one drives through never realizing it was ever a destination.

A distant memory are the horse-drawn, four-seated livery stable hacks that brought sightseers down the winding trail, now Route 64, from nearby Hendersonville in the late 1800s. No more do cheerful couples in crinolines and knickers frolic in the afternoon as they hike up to the actual bat cave down the road or venture into the village next door to gaze at the iconic monolith that protrudes from the mountain like a chimney.

Faded like hickory smoke drifted from a campfire are the echoes of a house full of hungry summer guests rushing into the dining halls of the dozens of boarding houses sprinkled throughout the mountains. For the most part, all that is left of them are the barely noticeable overgrown foundations, for no longer do whole families from South Carolina, Georgia, Florida and other southern states pile out of trains at the Hendersonville station and spend the summer at these forgotten refuges to escape the heat and yellow fever that ravaged the South in the last half of the 19th century.

Yet, the Reedy Creek still writhes its way north along Route 64 into this craggy mountain crossroads as does the Hickory Nut Creek that runs east down the gorge along Route 74A to the village. The Broad River sweeps down from the north along Highway 9 and meets the two rushing streams head-on in Bat Cave, swallowing them as it swings east on its rocky jaunt through the gorge before spilling into Lake Lure just beyond Chimney Rock.

Like a lot of places that seem to fade with time, Bat Cave managed to keep a finger on its underlying pulse. One could point to the Bat Cave Volunteer Fire Department as one of the main threads that held this sparse mountain community together. The three-bay station house with its stone facade sits on the south side of Route 74A, a couple hundred yards east of the jagged crossroads where Highway 9 radiates north, and Route 64 heads south to Hendersonville.

The thirty-five or so volunteers of this fire and rescue company stand ready to protect their corner of Henderson County with three engines, a 1,400 gallon tanker, a brush truck and a host of service vehicles. And on this fall day, they braced for what some of them feared was going to be an apocalypse—the main arteries were closed, houses evacuated, and high winds predicted for the weekend.

AT FIVE THAT MORNING, the two firefighters who had spent the night in their tents in the field across from the command center grabbed a quick breakfast at the mess tent before hurrying over to the tennis courts for a briefing of team leaders. There had to be a couple hundred firefighters packed in there.

The supervisor started off with a safety message. "Firefighting here in the mountains is different from what most of you are used to, and safety is our main concern. We've got steep drop-offs, falling timber, burning logs that roll downhill. And don't forget about the wildlife. We've had a couple of encounters with bobcats and bears."

Finally, the two men's names were called to join an 8-man task force. They were summarily briefed, then sent down to the Bat Cave Fire Department where the command needed a lot of fresh crews. Doug's force consisted of two engines, one from Denver, North Carolina, and one from Mountain Home, and another brush truck that came from the coast, all with 2-man crews.

At Bat Cave, Doug and his partner met up with the other

half of the A-RC-H team. They'd been sent there to work the night shift right after they had arrived. Doug swapped the pickup for the brush truck and went over to the station's mini-command post for a team briefing.

"Everybody get your radios set on foxtrot 3. That's where we're gonna talk to you," said the supervisor. "A lot of you guys are used to VHF and it's gonna be a little bit of a learning curve to use the Viper radios, but once you do, you'll see how much better it is. I'm going to be running back and forth getting the different teams what they need, so if you want anything, get on the radio."

He went over to a briefing map taped to the side of a truck. "Here's where I want you guys this morning. The Forest Service has a bunch of men in there right now and they've got a working fire. Get over there, lay down your hoses and help them out. The Bat Cave tankers will keep you supplied with water. Just radio when you need it and they'll come fill you up.

"I'm sending you men to what we're hoping is our last stand at this arm of the fire. We've got a half-dozen 'dozers in there putting in a firebreak just before it reaches Highway 9 and your job is to keep the fire out of there. We haven't had rain for forty-six days and everything's as dry as it gets. We're expecting a big wind event this weekend and we're in a race against time." He clapped his hands. "Okay, let's go. And stay safe."

THE FOREST SERVICE HAD BEEN unloading three bulldozers up on the far side of the Shumont wilderness all morning. They were working to establish a line on the fire's northern front that would finally shield the resort. One driver had come from Wilmington, one from Oklahoma, and one was from the Rutherford Forest Service office. They were waiting for James Ledgerwood, the Chimney Rock State Park supervisor, to get there after the morning briefing. He was familiar with the logging roads on that section of Shumont Mountain, since the state owned a big chunk of it.

Ledgerwood raced down the narrow asphalt road, pulled up and jumped out with a site plan the G.I.S. guy had just run off.

He slapped it on the hood of a truck and they all gathered around.

"Here's where you are," he said, pointing to a cross-hatched line. "You need to widen this logging road up there to fifteen feet, tying it to this one over here. One of our park rangers will direct the route and a Forest Service guy will tag the trees at eye level so you know where to go. The taggers know your equipment, what it can do and what it can't do, so they'll keep you out of trouble." He looked up and pointed to a trail running from the road to the top of a slope. "You'll be going right through there."

The guy from Wilmington shook his head. "Hey, I'm from the coast. I don't know if I can do this."

"Look, there's no dishonor in saying you're scared or not comfortable with it. We respect that," said Ledgerwood.

"Well, I'd like to give it a try. I just don't want you thinkin' I'm some kind of an expert."

"Okay, the guy from the Forest Service is going to be running the same size tractor as you. Follow his cat tracks and use your blade to clean it out. Just keep in mind, if he can go there, you should be assured you can get there, too. But if you're still not comfortable with it, let me know. Bulldozing on those rocks with that slope... you're putting steel on rock. And if you start to slide, you go right off."

The guy from Oklahoma spoke up. "I've done this kind of thing before. I'm pretty sure I can handle it."

"Good. You follow the Forest Service guy and make it wider." He turned to the guy from the east coast. "You follow behind them and clean it up. We've got another team widening this trail on the other side of the mountain. Hopefully, you'll meet up with them before dark tonight."

The superintendent started back to his truck. "We're getting strong winds later this week and they're gonna really need this line widened if they're gonna stop the fire before it hits the resort."

FERRELL BANKS MADE A QUICK INSPECTION of the now critical Highway 9 firebreak, and on his way back drove up to a state trooper at a check point and pulled down his window.

"How's the evacuation going?"

"We should have it complete by five. We're telling everyone they can shelter at Grace Lutheran Church on 6th Avenue in Hendersonville. The Bat Cave shelter had to close due to poor air quality."

Ferrell didn't want to take the time to drop in at the Bat Cave station since Brandon was going to a community meeting at the Rumbling Bald Resort, and one of them needed be on duty at the fire command. Brandon would be presenting an overview of the fire and what they were doing to fight it. With the predicted strong winds, he had felt it necessary to give the general public a heads up about the potential severity of the situation.

Ferrell swung onto the closed 74A and started toward Chimney Rock. The smoke was thick from all the backburning, ashes were flying, and fire apparatus was scattered all over. A mile and a half up, spotting Mike taking a break, he pulled up and got out.

Mike had taken off his hat and brush shirt and stood guzzling down a bottle of water. His dark brown hair glistened with sweat. Recalling the rumors that he and Annie were an item, Ferrell couldn't help thinking what a striking couple the two of them would make.

"How's it going?" asked Mike.

"Someone showed us an old logging road above Bat Cave and we've got 'dozers working like crazy putting a firebreak in there. If they get it in before the fire reaches Bat Cave, we stand a chance of stopping it at this end." He shook his head. "I sure hope we do. Our fire behavior guy is telling us with the winds they're expecting, if this fire jumps Highway 9 when it hits Bat Cave, with all the dry leaves on those mountains, it wouldn't surprise him if we see ten foot flames running at seventy feet a minute."

"What's happening up on Shumont?" asked Mike.

"We've got five 'dozers over at the north end trying to tie in that firebreak so we can cut off the resort. Every night we burn around whatever we've dug up, and all day we dump water on the line to make sure the fire doesn't jump the burnout. And where we can't get a 'dozer in, we're putting in hand lines. We don't know how we're going to tie it together before this wind hits, but we're trying our best." He tugged at his blond beard, "It's like that fire has had it in its head to wipe that resort out since the first spark." He looked up at Mike. "How's it going over here?"

"We've had a couple flareups, but we keep taking bites out of it and driving it down the road. I'll hand it to you, Ferrell, when I saw those flames on Round Top the other night, I didn't have a whole lot of faith your strategy would save that town. I would've started a backburn at the bottom of the mountain in Chimney Rock and let it run up instead of letting it come down the way you did."

"That was the first thing I considered," said Ferrell, "but it was too risky. At that stage, the fire was too explosive and there was too much fuel around those houses. I had to slow it down enough to give us time to clear it all away. We got lucky and got the retardant line laid down just in time to break the head of the fire. Instead of it roaring off the top of Round Top and throwing itself into the town, it crawled off the cliff and came down slow enough for us to get a grip on it."

"I don't know how you're coping with all that's going on," said Mike.

Ferrell scratched behind his ear. "I've been compartmentalizing both fronts like I'm fighting two different fires. The problem is they're happening at the same time. Thank God, the Buncombe County folks have been able to keep it off the plateau up on Shumont, but it's crawled along the ridge and gone north into no-man's land."

A horn sounded. "That's us," said Mike. "We're going back at it."

Ferrell got in his truck, and drove to Chimney Rock, viewing the charred burnouts on the side of the road. The big logs and stumps were still smoking. Just before the Flowering Bridge, he saw a Trooper handing IDs back to a couple in their car. Chimney Rock was still closed, but they were letting residents back on Boys Camp Road. Seeing the elderly gray-haired couple, the gravity of his mission struck home. All their cherished mementos collected over a lifetime were probably sitting in their house. This fire was a ruthless thief sneaking along the backyards of three communities, trying to get in and rob them. It had come right up to the back door of Chimney Rock, but they had been able to beat it back. He couldn't help wondering how long their luck would hold.

BRANDON HAD MADE SURE all the emergency management folks would be at the afternoon planning session so they could all get on the same page regarding the high winds expected on Saturday and Sunday, and the conference room was packed.

"Okay, let's start with the northeast perimeter," he began.

Ferrell went over to the briefing map on an easel and pointed to a crisscrossed line weaving between Shumont and the resort. "If we finish this firebreak and can hold it, we should be able to stop it here."

"What are the chances of getting it done by this weekend?" asked Brandon.

"We're working on it every day and doing burnouts every night," said Ferrell.

"If you don't get it in, what's the next trigger point?"

"If we lose it, it'll run right though the resort, and we'll have to fall back to Buffalo Creek Road, which means that there'll be a lot of houses in between that burn."

"And if we don't stop it at Buffalo Creek Road?"

"Then it's going to start burning on Youngs Mountain, and there's no way we can stop it from going up that mountain once it starts. Then we've got to drop back again and try to catch it at Bills Creek Road." He looked around the room. "And if we don't catch it there, it's going to go straight through to Route 40."

Brandon nodded. "Make sure we've got crews assigned in every one of those contingency locations and that residents to the north, especially Morganton, are notified that the fire might be coming their way. Now, how about Bat Cave?"

"We've got 'dozers putting in a firebreak before Highway 9

that we're hoping will stop it," said Ferrell. "If not, with these dry conditions, it could run all the way down the gorge; or if the winds shift, down Highway 9 toward Black Mountain. In that case, we'll fall back to Old Fort Road."

MORGAN LEFT THE MEETING and as he started to drive to the command post in the resort, he listened to someone from the Forest Service talk on the radio. "Our 'dozers have gouged out four more miles of checkline in here, but dang if I can figure out how we're gonna tie this thing together."

"Aren't those bear hunters helping any?"

"They're trying. They've driven me up and down every logging road in Shumont, but haven't come up with anything that'll work."

"Well if they don't, that wind's gonna be comin' and this fire's gonna run right through that resort."

Morgan was suddenly struck with the conviction that things really do happen for a reason. Just that spring, as if they didn't already have enough to do, the town had put in twelve miles of biking and hiking trails on the resort side of the mountain. Since rescue was part of his job, he had to spend a lot of time scouting out where the trails could go, figuring out how they'd get people out of there if they got hurt, how they'd reach them, what equipment they'd need, what equipment wouldn't work. Before then, he'd never had a reason to spend time in that remote northern area that he now knew like the back of his hand.

Morgan grabbed his radio. "Hang on. I think I know how it can be connected. I'll be right there."

With everything he'd been through and everything he'd put those firefighters through in the past fourteen days to protect the houses in there, he wasn't going to let them burn now. He was living on adrenaline and so worn out that he counted on his faith to keep him going. He pulled into the resort, got on an ATV and headed for the woods at the resort's upper end. The dire contingency plans they had discussed at the morning meeting if the fire jumped the line raced through his brain. Plan A, B and C, they called them.

He took a curve and spotted the ranger's truck.

"Come with me!" he shouted. Every one of the crazy paths they had blazed in there as they carved out the biking trails were clearly mapped in his head. They zigged and then zagged as he led them over a web of complicated connecting logging roads.

"First we get dragged all over tarnation by those bear hunters," said one of the Forest Service guys as they followed Morgan, "now we're taking a joy ride with this hotrod."

They came to a sudden stop behind Morgan and looked around. Right in front of them was the tail end of their firebreak.

"Well I'll be doggoned," said the ranger. "He's brought us right where we need to be in order to tie in the line." He quickly got on the radio. "Bring in the 'dozers. Ron Morgan will lead you where you need to go." He looked over and gave Morgan a thumbs up, then he got back on the radio. "And bring in a 20-man hotshot crew. We need to get the trail burned out and mopped up before those winds show."

THE MINUTE THE two men from the A-RC-H company arrived at the Highway 9 location where they'd been assigned that morning, they started throwing water on a fire raging down the mountain. Once they put it out, they spent the rest of the day running water in their brush truck to the Forest Service crews in the woods. By the time six o'clock rolled around, they were happy to be heading back to the Bat Cave station to trade off the brush truck with the other two guys from their station and grab something to eat.

Black with soot, they peeled off their brush clothes, left them in the truck and went in the station house. It was crowded, noisy, and overflowing with the kind of spirited camaraderie a squad can exude when they know they've been toiling at something important, even heroic. Firefighters who had just ended their shift enthusiastically heaped their plates with food the women's auxiliary had prepared.

Doug and his partner quickly got in line, and a rugged team of wildland firefighters came in behind them. They had taken off their brush shirts, but with their brush pants and logger's boots covered with red retardant, there was no question, they were one of the hotshot crews from out of state.

Doug's partner nudged him and whispered, "I think this is the twenty-person strike team from Alaska everyone's talking about. They've got them working in the wilderness up on the Shumont range. Three of them are women."

His partner, anxious to make friends with them, struck up a conversation with the guy next to him.

"Are you the crew from Alaska?"

"Yep."

"Where were you guys working today?"

"Up on Shumont. Man, what an air show they put on! At one point it got so crazy, we were on a peak and could see the planes flying below us."

"I want to work in fire," said Doug's partner, earnestly. "How do I get into this full-time like you guys?"

"Go for it," said the hotshot. "There's nothing like being in the fire world. If you move to the Southwest, there's fire everywhere. You can't miss it. And, it doesn't really matter where your base is. If you work for the National Forest Service, once you're in the fire season, you're all over the place. We're from Alaska, but we've spent as much time in the lower forty-eight as we did up there."

They started down the line, hungrily loading up sturdy paper plates with what looked like good old-fashioned home-cooked food.

"Can we sit with you?" his partner asked, as he nudged Doug to go along.

"Sure."

The hotshot team sat together in the long line of tables, accepting the guys from Davidson County as their own. They all knew what it was like to thirst for the challenge of fire. They'd been there themselves.

"What is it like fighting fires out west?" Doug's partner asked as he listened intently and barely touched his food. "Do you camp out in the woods?"

"We usually don't bother with tents. We get 10 to 15 minutes from the moment we wake up to get packed up, geared up, and on our trucks, so most of us just throw down a sleeping bag and pass out." He looked around the fire house's meeting room. "We don't usually get assigned to a nice fire camp like this."

"What is it like to work in the wilderness?"

"Well, one of the biggest challenges is staying mentally engaged. Wildland fire doesn't give you much warning that it's coming, so you've got to be aware and ready to move quickly. A forest fire is gonna do what it wants to do, so you've got to be flexible."

A team member spoke up. "Listen to him, kid. Mac's one of our best."

"The biggest aspect of the job is the physical part of it," Mac continued. "A couple of weeks ago we were in Arizona and had been working for two straight weeks digging a fireline and cutting down dead trees all around it. Then the fire got up in a tree and hopped our line, and we had to start all over again."

Groans rose around the table. "We remember that one!" someone yelled.

Mac smiled at Doug's partner and threw up his hands. "When things like that happen, you just have to 'embrace the suck.' To do this kind of work, you've got to be flexible, resilient, have a really strong work ethic. A good sense of humor doesn't hurt either."

One of the women shouted out, "A sense of humor is the most important thing. When a bunch of filthy, sweaty and exhausted firefighters are sleeping all together in sleeping bags, living on sack lunches in the woods, and showering in creek water, humor goes a *long* way."

"Fitness is important too," Mac added. "Our crew's ability to perform in demanding conditions for extended periods of time depends on every crewmember being physically fit. All potential hotshots begin intense physical training no later than ten weeks prior to the start of a fire season.

"My boots have melted walking through flames. I've had times where I can feel my nose hairs getting singed. We've all been trained for extreme situations, and we're there because we want to be. No one's in our crew by accident. Everyone of us really loves it and all the nutty things that go along with it."

"I think I might look into this," said Doug's partner.

"Wildland firefighting is an awesome and important job. You're not going to find many occupations, other than the military or maybe the Peace Corps, where you have this strong feeling of family and purpose; and at the same time, you get these incredible opportunities to see parts of the country you would never otherwise see. The mountain vistas I saw up on Shumont today seemed to stretch to infinity. It was awesome. I felt like I was on top of the world."

They all looked up at two women handing every firefighter a paper bag filled with homemade cookies. Messages scrawled with a magic marker read, "This package is made for you & sent with love! Thank you!" or "We appreciate you so much! Enjoy this gift of Love!" Someone followed behind handing out cards made by students from The Lake Lure Classical Academy. Surprisingly, these tired men seemed interested in reading them. The reassurance was taken to heart after a day of life-threatening hard work.

Exhausted, now that Doug and his partner were well fed, all they wanted to do was get back to the tent and flop on their cots. As they pulled off the road in Lake Lure, Cindy Balk, the owner of the beauty salon came out and invited them to stay in her place every night.

"It'll be a lot warmer than sleeping outside and there are two showers you can use. There are firefighters sleeping in the real estate office next door and they've been using the showers. I just leave the door unlocked when I go."

Seeing the woman get in her car and leave, they quickly gathered some things from the tent and hurried over to the beauty salon. Doug had never set foot in one before and the instant he entered, he was surrounded by the mysterious stratagems women use to primp and polish, from the scent of perfume to all the potions in delicate bottles and jars in fancy glass cases. The sheer variety amazed him. Going from the smoky, ashy mountains to this den of guile, he was struck by the contrast.

The salon had been a house at one time, so it had a series of small rooms, including a kitchen that now had a bank of hair-washing stations lined up across it. He took a long, hot shower and, too tired to set up his cot, he just threw his sleeping bag on the rug and got in. The generosity of the owner offering her cozy, warm little place for them to sleep, the hearty home-cooked meal served at Bat Cave, the bag of homemade cookies made with love, and the heartfelt words of thanks on the cards from the local kids touched his heart, and he fell asleep feeling welcome and appreciated.

PATRICK BRYANT, the inn's manager, stuffed the last of the tablecloths and trays into their van. They had just finished serving over 900 firefighters dinner and it took everything they had, and some, to do it. The fire had grown so large and the amount of responders so numerous the North Carolina Baptist Men and Women's Disaster Relief Ministry would take over tomorrow, serving all the meals, plus providing the bag lunches for everyone going out in the field.

Patrick shoved the last container into the van, closed the door and waved the driver off before heading over to the back field and looking out on the fire, something he had done every night.

Seven days earlier, he was looking forward to going into the off-season after a hectic summer catering to the vacation crowd. Down to a skeleton staff when Annie called, they somehow met the challenge. It took every resource they could put their hands on as well as the mustering of volunteers from the entire community. He smiled inwardly. Enlisting the evacuees staying with them to help make the bag lunches and serve the meals was a huge plus.

Operating under the stress of not knowing what the next hour would bring, had been the worst part of it; but everyone's commitment to make sure the firefighters were properly fed regardless of any personal sacrifices they had to endure, carried them over the finish line.

Day Thirteen

Thursday, November 17. THAT MORNING, INGLES served their last breakfast and the Lake Lure Inn their last coffee, and by afternoon the North Carolina Baptist Men were ready to take over with their full-sized commercial kitchen and refrigerated trailer. When the inn's 40' x 20' tent was in the way, the Baptist men each simply grabbed a pole and moved it. Home-based in Cary, NC, this nonprofit organization's purpose is to relieve the human suffering disasters cause by providing, among other things, hot meals, debris removal, child care and family assistance. They draw their volunteers from all over the state, and when they show up, bring their food with them.

LATE THAT AFTERNOON, Nancy Brown, the woman who ran the wolfdog refuge, was returning from feeding and walking the sixteen animals being kenneled in Flat Rock. Highway 9 was closed from Bat Cave to Shumont, so she had to take a detour and travel an extra fifty miles twice a day for the chore.

The crews the Forest Service was sending over to protect the sanctuary kept Nancy informed about the fire, as well as the those she'd run across working on the roads, so when she got the text about a meeting at the main Broad River fire station that afternoon, she figured she could skip it.

The fire station was located just off Highway 9, five miles north of Shumont and on the same road she had to use to get to the sanctuary. As she came around a curve and saw a long line of vehicles on both sides of the road in front of the station, she decided she'd better pull in.

She found a spot to park and rushed through the gray smoky fog to the fire station's adjoining community room. Sixty or so people listened to the chief inside where the smoke was almost as dense.

"A strong cold weather front with gusty winds that could reach 40 miles per hour will be moving through the area this weekend," the chief announced. "These winds are expected to start picking up tomorrow morning, so all of you should be on your toes and be sure to pay close attention to monitoring the fire."

As he continued with his report, Nancy Brown started to worry. An evacuation was beginning to look like a strong possibility. The minute she got back to the sanctuary she'd have to put in a call for another box of tranquilizing darts and pay whatever it cost to get them there overnight.

"Burnout operations on our section of the fire's containment line," the chief continued, "are almost complete and helicopters have been delivering large water drops to ensure that these burnouts don't jump the line. Be prepared to see even more smoke tomorrow due to the additional burnouts that will occur tonight."

The briefing finished, Nancy was making her way past a crowd at the door when a fireman stopped her.

"Don't worry, Nancy," he said. "We've got your back."

By the time she reached her truck, she was wiping tears. When she arrived at the sanctuary, she made the call for the tranquilizer darts, then sent word for all the volunteers to assemble at the lower parking area. "Invite those eight Forest Service guys from Texas, too."

She checked out her dart rifle as she made a call to the vet.

"It looks like we might have to bug out of here," Nancy told her.

"You're familiar with the agility course at the boarding facility," the vet said. "If you have to get out of there, drive your animals over here and take the fence down and pull your trucks in. We can leave the dogs crated there. We'll walk the ones we can and hose down the rest the best we can."

With that settled, Nancy started down the lane to the parking area. It would take a while for everybody to assemble, so she stole a minute to visit Mani, her canine soul-mate who she always referred to as her "heart dog." The instant Mani noticed her coming around the tree-lined lane, he howled the long, doleful greeting that defined his species. Nancy let herself in his cage and he gave her an enthusiastic welcome, licking her face and then butting his head against her to be petted.

He was a light buff color with fine dark streaks across his rump and outlining his ears. A pure white muzzle and eyebrows set off his dark eyes. The reason Mani touched her more than any other animal she had ever known was probably because he was her first wolfdog rescue as well as her first high wolf content dog. She cut her teeth in this field with Mani, and it wasn't easy. Either he loved you or he hated you. He only let six of her volunteers venture into his enclosure. The first couple of years he gave her a big challenge, even knocking food out of her hand when she came to feed him, but they finally came to terms and the experience helped her conquer her fear of wolves.

Together sixteen years now, he would sit in her lap and sleep with her when they were on the road or at an exhibition. He still stole cleaning rags and sticks from the volunteers he allowed in his enclosure, and he wanted a chunk out of Nancy's new boyfriend, but every time she looked into his beautiful wolf face, she melted.

She hugged him and gave his fur a final ruffling, then walked to the field where everyone had gathered.

"I just returned from a meeting at the fire station," she announced, "and they're saying we'll be getting big winds this weekend with strong gusts starting in the morning."

One of the volunteers, who two days earlier showed up out of nowhere, piped up. "I drove down to the barricade at Shumont Road this morning and saw fire engines lined up bumper to bumper for as far as the eye could see. It looked like they were getting ready for Armageddon."

"Does this mean we're going to evacuate?" someone yelled.

"I don't know," said Nancy, "but we've got to have a crate next to every animal and all the trucks have to be gassed up and parked nearby."

"If we have to go, are you going to tranquilize them?" someone asked.

"Only if we have to," she said. "I hate to do it. Three ccs will knock them down, but it takes seven to fifteen minutes to work. These are scary minutes because the animal can have a seizure while the sedative is taking effect."

"Don't you think we should get them all out of here while the getting is good?" someone spoke up.

"I haven't made up my mind, yet," said Nancy. "When you crate an animal up, it stresses them out. And then we'll have to deal with the aftermath of that. Darting is even worse."

Everyone fixed their eyes on a truck pulling in.

"Here comes Grizzly Adams," a girl announced.

Nancy clapped her hands. "Okay, everyone, let's get out there and get totally staged for evacuation."

She walked over to greet the imposing Forest Service hulk with a bushy red beard.

"I take it you've heard about the winds we're expecting this weekend," he said as he jumped out of his truck.

She nodded.

"I'm just gonna lay it on the line, Nancy. Once those gusts start up we're gonna be fighting this fire tooth and nail. This thing can run down the gorge, or down number 9, or run right over this way. These mountains generate updrafts that create a slope effect. Fire typically runs upward, but with the slope effect it can turn around and come right back at you. This place is one of the four areas in the world that they've identified that experiences this effect. You need to decide right now what you're gonna do so we can help you. If you decide to stay, we'll be here with you. If you go, we'll still be here."

Nancy thought for a long moment about the world of woe she'd be heaping on the animals if they evacuated. Then she considered what could happen if she didn't. She looked into the eyes of the man with the big bushy beard standing in front of her and knew he wasn't going to let the worst happen. She made up her mind.

"We're gonna stay," she said.

He left, and she yelled over to a group of volunteers, "Put on the pump and make sure that water tank is filled to the brim!"

SMOKE FROM THE now infamous Party Rock Fire was expected to linger over the Raleigh Triangle for another day before a cold front was expected to sweep in and push it away. North Carolina air quality forecasters had issued another Code Orange for the region and urged that children, active people, older adults and those with heart or lung disease limit prolonged or heavy exertion outdoors.

With downtown Raleigh socked in, sixty volunteer firefighters from Wade County prepared to pack a bus with their sleeping bags and backpacks and hop on, when the deputy director of the county Fire Services announced he wanted to say a prayer first. He was well aware that most of them had never fought a wildfire before and would be learning on the job, mostly clearing leaves and debris away from buildings and wetting down groundcover to slow the fire.

The men and women lowered their heads.

"Lord, we're so thankful for each of the firefighters that are here to help others in the western part of the state. Lord, please keep them safe and please help them get back to us the same way they left."

The firefighters were prepared to work 12-hour shifts at least until Wednesday, and through Thanksgiving if needed. They were joining another forty-three from Wake County who had left for western North Carolina earlier in the week and taken five fire engines and ten brush trucks with them.

A firefighter from Garner found a seat next to a fellow from a Fuquay-Varina company.

"I didn't know I was going to be sent over there 'til 6 hours ago. I didn't know what to pack, so I just threw in whatever I had to stay warm, extra socks and stuff," he told him.

"I volunteered to go," said the guy from Fuquay-Varina. "I figured this is going to be a once-in-a-career event. I'm only trained to fight structure fires, so this is going to be a great chance to learn what to do in the mountains."

"The way I see it," the guy from Garner said, "we've got to help our brothers."

Once the last firefighter had piled in, the county's Fire Services director jumped on and stood at the front of the bus.

"Okay folks, you're ready to roll. Take plenty of pictures if you can do it safely. There's a lot we can learn from this." He started to get off, then stopped, faced everyone and called out, "Be safe."

Day Fourteen

F riday, November 18. YOU COULD CUT THE tension in the air at the tennis court with a knife, yet when the burly incident commander with the no-nonsense gray brush cut came out to personally address the two hundred or so firefighters, he appeared calm and in charge.

Brandon's steady, mellow tone floated over the crowd. "The Party Rock Fire is the US Forest Service's number one priority in the country right now. We've got almost 1,000 firefighters—both wildland and structural—trucks and apparatus from over 200 fire departments, 250 Forest Service personnel, folks from 24 states... all working against this fire that's burning in three counties and threatening over one thousand homes. For the past twelve days, our 'dozers have dug over ten miles of firebreaks all over these mountains and we're now braced with everything we've got— with everything the state's got—to stop this fire.

"They're telling us we'll be getting strong wind gusts this morning. Our guys have finished putting in the firebreak on Highway 9 in Bat Cave, and they're working their butts off trying to tie all our lines together around the resort. If we hang tight and all work together, we've got a good chance to break the back of this fire when these gusts hit.

"But let me emphasize, safety is number one. We have a plan for both fire fronts if we have to fall back. So, if the fire crosses your line and you can't put it out, remember, you're never gonna catch it. Do not try to be a hero. Do not run it down. Good luck, everyone, and stay safe!"

They put the two guys from the A-RC-H fire department with the same task force they'd been with all week and sent them to Bat Cave again. As the two pulled up to the station and glanced down Highway 9, it looked like the command was getting ready for a fire of biblical proportions. Engines were lined up bumper to bumper all along the closed section of the highway until they disappeared from view in the haze of thick smoke. The harrowing site made Doug remember hearing what someone said when they walked into the Bat Cave fire station the night before. Seeing the Outback Steakhouse cooking dinner, the guy quietly uttered, "The condemned men ate a hearty meal."

The Bat Cave supervisor managed to make his briefing as unnerving as the one at the Lake Lure command center, telling everyone to brace for 40 mile per hour gusts by noon. Doug's task crew was put with a Forestry group along Highway 9 again, and they chased spot fires all morning. By nine, as promised, the wind picked up and so did the spot fires. Everyone hustled frantically to put them out, the intensity so great that a Forest Service ranger came out of the woods and told them, "If you see embers start up across this road, call us on the radio." He pointed down the road. "And go that way 'til you run into Black Mountain."

The Forester disappeared back in the woods, and Doug went over to one of the guys from the coast. "What do you think?"

The man raised an eyebrow. "When the Forestry boys get worried, it's time to get scared."

THE HUGE SMOKY MESS TENT was crowded. Had to be night shift guys, thought Annie as she entered. Holding a cup of coffee in one hand and a Styrofoam box with the breakfast she'd just helped herself to in the other, she found an empty folding chair between two husky firefighters and sat down. A couple of the men at the table recognized her from their check-in and said hello.

She wouldn't have been there except the logistics section had a lull after the morning shift was launched, and they insisted she take a break. Still, she tried hard not to get drawn into a conversation so she could go right back. Everyone in the structure division was on edge and they were sending anyone who walked in the door to either Bat Cave or the resort. She sat listening to the back and forth around the table as she ate.

"They ought to throw the book at whoever started this fire," said the guy across from her. "And if anybody gets hurt up there, they ought to lock 'em up for good."

At the end of the table someone said, "Fat chance of that happening. Under North Carolina law, someone who starts a wildfire can only be charged with a felony if they can prove it was set intentionally, or if it ends up burning a building or causing a serious injury. And if it only burns brushlands or woodlands or was accidentally started, then it can only be charged as a misdemeanor, no matter how much damage it does."

Another firefighter spoke up. "They're looking for someone right now. One of the rangers saw someone down in the parking lot by the hiking trails."

Annie snapped the lid of her unfinished meal closed, got up and started to leave.

"Hey, don't let us scare you away. You hardly touched your food," said a beefy guy with two stacked plates in front of him.

"I've got to go take care of something," said Annie, rushing out of the tent. She had to find Jack and go with him to the authorities before they found him. And if she couldn't find him today, she had to go and tell them what she knew so they could catch whoever did this. She wanted to kick herself. She should've done this days ago. She'd just been hoping beyond hope that Jack would stay under their radar.

Route 74A was closed all the way to Bat Cave, but she still had the keys to the station's pickup. If she borrowed it, they'd wave her through. She reached the truck, radioed logistics and told them she would be back in a couple hours, then took off.

The smoke was thick down the highway, and as she neared Bat Cave, there were so many engines lined up at the roadblock, it took a while to make the turn onto Route 64 toward Hendersonville. She drove over the bridge, hung a left, and was relieved when she spotted Terri's truck parked in front of her mother's house.

She pulled up behind it and raced in. Her mother sat in her rocker smoking a cigarette and looking more on edge than usual.

"Where's Terri?"

"She's all nervous about something happening to the dogs, so she took them to a kennel in Hendersonville. Blackie, too. Her truck's loaded with our stuff, so she took mine."

"Did you ask her if she knew where Jack was?"

"She said she didn't, but I don't think she's telling me everything."

They heard Mae's sputtering truck pull up. Annie raced to the window and pulled aside the curtain.

"It's her, Mom. Let me handle this."

Terri bounced in and Annie greeted her with a stern expression.

"Hi," said Terri, meekly. "Are you here to help us move to Jack's house? We've got everything packed in my truck. Your stuff, too."

"Not right now." Annie motioned toward the couch. "Terri, have a seat. I want to talk to you."

Terri went over and slid down on the sofa, not taking her eyes from Annie.

Convinced the guilty look on Terri's face meant she knew where Jack was, Annie sat on the arm of an easy chair and looked steadily at her.

"Terri, I've got to find my brother, and I've got to find him fast. Tell me where he is."

Terri looked away.

Annie gave her a narrowed-eye look. "He's in trouble, Terri, and not thinking straight. You've got to help me help him. Now where is he?"

"He made me promise not to tell anyone... especially you."

"Tell me, Terri."

She looked first at Mae, ashamed, then at Annie. "He had me drive him; but first, he hid his truck in the woods behind his house so you'd think he'd gone to Florida."

"Has he gone up to the bat cave?"

"No. He said that would be the first place you'd look."

"You drove him somewhere, didn't you?"

"Yes, but I don't know where."

"How far was it?"

"Not that far. Just in and out and all around. I didn't go the whole way with him. We unloaded his stuff at this dirt road and he told me to turn around and go back. It was real scary. I got lost and thought I was never gonna get out of there."

"Where? Terri. Where?"

She pointed. "Up there. Past the road block."

"On Shumont?"

Seeing Terri nod, Annie looked over at her mother. "He's gone to Uncle Luke's old place. Mom, they're worried the winds could shift later this afternoon and the northern arm of the fire will head straight for the resort. If that happens, it'll overrun Luke's cabin." Annie jumped up. "I've got to get him out of there!"

"Wait! I'm going with you," said Mae.

"That's insane, Mom. That road to Uncle Luke's is barely drivable. I might even have to get there on foot. You stay here."

"No. He won't leave. He's too scared. But I can tell him something that'll make him come out."

"Don't talk crazy, Mom." She stood up. "I'm going."

Mae jumped up. "And I'm going with you!"

Annie shook her head in frustration and turned to Terri. "Can you handle getting everything over to Jack's house if they tell you to evacuate?"

Terri nodded, looking remorseful. Annie gave her a quick hug. "It's okay. You just wanted to help. And don't worry, I'll bring him back."

Annie got behind the wheel of the truck and looked at her mother. "Are you sure you want to do this? It's going to be a rough ride."

"I'm sure. Let's go."

By the time they reached the Highway 9 roadblock, visibility barely reached twenty-five feet. White ash blanketed the landscape like a coat of new-fallen snow. Annie pulled up to an ash-covered officer with a bandana across his face.

"We're taking supplies up to the 'dozer operators," she said as she lowered her window.

He motioned for someone to let her through. Dodging hoses

lying all over and firefighters chasing cinders, it took forever to drive the two miles to Shumont Road. They pulled onto it and started climbing the steep, twisting road that would cling precariously to the side of the mountain until it reached the plateau and leveled out. They could see the whole south side of the road had been burnt out, but not the other. Annie could picture the heroic efforts it must've taken for the firefighters to hold that treacherous road as a firebreak.

"They've got trucks from every fire station in Buncombe County up here," said Mae as they passed a house with a fire engine protecting it.

The field behind the substation near the top was packed with every kind of apparatus and crawling with firefighters. The road swung north and Annie kept going until a cluster of trucks and engines blocked the way. She stopped next to two firefighters and pulled down her window.

"We're trying to get to Old Apple Wagon Road," Annie called out.

"No one's going in there," said one of the firefighters. "We've got an evacuation order in effect. You'll have to turn around."

Annie nodded, then threw the truck into reverse and backed out.

"What are you gonna do now?" said her mother.

"I know another way we can get to that road."

She drove a short distance back down Shumont and turned onto a dirt road, bumping along for a half mile until she came out again on the narrow Apple Wagon Road that had been widened with a 'dozer. The smoke was getting thick, making her nervous.

"Mom, you're gonna have to help me with this. We've got to turn off anytime now. Do you remember where?"

"Yes. By old man Marsh's place."

"Keep your eyes peeled for it."

They rode a few hundred yards when Mae cried, "There! There it is!"

Annie stopped and looked around. "This must be where Jack

had Terri leave him." She clenched her teeth and turned onto a steep, narrow dirt road that dropped off on one side. She barely crept along as it snaked along the mountain.

"We're supposed to come to another logging road right around here, aren't we?" her voice now sounding a little shaky.

"You're okay. Keep going," said Mae.

They started to make a tight turn around a huge boulder.

"I remember this! Jack and I used to climb it. We're almost there," said Annie.

The truck swept under tree branches in the thick of the forest, then came to a sudden stop. Ahead, a beaten-down foot trail leading to a cabin almost totally hidden by overgrown rhododendron convinced Annie that Jack was there. She jammed the truck into park, slapped the steering wheel, and said, "Let's go get him."

Her mother opened her door and let out a shudder. "I can't get out on this side. It's a drop off."

Annie got out and motioned for her mother to scoot over, then she helped her get down. The two women made their way up the steep foot path to the cabin. The ancient log door squeaked open and Jack appeared, looking haggard.

"For God's sake, Annie, things are bad enough without you dragging the old lady up here."

"Jack, you've got to leave."

He turned and disappeared into the cabin. Annie raced in after him.

"There're no time for this, Jack. If the wind shifts, the fire's gonna come this way. We gotta get out of here."

"Nice try, Sis. You almost sound like you know what you're talking about. If it gets this far north, the whole state's gonna burn."

He struck a match and lit a kerosene lamp, and despite the cobwebs and decade's worth of dust, the glow made the rustic one-room cabin with its hand-hewn log walls look almost homey. Jack pulled out a chair and dragged it over to Mae.

"Here, take the weight off your feet."

Annie sank onto another chair, and Jack sat on the edge of

the bed, making the metal springs squeal. Her fingers drummed on the table while she thought. There they were again, the three of them in the same desperate situation, only this time in a desolate cabin at the back of beyond with the threat of fire on the horizon. How she yearned for the safety of the world she had made for herself. She pictured the furry little eastern red bat resting its wings on her glove as she held it, and how good it felt to be taking care of it and its kind. She thought about the first dinner with Mike just two weeks ago and how happy and hopeful she'd been. Then she looked at Jack and the familiar bravado he displayed to disguise his fear brought her back to a world of dread and foreboding.

"Jack, the police want you to come in for questioning. The sooner you do it, the better. Once we tell the Lake Lure Police what you know, it's gonna help them find whoever did this. I'm gonna be with you the whole time."

She looked pleadingly at him. "Okay, Jack? You and me, together."

"I can't. I just can't take it, Sis. This thing's too big. I've got to wait it out here until they catch whoever did it."

"What are you talking about?! There's no 'waiting it out here!' This fire is unpredictable and can do anything at any moment."

"That's why I want you to get in that truck and get the hell out of here!"

"I get it, you're scared. Let's think this through. What's the worst case scenario? I mean the very worst. I just found out that in North Carolina someone who starts a wildfire can only be charged with a felony if it damages structures or causes injury and the authorities can prove beyond a shadow of a doubt that it was intentionally set. And if it only burns wildlands, then it can only be charged as a misdemeanor no matter how much damage it does." She pounded on the table. "But it's not going to come to that. If I have to, I'll work night and day to find the person who did this."

"Annie, stop! I'm not going! Now get out of here and take Mom with you."

Even in the darkened room, Annie could see Jack's eyes were bloodshot. She'd seen him like this once before when he was sixteen. A motel had burned to the ground in Black Mountain and he'd been questioned for eight hours straight before someone turned in the real culprit. She became numb with the realization that in the state he was in, there was no way she was going to get him to come out with her.

She abruptly stood up. "Okay. If you're going to stay, I've got to get you something from my backpack."

Annie ran out and returned with a small case. "This is my fire shelter. I hope to God you don't have to use it. It opens up to a foil shell. Find a clearing and open it up and lay face down. Hold it tight to the ground so smoke and heat don't get inside."

"Stop!" screamed Mae. "We're not leaving him!"

Annie became alarmed. Everything was spinning out of control.

"Jack, if you don't come with us," Mae threatened, "I'll tell them everything."

Annie's eyes darted toward Mae. "What are you talking about?"

"Nothing!" shouted Jack. "Now get her out of here."

"I mean it, Jack!" Mae screamed. "I'll tell them! I promise, I'll tell them."

Jack sat back in the bed and stared into space. Mae pulled out a cigarette and lit it with her shaky hand.

"He was more of a pig than a man," she spit out.

"Stop! I don't want to hear it!" shouted Jack.

"Who are you talking about, Mom?" asked Annie.

"That dirty old Sam Boswell. I was always in a pinch for money, so I had to give him favors."

Jack jumped up and went to the door. "I'm getting out of here. I can't listen to this."

He left with Annie staring disbelievingly at her mother.

Mae took a long drag and slowly blew it out. "What else could I do? Marooned way up there on Bluerock Mountain. You had just turned six and Jack was only ten. My Pa wasn't gonna help us none. He was too mad at me. That is, 'til the fire. Then

210

he was sorry.

"When the sheriff came, he had a welfare lady with him to take you kids. When he began forcing me to the door and you started screaming, your brother popped up and shouted, 'Don't take her. I did it!'"

"I don't understand," said Annie, bewildered.

"Jack saw the whole thing," said Mae. "He used to watch when I went over there. When the liquor ran out, that bastard would slap me around, and your brother would have to bring me back home all broken and hurt. That night he watched through the window. Sam slammed me against the wall and I fell to the floor.

"But I was just as mean as he was. I crawled over to him on my hands and knees and yanked his foot right from under him. He fell and hit his head on the cookstove. I tried to get him to come 'round, but he was dead. I knew no one would believe it was an accident, and the only way I could figure to cover it up was to burn the place down."

"Didn't he die of a heart attack?" asked Annie.

"That's the whole sad, stupid truth," cried Mae in a tortured voice. She took out another cigarette and lit it with the old one. "I never had to burn the place down. All I had to do was walk away from it. If only I had done that, none of this would've happened."

Annie was incredulous as her mother spoke. All the injustices her brother had suffered tore at her.

"You know how Jack could always act out as a kid," said Mae. "Watching him tell them how he did it, I would've believed it myself if I didn't know better. It was almost as if they wanted to believe him so they'd have a genuine arsonist they could keep an eye on."

The room grew dead still as Annie sat in the near darkness of the windowless cabin, crushed under the weight of what had happened to the darling little boy who'd had his easy smile stolen from him.

Annie wiped her nose on her sleeve and glared at Mae.

"Please don't look at me like that. I already hate myself,"

said Mae as she flicked her ashes in an empty tin on the table.

"How? Mom? How could you have let this happen to your little boy?"

"You think it was easy? To stand by when people looked at him like he was dirt? What else could I do? I was no good in those days and everybody knew it. They were waiting for an excuse to take you two away from me. I hadn't been the best mother, but God only knows what could have happened to you if they put you out in foster care."

She took a deep draw on the cigarette and slowly blew it into the air. "With that welfare lady dragging you across the room and you screaming for me, when Jack ran up and said he did it, I kept my mouth shut. I'll never forget the feeling I got in my gut for not saying anything. I've felt it a thousand times since. It makes me want to puke."

This was one of the only times Annie had seen her mother cry.

"That's what finally made me come to my senses. I had to live up to what my brave boy did for his little sister and his mama."

The room became ghostly quiet again with Annie aware of the total absence of bird calls, then the smell of smoke. She rose and said, "I'll go get Jack and we're gonna get out of here. Then you're gonna have to fix this, Mom."

Annie went outside. She knew where Jack had gone and she made her way up behind the cabin. Just as she thought, a beaten path led up to the rock she and Jack had named Simms' Pinnacle. Jack's silhouette was cast against the dusky sky. She went over and hugged him like she was never going to let him go, weeping in his arms.

"I see she's told you the whole ugly story," he said. He put his arm around her and looked off in the distance. "I've been coming up here every day, watching the jets fly out over the lake. One day the smoke was so dense I thought one of them was going to hit Youngs Mountain, but it pulled out in time." He squeezed her shoulder. "Come on, Sis, we better pull out in time or that fire's gonna get us."

"When we get back," said Annie, "we've got to go to the police, and Mom's got to clear everything up."

"No. I don't want anything to happen to her," he said. "I already paid for what she did. If they do anything to her now, it'll be like I went through all of it for nothing. I'll go in and talk to them. If they don't catch who did this, I'm sure wonder woman will."

He threw out a wry little laugh. "You were always my hero, Annie. The first night I came home from that place they put me in, I was so worried you wouldn't trust me. But, when you got in bed with me and said you knew I was a good boy and something must've just gone wrong, I was glad I said I did it, or they would've broken us up. Your belief in me all those years and all those times got me through it. Sometimes, with all the suspicion and mistrust heaped on me, I would actually start to doubt myself; and then I'd take one look at you and the way you were looking at me and know none of it was true. I love you for it, Annie. You were my rock."

Annie hugged him. "I'm so sorry this happened to you."

He put his arm around her. "Come on. Let's go get the old bag and get out of here."

Annie let out a little laugh. Up until now, she'd always felt Jack's sarcastic remarks about her mother were uncalled for.

They hurried back to the cabin where Mae waited outside.

"Do you need to pack anything?" she asked Jack.

"There's no time, Mom. I'll come back for everything later." He looked at Annie. "Get in the truck and I'll help you back it out."

They helped Mae scoot onto the passenger side, then Annie got in and buckled up.

"Mom, pull your window down and let me know if I'm getting too close to the edge," said Annie. She looked in the rearview mirror. Jack motioned for her to start backing up. She turned the wheels into the mountain at too sharp of an angle and rammed into it on her side.

"Go forward again," shouted Jack. "And come straight out."

She inched ahead and then stopped. "Mom, take a look and

tell me how much room I've got on your side."

Mae strained her head out the window. "A couple feet."

Good, thought Annie. She turned the wheel enough to coax the truck a foot away from the mountain and backed up.

"Stop!" yelled Jack as the truck's back wheel slipped off the road and hung in midair.

Annie froze until the truck stopped rocking. She looked over at Mae. "Mom, you said I had two feet!"

"It was just an approximation."

"Whatever you do, Mom, don't shake this truck."

Jack suddenly appeared at Annie's window. "Don't move, you two. I'm going to open the door, and then I'm gonna pull you out, one at a time. Mom, stay there 'til I tell you to move."

Slowly, Jack opened the door, grabbed Annie's hand and helped her out. "Go stand over there out of the way," he ordered. He carefully reached in the truck for Mae's arm and slowly pulled her toward him when he heard the truck creak. He stopped and listened, but only heard his heavy breathing. He started pulling Mae toward him once more, and finally inched her close enough to put an arm under her and swoop her out.

Annie went around to the back. The truck hung precariously over an abyss.

"That takes care of our getting out of here in the truck," she said.

Annie and Jack looked northwest where the smoke seemed to be coming from.

"Can you hear that?" asked Annie.

"Yeah. It sounds like a train's coming."

"We better get out of here fast," Annie said, "but I'm afraid the only way out is running toward it 'til we get to that road that goes up to the plateau where it's safe."

"If we didn't have Mom," said Jack, "we could try working our way down the cliffs and head for Buffalo Creek, but there's no way she can make that descent."

"We've got to go up Apple Wagon and then climb up the first dirt road we come to," said Annie. "And we've got to get there before the fire."

They started off, and it was fairly easy going until they got to Apple Wagon. The severely torn up road was almost impossible to traverse on foot. Mae kept stumbling and twisting her ankles. Her knees were scraped and she could barely walk.

Jack stopped. "All right, Mom. I'm going to have to carry you on my back."

She slapped his hands away. "No! Leave me! I'm too old and I can't make it. You two go on and save yourselves."

"No Mama. I've carried you my whole life; I'm not gonna give up now." He looked at Annie, "Help me get her on my back."

The two hoisted the crying Mae on Jack's back and they trudged onward. They came around a curve and stopped dead as they eyed the burning embers shooting through the smoky, orange air. Annie pulled her shirt up over her nose. Flames lashed the horizon and the roar grew deafening.

"We should be getting to that dirt road that leads up to Shumont any time now," said Annie, her voice shaky.

"I hope so," said Jack.

They tramped on until the smoke got too thick to breathe. "Stop!" shouted Annie. She stripped down to her sports bra, and frantically ripped her shirt into two pieces. She quickly fashioned a mask for Mae and then herself. Jack put Mae down, took off his shirt and covered his nose and mouth.

"We got to get out of here," he said.

They got Mae up on his back again and took off at a faster pace. Suddenly, Jack yelled as he fell to one knee.

"Let me off!" Mae screamed.

"No. If I let you down, I'll never get you back up again."

Annie grabbed his arm and helped him stand.

"Are you gonna be okay?" Annie shouted over the roar of the fire.

"I twisted my ankle. I need something I can use as a cane."

"Use me!" Annie yelled. She put her arm around her brother's waist and every time he took a step she felt his muscles tighten from pain. Fire had reached the edge of the road on one side. Annie knew if it jumped across before they hit the dirt road they were doomed. The two kept climbing, with Annie urging, "Keep going! We got to get to that road!"

The road made another twist and the sight ahead made Annie's heart pound against her chest. The north ridge was ablaze with spot fires burning everywhere. Flying embers streaked in front of them. Ahead in the distance she could barely make out a clearing. It had to be the road. Suddenly she heard what sounded like a gunshot and she snapped her head around. A snag had fallen across the road behind them. In a matter of moments, it would flash into something big.

The small family struggled up the slope, ignoring the swirling glowing cinders and the solid wall of fire creeping along the ridge. The ear-splitting noise was like an echoing explosion— trees popping, snags crashing down, and most threatening of all, the roar of flames.

Her head down, Annie could see a small trickle of a stream next to the road. She struggled to breathe. Her throat felt like it was ripped open, and a sickening fear that they weren't going to get out of there gripped her. "Stop!" she screamed. She tore off the rags from everyone's face, quickly soaked them in the stream, then feverishly put them back.

Suddenly a massive burning snag crashed inches in front of them! Annie's heart pounded and her mouth went dry as she helped Jack hobble around it. A strange and sudden gust hit the north ridge. In seconds, a massive inferno exploded and roared down the mountain like the gates of hell had opened.

MIKE HAD SEEN ANNIE whiz by in a fire station pickup when he was walking along Highway 9 checking on a crew. He'd been keeping an eye out for her to come back through, and had grown concerned when he wasn't seeing her. He didn't know what she would be doing up on Shumont, but he had his suspicions. He went over to the Forest Ranger he'd been working with and told him he'd be back in a few minutes, then took off in his truck down the road to the Shumont barricade.

He pulled down his window and spoke to the officer. "Did you let a pickup from the Lake Lure Fire Department go up?"

"Yeah. The girl driving it said she was delivering supplies to the dozer operators."

"Has she come out yet?"

"I don't know. I just got back from a break, but I'll find out for you." He got on his radio. "Jerry, did a pickup with two women come off Shumont when you were here?"

"I can't say," came over the radio. "There were so many fire trucks going in, I didn't pay attention to the ones coming out."

The officer looked at Mike and shrugged his shoulders.

"I'm working with the Forest Service," said Mike. "Can you let me through?"

The officer nodded and let him go.

Shumont Road is dangerous enough on a clear day, but the thick smoke now made it harrowing. He made his way up, neared the substation and looked for the truck Annie was driving. With so many vehicles, it took him a while to establish that she wasn't there. He continued up the road until he hit a fire truck blocking the way.

One of the firefighters came up to the window. "Sorry, nobody past this point."

"Did you see a woman in a Lake Lure Fire Department pickup coming through here?"

"About an hour and a half ago. We sent her back."

Mike looked around and saw two dirt roads someone could turn onto. "You didn't see her go back and take one of those roads, did you?"

"No. I watched her drive back past the substation. She's long gone by now."

Mike bit his lip and racked his brain trying to remember when he could have missed her truck on her way back. Remembering a couple of moments when she could've slipped past him, he said goodbye and headed back to his position on Highway 9.

Jeff Sanford, another volunteer, overheard the conversation and went over to his partner and said, "Why'd you tell him you watched her go all the way back to the substation? Right after you talked to her we got that call from the base to go pick up that old guy who finally decided he had to get out of here. We never looked back."

"Don't be such a nitpicker, man. If I'd said we didn't see where she went, how was that going to make us look?"

Jeff shook his head. "I know that girl. She's a volunteer over at Lake Lure. I took a class with her. She takes care of bats. And it looked like she had an older woman in the truck with her." He walked over to an UTV and got on.

"Where are you going?" shouted his partner.

"I'm gonna take a run down Apple Wagon Road. It's pretty torn up. If she got on it, she could be in trouble."

"You better make it quick. That fire's gonna be running over that area any time now."

He took off down the road, but after fifty feet, it turned into a ripped up firebreak and he had to make his way over it as best he could. He decided to go as far as the dirt road that people used as a shortcut to Apple Wagon. As the road began to descend, he could hear the roar of the fire coming across the mountain. A gust of wind sent ash and embers flying. This wasn't a good idea, he thought. He better get out of there. He wasn't far from that dirt road. He could turn onto it and climb back up to the plateau.

He finally reached it and was about to turn off when a nagging thought entered his mind. There was another logging road up ahead of that one. He better go that far and then he'd be sure he'd done everything he could to help the bat girl if she were out there. He drove farther down and when he saw a flash fire up ahead, went as fast as he could to reach the road. Just as he was about to swing onto it, he saw something moving in the smoke. He slammed on the breaks and skidded to a stop. It was the bat girl! A man limped alongside her, carrying the older woman on his back.

AFTER THE WARNING FROM THE ranger, Doug and his partner kept one eye on the woods and one eye on Highway 9 as they ran water to the forest rangers and battled each flame with every ounce of strength they had left. Around five, someone on the Bat Cave radio frequency reported that the wind was dying down, making them hopeful.

A bad flare-up rose from a fire that had been crawling along under the matted debris. As they fought it, they noticed the flames were now going in a different direction, telling them the wind was shifting and the fire was starting to burn back on itself. For the next half hour, they listened intently to the traffic on the radio, confirming that everyone's positions were holding. Everyone held their breath and kept their eyes peeled for embers, when an announcement came over the radio. "Well, folks, so far, our lines are holding. We just might have killed it in Bat Cave." The shout that ensued—one packed with relief, accomplishment and gratitude—reverberated all the way down Highway 9.

However, what was good for one arm of the fire, was threatening a catastrophe at the other.

WHEN GARY WILSON got a call from fire command specifically requesting that he personally attend the six p.m. briefing, he knew something had to be up. He was the fire chief of the all-volunteer Fairfield Fire Department that abutted the resort, and when he arrived at the briefing and looked around he couldn't help noticing that a fire chief from the county to his north was also present. Not a good sign.

When the Incident Commander stood up to kick off the briefing, Wilson suspected they were headed for trouble. Then when Brandon said their weather forecasters were calling for 30 to 40 mile per hour winds with 60 mile per hour gusts on Saturday, he grew concerned. Then, when the commander added that if they did get them at that speed, they weren't going to be able to hold the fire, he was in shock.

"The winds have shifted to a northeastern direction and the fire is now running back across Shumont Mountain, reburning and putting itself out as it rolls across that range. However, it's spearheading a new burn headed toward the resort."

Brandon looked at Wilson and Jim Howell, the chief of the Bills Creek Fire Department. "You have to go back and start evacuating everyone in your district all the way to Bills Creek Road."

As Wilson drove back to the station a few hundred yards up

the road from the entrance to the now evacuated Rumbling Bald Resort, he looked at the burning mountain rising up beyond the resort's golf course, and all he could think of was that there were 400 houses between it and Bills Creek Road.

He pulled up on the golf course's driving range abutting their station house. They'd been using it as a parking lot since the start of the fire and had crammed as many as fifty engines in there at one time. The screens that had kept golf balls from hitting the stationhouse had been torn back and flapped in the wind.

Four engines stood lined up, ready to pull out. He got out of his truck and watched them turn up Buffalo Creek Road that ran along the bottom of Youngs Mountain. If a fire got started in that steep, dry wilderness, he was sure it would run up it like an Indy 500 racecar. A sheriff's car and two highway patrol cars, responding to his call to help with the evacuation, came speeding down the road and pulled in.

He went into the station's crowded meeting room and his crew gathered around him.

"Well, everyone," he announced loud enough for all to hear, "the Forest Service just delivered a doomsday forecast. They're expecting 30-40 mile per hour winds tomorrow and have pretty much guaranteed if we get them, the fire's going to run right through to Bills Creek Road, so we've got to get everyone evacuated between here and there tonight."

A muffled roar rose. Almost everyone in the room had a home within the threatened area.

"What else did they say?" someone shouted out.

"They didn't sugarcoat anything. They came straight out and said here's where the fire is, here's where it's spreading, the winds are supposed to shift in the direction of Buffalo Creek Road with 60 mile per hour gusts. If that happens there's no way we can stop it. It'll outrun us all the way to Bills Creek, and we'll try to stop it there."

He clapped his hands. "Okay, everyone, we've got to round up folks and set up teams to go knocking on doors. There's a good four hundred of them, and it's gonna take all night."

Just as the chief finished, a strike team from Texas came into the station to eat dinner. They had been burning out and mopping up on the hiking trails in the woods above the resort where the fleet of 'dozers were connecting the firebreaks. Someone asked them if they had heard that winds would be coming in the morning.

One of the hotshots nodded and said, "Yeah, we heard. That's why, even though we've been at it since six this morning, we're going to go back at it again after we eat."

Later that night, Wilson sat drinking his umpteenth cup of coffee. He looked around the meeting room jammed with cots and sleeping firefighters and wondered what might happen to it. He'd been the volunteer fire chief for the thirty-five years since the fire department was established. Now retired from the resort's security department, he was still at it, along with 26 other volunteers.

He studied the wall display showing various knots, then the bank of photos from some of their fund-raising events someone had posted on a board. It wasn't a fancy firehouse. In fact, starting from nothing in 1981, they had cobbled it together by whatever means they had.

They started out leasing space in the resort's maintenance building now at the rear of their station, and for two years parked their engines inside the building at night and pulled them out in the daytime so the resort's maintenance crew could work. Next, they secured a low interest loan for $50,000 and built their 5-bay fire station at the front of the building. Finally, they got a lifetime lease on a pole barn between the maintenance department and the fire station that the resort no longer had a use for and turned it into a meeting room at a cost of $70,000.

He looked around and all the love and community spirit that had built the place flooded over him. How he would hate to see the place destroyed. A handful of firemen and officers walked in, interrupting his reverie. They helped themselves to coffee and some brownies and came over to Wilson's table, exhausted.

"How's it going out there?" Wilson asked as they pulled out chairs and sat down.

"My team finished going door to door in the Apple Valley

subdivision," said a woman, "but Dave is still driving up and down every street with the engine's loudspeaker on, telling them they've got to get out."

"If no one was home, we posted a notice on their door," said another volunteer. "A couple of them asked why they had to leave when they were going to start letting residents back in Chimney Rock, and I had to explain to them that the fire had changed direction, circled around and was coming back at us. When I ran across anyone who said they weren't gonna leave, I warned them they may not live through it if it gets as bad as what they're saying. And if they still insisted on staying, I did just like you told me. I got the name and phone number of their next of kin."

Day Fifteen

Saturday, November 19. BY SIX THAT MORNING, the Fairfield Fire Station looked like a staging area in a combat zone. Engines from all over the state were either parked at the ready on the driving range or were zooming in and out on their way to their two fallback positions.

The firefighters were aware that the National Weather Service had issued a Red Flag Warning that would be in effect until six p.m., and were prepared for a grueling shift. The noise level in the packed station was so high the chief decided to go out and check on the situation at the driving range. Outside, three men walked up to him and introduced themselves as chaplains from the Billy Graham Ministry.

"Can we do anything to help you guys?" one of them asked.

"Well," said Wilson. "We've got plenty of resources and plenty of food, we're good there. How about a prayer that these winds don't increase the way they're saying they will."

"There's nothing wrong with that," the man responded. "God stilled the winds in the disciples' boat on the Sea of Galilee to keep them from drowning. I don't know why he can't do it here."

About a dozen firefighters gathered around him as the man said a prayer for everyone's safety and for the winds not to increase. Wilson stood, head bowed, knowing he'd never forget that moment and that prayer for as long as he lived.

THE GUYS OVER AT the Fairfield Fire Department weren't the only ones praying that morning. Everyone at the command center was on pins and needles and asking God for help. It seemed ironic to a lot of the folks in the command center that with all the firefighters and resources they had gathered from all over the US, in the end, everyone was putting their faith in getting out of this mess in the hands of God.

Ferrell barreled down 74A from Bat Cave. Lake Lure was still closed to visitors and through traffic, but cars were lined up at the barricades with people milling around as the Highway Patrol issued re-entry passes to Chimney Rock's business owners and residents. Ferrell pulled into the lot and hurried into the town hall where Brandon was waiting for his report.

"Well?" he asked.

"Bat Cave is holding," said Ferrell.

A murmur of relief rippled across the room.

"It's burning back on itself and should lay down good enough for our crews to start mopping it up in the next couple of days."

"Do you think we can lift the evacuations over there?" asked Brandon.

"Give me 'til noon tomorrow," said Ferrell. He noticed the wind charts scattered on the table. "How's the other end holding up?"

"Every once in a while they're getting a gust in the 40 to 45 mile per hour range, but so far everything's holding."

Every time a phone rang or a voice came over the radio, Brandon gave it his full attention. He knew they were one phone call away from someone reporting that the fire had jumped the line. And if it did, as the incident commander he would have to be the one to pull the plug on the resort and all the other developments between it and Bills Creek Road. Braced for it to happen, he had to keep staving off the sickening kind of feeling he imagined one must get when they have to take someone off life support.

"Have you heard from Raleigh about our relief shift yet?" asked Ferrell.

"They're pulling a Type 1 team out of Oregon," said Brandon. "They'll start arriving on Tuesday and take over on Wednesday. I'm preparing a transition plan for them now."

It went without saying that after more than two weeks of the non-stop battle against the fire, they both looked forward to some relief. A human body can only take so much stress; yet neither of them relished leaving a disaster in their wake.

"I'm going over to the resort," said Ferrell on his way out the door.

Driving down 74A, Ferrell felt confident they had killed the fire in Bat Cave. His strategy and the bulldog tenacity of scores of firefighters doing their job hell bent for leather had made it happen. But who would remember that if 400 houses burnt to the ground?

He drove to the resort recalling the reactions to stress that the Forest Service warned against. Two of them stuck out. What they called target fixation or locking into a course of action whether it makes sense or not, and just trying harder, was one of them; and the escalation of commitment, or accepting increased risk as the end of a task gets nearer, was the second. He thought over those two caveats and decided he and Brandon were okay on both accounts. Their last ditch strategy to stop the wildfire before it hit the resort made sense. They had made the firebreak wide enough and had set experienced wildland firefighters on the scene. And as far as accepting increased risk was concerned, he was going to be standing by that firebreak all day, and the minute it looked like things were going bad, he would pull everyone out.

He continued to the resort, allowing himself a modicum of optimism. After all, how many times on this fire had their meteorologists been wrong? Maybe 45 mile per hour gusts were the worst it was going to get. Heck, they had enough seasoned forestry guys on the line to tackle that. With all the crews in the woods chasing embers, they just might make it. Suddenly, the vision of sustained 60 mile per hour winds and hundreds of scattered spot fires on bone dry fuel exploding into giant flashovers, like happened up on Rumbling Bald Mountain Thursday night, gave him a brutal dose of reality.

He made his way along 74A and took the turn onto Bills Creek Road. When he got two miles up and took a left onto Buffalo Creek Road, he threw a wave to the firefighters standing solemnly next to their engines like centurions. It was eerie driving through the deserted countryside with rolling golf greens lying on both sides of the twisting road and not a golf cart in sight. Because of all the winds the day before, the smoke had lifted and the air was almost clear, belying the threat standing on the community's doorsteps.

Buffalo Creek Road made a 90-degree turn with the creek and started running north. He passed the entrance to the resort a few feet away, pulled up to the Fairfield station and went in. The tension in the crowded, noisy room was palpable, and he could read concern on the faces of those serving the breakfast. A couple of hotshots were rushing out with piles of Styrofoam boxes and a case of water.

"Where are you guys working?" he asked.

"Right up the road in the woods by the hiking trails," they shouted as they hurried out.

A woman came running from the kitchen with a cardboard carton.

"They left already?" she asked Ferrell, disappointed. He nodded. "I just packaged up a bunch of brownies for them."

"I'll take them," Ferrell said. "I'm going over there after I grab something to eat."

He looked around for the chief and, not seeing him, got in the food line. He hadn't eaten since last night and needed to get something in his stomach. News about the quality of meals being served at the various station houses traveled fast among the firefighters. When word got out that many of the top restaurants in Hendersonville were serving dinner at Bat Cave, a lot of the guys started going over there to eat; but there was something about the down-home meals served by the Fairfield Auxiliary that gave Ferrell the comforting feeling of sitting at the dinner table with family, so he dropped in there to eat whenever he got the chance.

He wolfed down a heaping dish of scrambled eggs, bacon and homemade biscuits and gravy, then grabbed the box of brownies and took off for the woods. As good as the breakfast was, by the time he got out of the parking lot, he couldn't remember what he had eaten. After so many days of ceaseless stress, he had gone past the living-on-adrenaline phase and was now operating on autopilot. His mind was keen and his goals clear and compelling, but every shred of concern for his personal well-being had gone by the wayside days ago. He just concentrated on getting enough sleep and food to keep doing his job.

He drove up the road to the hiking trail turnoff. Bulldozers were being loaded on their trailers, and Ferrell figured his boss was having them sent to safer ground. There had to be over a million dollars in equipment. Plus, if the fire got away, they'd need them over on Bills Creek. Heaven help them, he thought. If it ran past Bills Creek, they'd need them in Morganton.

The woods along the parking lot were torn up with the devastation reaching fifty to sixty feet deep in places. Brush trucks with two-man crews at the ready were stationed all along the scarred, limb littered, torn-up four miles of new fire break. Ferrell knew most of these Forestry folks, and as he drove along, he could sense the tension. Everyone was watching the terrain and acutely aware of every breeze. Every firefighter knew that this line was either going to be the end of the Party Rock Fire, or the beginning of a firestorm, the likes of which no one around there had ever seen before. Moment to moment, every person on the line stood ready to fight and prepared to run.

The fire moved closer and closer to the line as the day went on, and every time the wind whipped up, they'd hold their breath, fearing the big winds were coming and this would be it. Yet, through the day it kept doing the same thing: gusting, then dying down long enough for them to frantically beat down any embers that crossed the line.

All afternoon, Ferrell rode up and down the checkline, going from one area of concern to another, checking with crews, seeing how it looked with his own eyes, and constantly asking himself if they were all in a good spot, could they get out of there in time?

He kept calling the command center for the weather forecast. The way they dangled at the mercy of the weather put him more on edge than he thought was possible to endure and still be able to lead. Every time a report of a spot fire came over the radio, the whole line tensed up until they heard it was out cold. Every once in a while the fire would hit a spot in the woods heavy with debris, and flames would spike to ten feet, but as the afternoon went on, it kept at two to four feet.

By four-thirty, Ferrell was getting a sneaky feeling the line just might hold and he couldn't wait for five o'clock to come when the humidity would begin to increase. When he got a call from command and was told the winds wouldn't be as bad as they had thought, but to keep vigilant, he actually allowed himself to feel confident they were going to hold it.

Fresh crews started arriving for the shift change, relieving the guys on the line. Before he sent the new crews out, Ferrell gave a briefing and safety talk that ended with a heartfelt message: "If we can hold it overnight, people, we've got a chance of containing this thing by morning." Normally, he never would've let such a prediction color his briefings, but he knew fire. And by now, he knew this fire. The monster was getting tired. It had hungered for that big wind to give it the strength to consume the resort it'd had its eye on since day one, but it wasn't getting it. Ferrell watched the fire he'd been fighting for fourteen grueling days angrily paw at the edge of the checkline like an enraged beast, and he could see it didn't have the strength to escape the barrier without the wind. They had caged the dragon, and if they could keep it there, and these winds didn't show, it would be slain.

He stood there, shaking hands and thanking the men as they came off the line. For the first time since the fire started, a feeling of elation was seeping into his being. He could see a glimmer of it in the eyes of the men, but no one said anything. They didn't want to jinx it.

A million times he had asked himself why he and his fellow firefighters did this kind of work. Why they kept pushing their bodies to the limit. Why, in the words of the Incident Response Pocket Guide, they kept "working to accomplish difficult tasks under dangerous, stressful circumstances." As he shook the firm hands of the exhausted, sooty, ash covered men, the feeling of brotherhood took hold and he knew why. In spite of the risk to themselves, they were all driven by an inherent desire to help their fellow man. He was filled with pride to be counted amongst them, and was humbled and honored to have led them.

Day Sixteen

*S*unday, November 20. "PARTY ROCK FIRE Containment Lines Hold Overnight," headlined a press release the command was about to issue. It gave Brandon a surge of emotion like nothing he had ever felt before. Gratitude was 90 percent of it. Over the last fifteen days he had the honor of leading a team of firefighters up against one of the most complex fires the state had ever seen. He'd never forget them. And thanks to the National Incident Management System, he had been given access to every emergency response network in the entire USA. The system was designed to enable every organization, both private or public, to operate together during a homeland incident, and it succeeded.

He'd been in the fire business for 27 years now and was planning on retiring soon. Three weeks ago he never would've imagined that at the tail end of his career he'd land as the Incident Commander of a fire that would go down in North Carolina wildland history. Yet, it had happened. Yesterday, he had feared it would leave a sad notation on his record, and now twenty-four hours later, he was getting ready to turn over a contained fire to the Oregon team to mop up. They'd gotten the job done.

He got up and walked through the command center to the back door and went outside. He looked out over the lake at the massive granite range that sprawled along the western horizon, then at the huge bald protrusion they called the Party Rock, now cast reddish by the rising sun. As he stared at it, he could picture the Rutherford County ranger on that first night, jumping aside as a burning snag rumbled down the mountain and flew off that cliff. He recalled the men in the boulder field at the bottom dodging them as they came crashing down. He saw the folks from a small town on the coast, who didn't own lightweight wildfire turnout gear, sweating it out in hot bunker pants while raking leaves from around a house, their jackets off and suspenders hanging from their hips. He could envision a 20-man hand crew walk single file in black logger boots through the lonely, gray, ash-covered forest with heavy packs slung on their backs, their rakes held horizontally in front of them—a continuous line of yellows and greens. He watched their helmets bobbing along in a row, and listened to the sound of their marching fade as they disappeared into the smoke.

Brandon was suddenly shaken from his reverie by Gary Wilson, the Fairfield Fire Department's chief, who came in with an invoice he needed processed. Brandon recognized him and shook his hand.

"I hear you guys are getting ready to pack up and go," Wilson said.

"Yeah. An Incident Management Team from the Oregon Department of Forestry is on its way. Tomorrow the folks who will be taking over our positions will shadow us as we go through our briefings, and Tuesday we'll shadow them as they do their presentations. That way, we'll have a smooth hand-off, and Wednesday, we're out of here."

"As long as I live," said Wilson. "I'll never stop thanking all the organizations and individuals who brought food, water, drinks and gift cards to our station, or the fire departments that came from all over and stayed to defend us no matter how bad things looked."

"That goes for all of us," said Brandon.

"Well, I hope you'll come back and see us sometime. We've got a good poker game going every third Thursday."

Brandon shook his head. "Thanks, but I'm afraid this fire business is all the risk I can stand."

The men parted and Brandon headed out for the tennis courts. It was time for the crew leader briefing, and he wanted to address them personally.

He went to the front of the crowd of about a hundred and spoke in his now familiar, confident style. "With the winds gusting up to 45 miles per hour yesterday and last night, we sure were tested," he told them, "but I'm pleased to announce that the fire did not cross our containment lines, and its footprint remains at 7,171 acres for the second day." A cheer rose, and Brandon let himself enjoy the merriment before continuing. "We're gonna get windy conditions and low humidity again today, so you've got to keep on your toes. We've got 925 firefighters working this fire and if we can hold it one more day, we're gonna start sending you folks back home." Another cheer rose.

After everyone enjoyed a hearty laugh and a wave of high fives, the men disbursed and Brandon crossed the field to the town hall. Inside, he spotted Chief Brent Hayner of the Broad River Volunteer Fire Department. He was talking with a member of the command who was helping put together numbers for the transition plan they would be handing to the Oregon team.

Hayner looked over at him and Brandon crossed the room and shook his hand.

"So, you're leaving," said Hayner.

Brandon took the papers his team member was handing him. He scanned them saying, "Yep, my two-week mountain holiday is coming to a close."

Brandon studied Hayner's report. "I see every one of the twenty-one fire departments in Buncombe County sent men and apparatus to protect the houses up on that mountain of yours."

"There's no words for the support we've gotten from them," said Hayner. "Nor for the more than a hundred companies from all over the state who've helped us at some point. You guys in Rutherford and Henderson counties may have been the sweethearts of the media with all your Kodak moments, but we've had some amazing and unforgettable moments on Shumont, too."

Brandon looked at Hayner. "Everyone in the command center respects the way you folks were committed to providing the same care and mitigation for every structure up there, from the tiniest cabin to the biggest estate. I call it an awesome job."

ANNIE WOKE IN HER CHILDHOOD bed early that morning, her throat raw and her eyes sore from the smoke the day before. Even though they were only in the substation up on Shumont long enough for her mother to settle down over a glass of iced tea, Annie felt the exuberance in the air over the fire holding in Bat Cave. She read it on everyone's face and in the way they moved, their formerly frenetic pace morphing into a proud stride.

She rose from her bed, and losing her balance, fell back down again. The terror of almost perishing in a fire the day before had taken a lot out of her. Wearing one of her old T-shirts, she got up again, went to the kitchen and put on a pot of coffee. Her mother must still be asleep in her room. She expected to find Jack asleep on the couch, but when she saw he wasn't there, she looked over at Terri's closed door.

Annie decided to let everyone rest for another hour, then she and Jack would have to go to the police. Afterward, she'd have to face Morgan and tell him about the truck. She wanted to say something about it last night when she called about not coming to work in the morning, but didn't want to give the volunteer she spoke to bad news after listening to her happily babble on about how they stopped the fire from reaching the resort, and how if they held it all night they'd be sending people home.

She sat with her legs pulled up, drinking her coffee and thinking about the fire. The past two weeks felt like a bizarre dream. She could barely remember them, except for the nights she spent with Mike. She started to relive the feeling of being in his arms, and quickly shook it off. She felt ashamed, as if she'd been sleeping with the enemy. He'd called her three times last night but she let it ring.

After Jack goes to the police, Mike will hear about it soon enough and stop calling, she told herself. Then she thought about Morgan. She wouldn't be able to stay on with the fire with everyone suspecting that her brother started it. Besides, it was time to get back to the bats. The annual surveys were coming up, and she would have to get ready to count them in caves throughout the state in January and February. Her fellow scientists were anxious to see the numbers.

She perked up her ears. Was that a vehicle pulling up to the front of the house? A car door slammed. She jumped up and ran to the window. Mike walked towards the door. She leaned back against the wall and listened to him knock. It stopped, then he knocked again, louder, more urgent.

Mae came running from her bedroom in a robe. "What's going on out here?"

"Mom, it's Mike. I don't want to talk to him."

"I don't understand," Mae said. "Why does Mike want to talk with you this early in the morning?" Mae's eyes roamed the distraught expression on Annie's face. "You and Mike?"

Annie nodded. "But it's over, Mom. He thinks Jack did it."

Mike knocked again.

"Good Lord, girl," said Mae. "What a mess."

"Well it's gonna get a lot messier once Jack goes to the police. So please go to the door and get rid of him. I never ask you for anything, Mom, but you have to do this for me."

Flustered, Mae clutched her robe closed and went to the door. Annie pressed herself against the wall and listened as Mae put on a smile and opened the door.

"Well, land sakes, if it isn't Mike McNeil! I'd ask you in, son, but I'm not even dressed. Now, what can be bringin' you here so early in the morning?"

"Hello, Mae. Is Annie here?"

"No, my boy, I'm afraid she's not. She's probably down at that fire center. She practically lives there these days."

"The next time you see her or talk to her, please ask her to call me."

"Sho' nuff, sweetheart. I'll be happy to."

She stood at the door and waved at him as he drove away. Finally, she turned to see Annie with her head in her hands, crying.

Mae went over and hugged her. "Oh, baby. You've loved that boy since you were a kid. I've messed up your life, too."

Annie shook loose and quickly wiped her eyes with her hands. "No, you haven't messed up my life, Mom. Because I'm not going to *let* anyone mess up my life."

They heard Terri's door open and looked over. Jack stood there, bare-chested and in jeans.

"What's going on?" he asked. "Who was that at the door?"

"It was nobody. You better get ready so we can go."

"Okay, I'll shave and get dressed," said Jack.

"I'll get ready, too," said Mae.

"No, Mom. You barely made it through yesterday, and you're getting too old for this kind of stress. It's my turn. You stay here with Terri. We'll phone you. And I'll tell you, Mom, this is going to be the last time this is gonna happen to us 'cause I'm getting him the hell out of here."

Annie was driving Mae's beat-up truck, but by now, the road patrol folks at the Bat Cave barricade knew her by sight. She pulled up and said hello, anxious for news.

"How's the fire on the other end?" she asked.

"It's holding. Thank God we never got those winds."

"You've been putting in a lot of time on this fire, haven't you," she said.

"Sixteen hours a day that first week, and I haven't had a whole day off since it started. But it looks like it might be coming to an end. They're going to open the road up all the way to Lake Lure starting tonight at midnight. Tomorrow, they'll even be running the school buses through. I'll bet anything the fire tourists will be here, walking through the burned out woodlands. I hope they don't. There's plenty of standing dead trees that have been badly burned and can fall without warning and kill somebody."

"I'm glad to see the smoke has lifted," she said.

"Those winds blew it away." He gave a little salute, wished her good luck and waved her through.

Charred trees smoldered all along the blackened north side of the road with fire trucks standing guard. As they neared Chimney Rock, Annie and Jack hardly noticed all the parked cars in front of the stores as if the fire never happened. At the same time, folks ran in and out of the stores unaware of the beat up old pickup sputtering its way through the village with the two siblings sitting quietly with their thoughts, bracing for the drama ahead.

The barriers had been taken down in Lake Lure, but the town still swarmed with firefighters and engines. Annie pulled onto the vacant field next to the beauty salon and got out. She clasped her brother's hand. "You okay?"

"As okay as I'm gonna get," he said.

They crossed the street and started walking toward the town hall. Several firemen said hello to her as they passed, and she wondered what they would be thinking about her after they heard the rumors about Jack. Annie felt her heart thump in her chest as they neared the part of the building that housed the police. She took a deep breath and put on a resolute face. How would it look for Jack if she got weepy? They went in and asked the receptionist if they could speak to the chief.

They were invited to take a seat, but Annie and Jack stood and waited. A door opened and the chief came out and introduced himself.

Jack offered his hand and said, "I'm Jack Simms. My sister said you were looking for me."

"Yes, come with me. I need to talk with you."

They followed him in and were shepherded to a small, barren room they used for interviews.

The chief left them for a moment and came back with a folder.

"I understand from the park ranger that you were on the hiking trail the day the fire started," he said as he came back in and shut the door.

"Yes, sir. I was."

He pulled out a chair, sat down across from them and took a minute to study the file. "The park ranger says here that you were in the parking lot next to the state's hiking trails around 1:30 p.m. on November 5. Is that correct?"

"Yes, sir."

"Were you up on the Party Rock that day?"

"Yes, I was."

"Good. We're getting somewhere. We think we've caught the kid that started the fire and need as many witnesses as we can get to corroborate that he was up there. Can you describe anyone you might have seen there?"

Jack hunched forward. "Three teenagers came up as I was leaving. I remember one of them pretty clearly. I'm sure I can recognize him if I see him again."

The chief pulled a piece of paper from the file and laid it on the table. Jack looked at the six photos and put his finger on one.

"That's him!" said Jack, almost breathless.

"Good," said the chief. "This case is being handled by one of the State Forest Service's fire investigators. We're just helping them with local contacts. They're gonna want to get a statement from you. You're a hard guy to find. In fact, if you hadn't had that conversation with the ranger about your chair caning business in Bat Cave, we might never have located you."

"How did you find who started the fire?" asked Annie.

"Stephen Tillotson, a Chimney Rock Park ranger, was on 74A in Lake Lure when he heard the fire report over his radio. He knew anyone coming down the Party Rock trail would wind up on Carsons Road so he hightailed it over there and got the names and driver's license numbers of four different parties coming off the trail. But that's all I can talk about right now."

Jack gave him his contact information and the two left.

"I can't believe it," Annie said after they got out. "You *were* under their radar. It happened too long ago."

"Maybe so, but I'm still getting the hell out of here," said Jack. "I've had enough of this. I want to have a good life. Come on, I'll walk you to your truck."

She stopped and turned to face him. She gently swiped a shock of blond hair that had fallen across his forehead. "My darling Jack. If anybody deserves a good life, it's you."

"You, too, Sis."

She hugged him and said, "You better get home and give Mom and Terri the good news. I'm gonna get my truck and go home."

He started to leave and she grabbed his hand.

"So it's you and Terri?" she said.

"Yeah. I like her. She's had a tough life like me, but she's a survivor."

Annie let out a grunt, "Aren't we all?"

As she watched her brother walk across the parking lot, the weight of everything that had happened to him came crashing down on her. She tried to hold back tears, but couldn't keep them in. She ran behind a fire truck and openly wept. A fireman must have heard her for he peeked around the corner, then came over to her, and she fell into his arms, sobbing.

He held her until she finally stopped, then pulled out a handkerchief.

"Here."

She took it and wiped her face.

"Go on, blow your nose."

She whimpered, then blew her nose. She tried to give the handkerchief back, but he wouldn't take it.

"You keep it. There's a bunch of them over in the donation tent. They got everything in there. Shoelaces, lip balm, socks, you name it."

She hugged him again. They'd both seen so many people break down she started for the mess tent while he climbed back into the truck as if nothing unusual had happened. But she didn't want to go see Morgan with puffy eyes. She'd get a cup of coffee and some breakfast first. She got in line outside the tent behind some guys with a Morehead City Fire Department insignia on their T-shirts.

A man, possibly their task force leader, rushed up to them.

"Let's hurry up and chow down, everybody. After you eat, we've got to go over to logistics. They're releasing us at noon."

A shout rose from the group.

Annie listened to their banter as the line slowly moved closer to the tent entrance.

"My boots are so burned, I don't know if I should save them as a trophy or just throw them out," one of them said.

"Stop carping about your boots. Our brush truck's gonna need new tires, bearings, brakes, the works," said another.

"I won't be sorry to say goodbye to sleeping in that tent every day," he added. "I had to use earplugs to block out the noise of those generators, diesel engines, and those darn beeping truck back-up alarms."

Waiting in line, the realization that Jack was going to be all right took hold of Annie. As she sat at a table eating, a strange melancholia swept over her. She could tell these were symptoms of PTSD and she had to shake them off. Their escape from the fire yesterday on top of everything else was taking its toll. Once she left the fire command and got a couple of days rest, she'd be okay. That's all she needed.

She made her way to the structure division tent and spotted Morgan across the room talking with the logistics guy. She waited until he was free and went over.

"I thought you were going to take the day off," he said.

"I am, but I need to talk to you. Can we go outside?"

He ushered her out and asked if she wanted a cup of coffee.

Figuring that was firefighter speak for "tell me what's on your mind," she said, "I took the company's truck up to Shumont and it's hanging over a cliff. That is, if it hasn't been burned."

"I'll take care of it. We'll get it towed out of there once things quiet down. You'll just have to meet the driver and show him where it is."

"I'm sorry," she said. As she continued, she knew if she looked him in the eye, she'd break down. "I'm not coming back. Now that the fire's winding down, I'm needed more at the Wildlife Resources Commission."

"You've done a yeoman's job. More than we had any right to ask. You know that, don't you?"

"How much longer do you think you'll be tied up with this?" she asked.

"A couple weeks. That whole range has to be mopped up. Everyone wants to get back in their homes at the resort, but they're predicting more gusty winds so we need to see what the fire does tonight. But I'm not too worried. We've got areas that are still smoldering and occasionally flaring up, but nothing's getting away from us."

Annie wanted to hug him, but knew if she did, the both of them would break down, so she just said goodbye and turned.

"Mike's leaving us, too," he called out after her.

She ignored him.

"You know he's been looking for you, don't you?"

She bit her lip, threw up her hand, and kept walking.

PART THREE

Not to Be Grieved by Blame

T uesday, November 22. FIRE TRUCKS WERE STILL scattered all over the town and along 74A leading into Chimney Rock, and Tent City still loomed on the skyline, but with the lines holding for three days now, and Thanksgiving just around the corner, Lake Lure started to take on a holiday atmosphere. With the roads open and all evacuation orders cancelled, evacuees settled in to spend Thanksgiving in their own homes.

At the fire command, Brandon's people were getting ready to leave, the team from Oregon had arrived, and resources of every kind were starting to be sent home. The front entrance of the town hall had even opened for business, with people being warned to use caution due to the heavy fire and emergency vehicle traffic.

Noises tried to wake Annie asleep in her own bed, but she kept rolling over and sinking back into oblivion. A door slamming downstairs finally succeeded. She looked around and tried to think what day it was, but ended up unsure. Dirty dishes were stacked on her night table and a couple of scrunched up popcorn bags lay on the bed.

Suddenly, her bedroom door was nudged open. Blackie bounded in and jumped on her bed, purring. Moments later, her roommate appeared in the doorway.

"It's about time you got up. You've been dead to the world for the past forty-eight hours," said Terri. She flounced over to the night table in a short, ruffled denim skirt and started gathering up dishes. "At least you've been eating."

Annie sat up and fluffed up an extra pillow to lay against. "Are you moving back in?"

"No." She glanced away. "I'm staying with Jack."

"I'm glad," said Annie. "You guys are right for each other."

Pleased with Annie's response, Terri plopped down on the edge of the bed. "Now that we've got that over with, what's going on with you and the incredible hunk?"

Annie pulled up her legs, hugged them and rested her chin on her knee. "It didn't work out."

"Your mom told me it had something to do with Jack," said Terri.

"He thinks he's an arsonist," Annie snapped.

"Well, you can't blame him. From what Jack tells me, so does everybody else."

"Yeah, but I don't want to be in love with *everybody else*."

"So, go tell him the truth."

"It's not that easy, Terri. How can I tell him my mother let her son take a beating all his life for something she did? I could never do that to her. We've got to keep it in the family—as long as she's alive, anyway. Right now, no matter what I do, Mike will end up despising one of them. Besides, he comes from such a straight-laced family, we'd never fit in. Nope. Long term, it's not going to work. I know what I want for long term, and I'm not going to settle for anything less."

Annie sat with her thoughts for a moment. "You know, by the time I was ten it never really bothered me what people would say about Jack because I knew how good he was. After a while, I don't think it even bothered him. The fear of being accused of setting the next fire was what got to us. But when Mike wouldn't believe me when I told him Jack would never have set the Party Rock Fire, it really hurt. It poured salt on every wound. I could see every nasty look, feel every sneer."

Annie wiped a tear. "When we were kids, we used to live up on Bluerock Mountain. I don't remember much, mostly the little critters I kept, and Jack. No matter how bad things got, I'd look up at that cocksure grin of his and feel safe. Whenever I got hungry, he'd come up with a way to get us something to eat. He'd take a chicken down the mountain and sell it, or some eggs.

"When Mom would rock me in her chair at night, sometimes she would tell me stories of olden days with knights and ladies, and I always pictured Jack as the prince who would slay the dragons. But he went away for a while after the fire, and when he came back he wasn't the same, mostly something about his smile. We had moved into the river house by then, and I felt Jack and I had traded places; little by little, it was me who was taking care of him."

They both looked up at the door. Jack stood grinning, his arms bracing the doorway.

"I put your equipment back in your office and Mom's got your kitchen cleaned. She's stuffed the refrigerator with food, too."

"How long has Mom been here?" asked Annie.

"We all came together," said Jack as he moved aside to let Mae in with a tray. Annie couldn't help wondering how much of her conversation with Terri her mother had overheard.

"Here's your favorite," Mae sang out. "Homemade macaroni and cheese."

Jack put his hand next to his mouth as if he didn't want Mae to see his lips move and whispered. "It's from a box."

Unfazed, Mae put the tray on the bed next to Annie. "Well, I did make it at home."

"Any news about the fire?" asked Annie as she picked up the dish and dug in.

"It's stopped growing and it looks like they're ramping down," said Jack. "The gang that's been here is leaving. I saw them on TV yesterday, thanking everyone. Boy, are they a tough lookin' bunch."

Annie chuckled. *"Ooh, yeah... they're tough, all right."*

"A new group from Oregon is taking over tomorrow," Jack added.

Annie finished the last of the macaroni and Mae whisked away the tray while Terri got the last of the dishes on the bedside table before going downstairs.

"When are you going back to being bat girl?" he asked as he sat down on the bed.

"Next Monday."

"By the way, I went up to Uncle Luke's place and we lucked out. The fire just missed it."

"The fire chief will be happy to hear that," said Annie.

"He was. I had the truck towed out of there, and once we got it to Shumont Road, I drove it to the station. I put your backpack and fire shell in the kitchen."

"I love it when you take care of me, Jack." She squeezed his hand. "But, it's not just you and me anymore, is it?"

"Nope. I got myself a girl."

"It's funny," said Annie. "When Terri told me about all the crazy schemes she came up with to survive on the streets at fifteen, I could see myself doing the same thing if I didn't have you and Mom, and I knew we were going to be friends forever."

"Come on! We got to get going!" Terri yelled from downstairs.

He rose, gave Annie a kiss on the forehead and rushed out, yelling that he'd see her on Thanksgiving.

Annie lingered in bed for a while, then got up and went downstairs and strolled through the rooms she loved. A wave of gratitude to her brother firefighters who had saved it rolled over her and she had to fight off getting weepy again.

Seeing the mountain of equipment and records stacked on the floor of her office, she started sorting things out, then stopped. She was too worn out. She'd do it another day. She went in the kitchen and looked around. For all her mother's shortcomings, she knew how to make a place sparkle. She opened the refrigerator, and it was as if her mother had made a list of her favorite foods and gone to the store and bought them.

She grabbed a yogurt, found a spoon and strolled around eating. Where was her phone, she wondered? Her backpack leaned against the wall. It had to be in there. She quickly retrieved it, but as she suspected, it needed a charge.

She went to her bedroom and plugged it into its usual spot on her bedside table. In moments, she heard text message beeps. She sank down on her bed and started to read them. There was one from Bruce Button saying he was still trying to get hold of his friend who was with the F.B.I. She jotted a quick text thanking him and telling him everything was okay and she didn't need to talk with him anymore about Jack.

The messages from Mike had to be from when she was up on Shumont two days ago. She could tell he had been worried about her, and oddly, Jack, too. She didn't want to go back to sleep, but a yearning in every part of her made her slip between the sheets and sink onto the pillow.

She woke in the dark. Someone was knocking on the kitchen door. Her cat stood at the foot of the bed, his back arched. The knock came again and Blackie took off. Annie pulled the blanket aside and slowly rose. Again, the knock. Cautiously, she went down the stairs. She could see a figure through the glass pane on the upper half of the door. Nothing but a dark shadow, but she knew who it was. She quickly leaned against the wall so he couldn't see her.

The screen door squeaked open and he tried the doorknob. It was locked. Her heart beat wildly.

"Annie, I know you're in there. Please let me in."

Her breathing became heavy.

"Annie, your mother came over tonight and told me everything. I'm sorry I didn't believe you. Please forgive me."

All became quiet.

"I'm leaving tomorrow for a fire in the Chattahoochee River Preserve. I'll be gone for a week, unless we put it out sooner. Take care of yourself, Annie. I love you."

The screen door squeaked closed, then moments later a truck door slammed shut. She ran to the door and watched him pull away. She closed her eyes and felt him wrap his arms around her and pull her close and whisper that he loved her.

THE NEXT DAY, ANNIE was beginning to feel like herself again. However, she still smelled smoke even though the air was clear. Every once in a while she'd think she saw something move or come careening toward her, and then get concerned when she realized it never really happened. She had a case of PTSD, and she had to get over it before she started surveying all the caves. There were a lot of places she'd have to climb into that could pose a danger to her and her partner if she weren't in top form.

She worked in her office all morning, but found it hard to concentrate. The only thing she seemed to be able to keep her mind on was Mike's dozen or so text messages. She didn't respond to any of them, just kept reading them over and over. Terri stopped by to pick up something she had left behind, and over a cup of coffee, Annie told her that her mother had overheard their conversation and gone over and told Mike what had happened.

"So where do you stand with him now?" Terri asked.

"Nowhere, really. I don't think I can ever forgive him for not believing me. If he had, it would've been like he was on our team."

Terri left, and Annie went back to her computer, but was finding it hard to wean herself from the fire. For the second time that day, she pulled up the Lake Lure website for an update.

"An aerial infrared image of the Party Rock Fire taken last night still shows some areas of isolated heat, such as smoldering stumps or large downed trees," the press release read. "The strong winds during the past three days have also blown a lot of leaves into the containment area and have had to be extinguished. Other hot spots that were well within the fire's interior, have been allowed to burn out on their own. Residents may see what appears to be small campfires in the nights ahead, but are asked not to call authorities unless they believe what they are seeing poses an immediate threat to life and property."

Annie chuckled. She pitied whoever was answering the phones these days. They had to be spending most of their time jotting down baseless reports and calming people down.

She worked in her office all day, mostly answering emails, and decided she would run into Chimney Rock for a quick hamburger. She pulled up to the Riverwatch restaurant and walked in. The place was packed with firefighters and townspeople alike. Instead of waiting for a table, she decided to sit at the bar where she couldn't help overhearing the man next to her talk with the bartender.

"See those firefighters over at those two tables," the man said. "I want their tabs put on my bill."

Annie sat there trying to hold back tears, but in seconds they streamed down her cheeks.

The man tossed his head toward Annie. "I bet that one was working on the fire, too," he said.

Annie smiled weakly through a sniffle.

"Put her bill on mine, too," he said.

She wiped her nose on her sleeve and laughed and cried at the same time. Finally, she pulled herself together and said, "I'm sorry. I'm kinda on an emotional rollercoaster."

"That's all right. You folks have been through a lot."

Halfway through her meal, Annie heard the bartender tell the man no one was letting a firefighter pay for their food, and she got weepy again.

"And if they make it to the cash register without anyone picking up their tab, we don't ring it up," he added.

Annie left the restaurant worried that she might have more than just a mild case of PTSD. Thankfully, she had the week off. She had to do something to calm herself. She slipped onto the front seat of her truck, pulled out her phone and sat for fifteen minutes, reading Mike's texts.

ANNIE WASN'T HAVING much luck weaning herself from news about the fire. In fact, it had become addictive. On waking this Thanksgiving morning, the first thing she did was boot up the Lake Lure website and read a statement from Link Smith, the incoming incident commander from the Oregon team.

"We've had a ton of help come to Oregon from North Carolina during the fire seasons between 2013 and 2015," the press release read, "and it's an honor to be here to serve on this fire and repay what so many of you have done for the people of Oregon."

She scanned over the rest of the release. The fire's footprint was still holding at 7,171 acres with no one hurt and no houses destroyed. They were planning on using handheld infrared scanners that could see through leaf litter and detect hidden heat, then go through the methodical process of gridding to make sure every piece of ground along the fire's perimeter was free of active fire. Annie sighed when she read: "The smoke in the area this morning is from other fires, not the Party Rock Fire." Hopefully that tidbit would save them from a few distraught calls.

If she could break away from her mother's house around six that night, she wanted to run up to the command center and help the North Carolina Baptist Men serve all the firefighters a Thanksgiving dinner. Annie was suddenly pleased with herself. She had pictured them spending their Thanksgiving raking through smoky leaf litter and hadn't burst into tears. Maybe she *was* getting better.

She arrived at her mother's house just after noon. The instant she opened the kitchen door the aroma of a turkey roasting in the oven and an apple pie cooling on the windowsill enveloped her in the comforting aura of being home for the holidays. Mae worked on a salad at the sink. Annie, seeing the dining room table hadn't been set yet, got busy putting out plates.

"Well, aren't you going to ask me?" said Mae.

"Ask you what?" said Annie as she set the last plate down.

Mae stopped slicing a cucumber and faced her. "He loves you, Annie."

Annie strolled over to her mother with her arms folded.

"Okay. I'll ask you. Just what did he say when you told him you practically ruined Jack's life!?"

"Frankly, Annie," said Mae as she went back to her salad, "he couldn't care less about me. He's only interested in you. You've got to lighten up, baby. Things aren't always black and white. You've loved that boy forever, and now you mean to tell me you can't forgive him for being like everyone else in this town?"

A cry made them look out the kitchen window. Terri was on the old tire swing with Jack pushing her. It made the two women smile.

"It's good to see them so happy," said Mae.

Minutes later, Terri came running in screaming, with Jack chasing after her. Mae was taking the turkey from the oven and almost dropped it.

"Lordy, are you two going to be carrying on like that all afternoon?" said Mae. "Get yourselves over here and help me with the dinner. Jack, start mashing the potatoes."

All through the dinner, to everyone's delight, Jack continued in a jovial mood.

"Now, Terri, you may think my sister is a sweetheart, but I want you to know she was the terror of Edneyville Elementary."

Annie looked at Terri and rolled her eyes. "They loved me at Edneyville Elementary."

"Maybe before Stinky," said Jack.

And, as if Terri knew Jack expected her to respond, she asked, "And just who is Stinky?"

"Wait a minute," interjected Annie. "Let me preface this little tale with the fact that I may have only been in the third grade, but I had read all about skunks and knew that when they were very young they didn't spray."

"*She* may have known that," said Jack waving a finger, "but nobody else on the playground did. And when she caught the little critter and started showing it around to everyone, all hell broke loose."

"When the school called me to come and get her and the skunk," said Mae, "I didn't know what to do 'cept take it to the vet. He had to remove the musk glands in the parking lot outside his clinic."

"That episode was just the first chapter in 'The Adventures of Stinky,'" said Jack. "He'd run all over the house at night and sleep all day. His favorite spot was behind the refrigerator."

Annie giggled. "One day, Mom was on the porch with a couple of Jehovah Witness missionaries bending her ear, and Jack coaxed Stinky from the fridge and shoved him onto the porch."

"They sure got out of here fast," laughed Mae.

As Jack and her mother went through a litany of Annie's adventures with all the wild creatures she had befriended, a feeling of peace took hold of her. She saw the love in Terri's eyes as she listened to Jack drag out the rest of the old family stories, brush them off and give them a new shine, and she knew she didn't have to worry about her brother anymore.

The meal now finished, everyone was helping clear the table when Mae's phone rang. The pleading expression on Mae's face as she handed it to Annie told her who it was and she shook her head.

Mae put her hand over the receiver. "Talk to him, baby." Then she handed Annie the phone again. "Go on. Talk to him."

Annie put the phone to her ear.

"Is that you, Annie?"

"Uh-huh," she barely whispered.

"It's been raining all day and I'm coming home tomorrow. I should be there around six. I want you to be waiting for me."

She said nothing, just put the phone in the cradle and went over to the front window, looked out and thought about what

Mike had said. Was he giving her a subtle warning that this was his last plea? Would this be her last chance?

Jack came up from behind her and handed her a coat.

"Come on. Let's take a walk," he said.

They went out and strolled over to the river. It had grown dark, and light from a lone street lamp ricocheted off the boulders as the water danced over them. The familiar breeze came sailing through the gorge, swirling Annie's ponytail.

"Mom and Terri told me about Mike," said Jack.

"That was nice of them," said Annie as she brushed her hair from her face.

"Don't be that way, Annie. They're worried about you. They don't want you to make a mistake you'll regret for the rest of your life."

"Can you smell the smoke?" Annie asked.

"Yeah, I can smell it," said Jack.

"Good. So, it's not my imagination. They say it's coming from a fire in McDowell County." She kicked a stone into the river. "I'm afraid from now on, every time I smell smoke, I'll think of the Party Rock Fire. I'll never forget the sight of that dragon spitting out flames and writhing along the Bald Mountain ridge in the dark of the night."

They strolled along the deserted lane until Annie said, "Jack, I saw the whole thing up close, the biggest battle between man and the forces of nature I hope I'll ever see. And the way they fought it was a thing to behold. After watching them for two weeks, I can truly say that anyone in North Carolina can go to sleep knowing that if there's a fire, there are people who will do everything humanly possible to keep them safe. I'll never forget this fire and the privilege of working with the best of the best for as long as I live."

He put his arm around her shoulder and pulled her close as they continued up the lane. "So, you're going back to being a bat girl on Monday?"

"Yeah. That's where I belong. I don't think I was cut out to be a firefighter. When I signed in all those men and women about to walk into danger, my heart went with them. No matter how dead tired I was, I couldn't go home 'til I checked them all back in again. I had to be sure they all came back. I don't know how those guys that ran that fire bore up under the responsibility of putting all those lives on the line. Maybe that's why they started every briefing with a safety message and ended it with an order to stay safe."

"So, what are you going to do about Mike?"

"I don't know. He really hurt me."

"That's because you love him," said Jack. He laughed softly. "I remember the first day Mom took you over to that big house of theirs and you came home and told me you were gonna marry him when you grew up.

"I'm sorry I ever said that. I've had it thrown in my face so many times it isn't funny," said Annie.

"Sis, I want you to know I'm going to be all right from now on. I bought a ring, and I'm gonna ask Terri to marry me."

"I'm glad," said Annie.

He stopped walking and started to turn around. "Come on, let's go back."

"I'll never forget the Party Rock Fire for as long as I live, either," he said. "It changed everything. I've decided that I'm not going to let what happened up on Bluerock Mountain drive me from the place I love. Now that you and Terri know what really happened up there, I feel safer and more at peace. Sorta like, with you two by my side, I can handle anything that comes along. Besides, if they didn't come after me for this fire, I'm pretty sure I'm in the clear."

"I can't believe I'm saying this," said Annie, "but I think you're right." She let out a bitter little laugh. "I just wish I thought that two weeks ago."

"Annie, you know what I'd like to see?" He didn't wait for an answer. "You and Mike together. It would be like you aren't letting what happened on Bluerock Mountain drive you from the man you love. Like we aren't letting it control where our lives are headed."

Jack stopped walking and looked at her. "Mom says he's a nice guy. Give him a break."

MIKE PULLED OFF I-85 in Spartanburg and headed north on Route 26. He glanced at his clock and figured he should be home by six. The big misstep he made with the girl he wanted to spend the rest of his life with stung every time he thought about it, and he wondered if she would be waiting for him at the house. If her truck wasn't there, maybe he should give it one more try and go find her.

He was sure she loved him; they just had to get past this thing about her brother. Then he thought about how strong-willed and determined she had to have been to come from such a tough childhood, and then go out and make something of herself the way she had. It was highly possible that if she set her mind against him, nothing would change it. No. If she's not there, I'm not chasing her. She knows I love her, and it's now up to her to decide what she wants to do about it.

He pulled off the highway and got some gas, but before he took off, checked his texts one more time. As he feared, there was nothing from Annie, and he was back on the road when his mother phoned.

"Hey, Mom," he said, "how was turkey day at the McNeil's?"

"How do you think? My only child missing from the table and out starting fires."

"Mom, I wasn't starting this one. I was putting it out."

"Hopefully, next Thanksgiving we'll have a baby at the table."

"Something tells me this conversation is leading somewhere," said Mike.

"Mabel Whiteside phoned yesterday. Believe me, they don't call her the town crier for nothing. When she said a tall, gorgeous blonde spent four nights at the house, I figured you were having a fling. But when she said she drove what looked like a plumber's truck, I knew it was our Annie."

Mike groaned.

"Your father and I are simply over the moon, son. But this kind of gossip isn't good for the family name. You've got to nip it in the bud and get married right away."

"Whoa! Mom. Not so fast."

"Fast!? You're almost thirty-five, son. What are you waiting for? Am I never going to be a nana?"

Mike rolled his eyes and listened to his mother go on. "Your dad thinks her family can be a bit of a problem. He's thinking about up the road when you get into politics. But I told him not to worry, I've got plenty of time to gloss things over. Tell me, is Mae still drinking?"

"Mom, I want you to stop this. I don't want to see you disappointed."

"Disappointed!? Michael Samuel McNeil, I have no intention of being disappointed! You get busy and win that girl over, you hear me?"

The closer he got to Lake Lure, the more his mother's call bothered him, and the more he yearned for Annie to be waiting for him. He drove through Bat Cave, then Chimney Rock, and when he passed the command center in Lake Lure and saw it was beginning to ramp down, a pang of melancholy hit him. He would never forget the busy, stinky, noisy Tent City. With all the generators, tractor trailers, portable light towers and tents, it had the atmosphere of a huge carnival hectically preparing for the next show. But most of all, he'd never forget all the firefighters who came to save that little mountain community.

He made a left onto his road and wound around the lake until he pulled into his driveway and saw that Annie hadn't come. Disappointed, he stripped in the laundry room and took a shower before going upstairs. He put on a pair of jeans and a sweater and realized he hadn't eaten since last night. There was nothing in the fridge, so he took out a beer, went to the window and looked longingly toward the end of the driveway.

He stood at the window for several minutes hoping she'd pull in, when her truck suddenly appeared. Quickly, he stepped far enough back from the window so she wouldn't see him, but where he could still see her.

She jumped out of the truck and energetically hurried over to the tailgate, just as she had the first time he laid eyes on her all those years ago. He watched intently as she took out her duffle bag and what looked like a carrying crate. Seeing her struggle with the two hefty items, he could hear his father say, "Go help her, son," but he didn't move. The determined way she was unloading was sending a message, and he didn't want to interrupt it.

He listened to her come in downstairs, then set his eyes firmly on the staircase. A black cat appeared from below and cautiously stepped into the room. Mike couldn't suppress a grin. He was getting the message.

Annie came bounding up the stairs and hoisted her backpack onto the sofa table without making eye contact with him. She unzipped one of the pockets, pulled out a book and faced him, hugging the book in such a way as to show off the cover. The teasing way she had gone about it made him try to grab her, but she quickly stepped back, still coyly displaying the cover.

"Oh, so you want to play, do you?" he said laughingly as he tried to grab her again.

This time she agilely jumped up on the couch, making him laugh. Her ponytail tumbled across the book she was still holding as she looked down at him with a coquettish smile.

"Okay. You got me. I can see the only way I'm gonna get my book back is if I take you along with it," he said as he swooped her up in his arms and carried her upstairs to his room. He let her down and lovingly brushed his lips across her forehead. "You know, if we keep meeting like this, the neighbors are going to talk." He kissed her cheek, then her ear. "In fact, gossip has already hit DC."

"We can't have that," said Annie.

"I guess we're just gonna have to get married," said Mike.

"We have no choice," she said. "It's the call of the wild."

❧❧

FIRE COMPANIES

Following is a list of the 225 North Carolina fire companies that came from 56 counties to fight the Party Rock Fire that burned 7,171acres. It is considered to be the largest call for mutual aid the state had ever seen and resulted in no lives or structures lost.

I apologize for any companies that may be missing or misspelled.

Fire Department	County
Aberdeen	Moore
Advance	Davie
Albemarle	Stanly
Allen	Cabarrus
Altamahaw-Ossippe	Alamance
Apex	Wake
A-RC-H (Arcadia-	
Reedy Ck.-Hampton)	Davidson
Arch	Livingston
Ashford-North Cove	McDowell
Asheboro	Randolph
Asheville	Buncombe
Aurora	Beaufort
Bahama	Durham
Bakersville	Mitchell
Barnardsville	Buncombe
Bat Cave	Henderson
Battleboro	Nash
Bay Leaf	Wake
Bear Creek/	
Swansboro	Onslow
Beaufort	Beaufort
Big Marsh	Robeson
Bills Creek	Rutherford
Biltmore Forest	Buncombe
Black Mountain	Buncombe
Bladenboro	Bladen
Bladen County FD	Bladen
Blounts Creek	Beaufort
Blue Ridge	Henderson
Bostic	Rutherford
Broad River	Buncombe
Buffalo	Cherokee, SC
Bunyan	Beaufort
Carolina	Mecklenbrg.
Carrboro	Orange
Carthage	Moore
Cary	Wake
Cedar Grove	Orange
Central FD	Davidson

Fire Department	County
Central Rural	Stanly
Central School	Iredel
Chapel Hill	Orange
Charlotte	Mecklenburg
Cherry Mt.	Rutherford
Chimney Rock	Rutherford
Chocowinity	Beaufort
Clark's Neck	Pitt
Clarkton	Bladen
Cleveland No. 3	Cleveland
Cleveland No. 7	Cleveland
Cliffside	Rutherford
Climax	Guilford
Columbus	Polk
Concord	Cabarrus
Courtney	Yadkin
Cumberland Road	Cumberland
Currituck County FD	Currituck
Cypress Point	Moore
Dana	Henderson
Deep River	Lee
Denver	Lincoln
Dudley Wayne	Duke Pike
Durham, City of	Durham
Durham County FD	Durham
Durham Highway	Wake
Dyartsville	McDowell
Eagle Springs	Moore
East Bend	Yadkin
East Howellsville	Robeson
East Side	Stanly
Eastern Wake	Wake
Edneyville	Henderson
Efland	Orange
Ellenboro	Rutherford
Elizabethtown	Bladen
E. M. Holt	Alamance
Etowah Horseshoe	Henderson
Elon	Alamance
Enka-Candler	Buncombe

Fire Department	County
Fairfield Mountains	Rutherford
Fairview	Buncombe
Farmer	Randolph
Farmville	Pitt
Faucette	Alamance
Fire District 13	Guilford
Fletcher	Henderson
Forbush	Yadkin
Forest City	Rutherford
Fountain	Pitt
Franklinville	Randolph
French Broad	Buncombe
Fuquay-Varina	Wake
Garner	Wake
Garren Creek	Buncombe
Gastonia	Gaston
Gerton	Henderson
Glenwood	McDowell
Goldston Rural	Chatham
Gray's Creek	Cumberland
Green Creek	Polk
Green Hill	Rutherford
Green River	Henderson
Greensboro	Guilford
Grimesland	Pitt
Guil-Rand	Randolph
Guilford No. 13	Forsyth
Halifax	Halifax
Harmony	Iredell
Harrisburg	Cabarrus
Haw Creek	Buncombe
Haw River	Alamance
Healing Springs	Davidson
Hendersonville	Henderson
High Falls	Moore
High Point	Guilford
Holly Springs	Wake
Hot Spring	Madison
Horneytown	Forsyth
Hubert	Onslow
Hudlow	Rultherford
Idlewild	Mecklenburg
Jacksonville	Onslow
Kernersville	Forsyth
Kannapolis	Cabarrus
Knightdale	Wake

Fire Department	County
Lake Lure	Rutherford
Leicester	Buncombe
Leland	Brunswick
Lemon Springs	Lee
Lewisville	Forsyth
Locke	Rowan
Lower Currituck	Currituck
Matthews	Mecklenburg
Midway	Davidson
Mill Spring	Polk
Mills River	Henderson
Monroe	Union
Morehead City	Carteret
Moore County	Moore
Mooresville	Iredell
Morrisville	Wake
Mountain Home	Henderson
Moyock	Currituck
New Hanover	New Hanover
North Lenoir	Lenoir
Norwood Center	Stanly
Number 3	Cleveland
Number 7 Township	Craven
Old Fort	McDowell
Onslow County	Onslow
Orange Rural	Orange
Pamlico	Pamlico
Parkton	Robeson
Parkway	Mitchell
Pinecroft-Sedgefield	Guilford
Pinehill	Hoke
Pinehurst	Moore
Piney Green	Onslow
Pleasant Garden	Guilford
Pleasant Grove	Duplin
Pumpkin Center	Onslow
Puppy Creek	Hoke
Raft Swamp	Robeson
Raleigh	Wake
Red Oak	Pitt
Reelsboro	Pamlico
Reems Creek--Beaverdam Dist.	Buncombe
Reems Creek	Buncombe
Reynolds	Buncombe
Riceville	Buncombe
Rolesville	Wake
Rocky Mount	Edgecombe

Fire Department	County	Fire Department	County
Rutherfordton	Rutherford	Upper Hominey	Buncombe
Salisbury	Rowan	Valley Hill	Henderson
Saluda	Polk	Vienna	Forsyth
Sandy Marsh	Rutherford	Wadesboro	Anson
Shelby	Cleveland	Wake Forest	Wake
Shepherds	Iredell	Wake-New Hope	Wake
Shiloh-Danieltown-		Wallace	Duplin
Oakland	Rutherford	Warsaw	Duplin
Shingle Hollow	Rutherford	Weaverville	Buncombe
Simpson	Pitt	Wendell	Wake
Skyland	Buncombe	West Buncombe	Buncombe
South Iredell	Iredell	West Area	Cumberland
Southern Pines	Moore	West End	Moore
Southmont	Davidson	Western Carteret	Carteret
Spindale	Rutherford	Western Wake	Wake
Spring Lake	Cumberland	White Lake	Bladen
Statesville	Iredell	William R. Davie	Davie
Stony Hill	Wake	Wilmington	New Hanover
Stoney Point	Cumberland	Wilson	Wilson
Summerfield	Guilford	Wingate	Union
Sunnyview	Polk	Winston-Salem	Forsyth
Swannanoa	Buncombe	Winterville	Pitt
Tabernacle	Randolph	Woodfin	Buncombe
Tramway	Lee	Wrightsville Beach	New Hanover
Troutman	Iredell	Yadkinville	Yadkin
Tryon	Polk	Yanceyville	Caswell
Unionville	Union	Zebulon	Wake

❧❧

County & City Resources of Special Note:

Buncombe County: Sent Fire Marshal's Office along with Numerous Chief Fire Department Officers

City of Charlotte: Task Force with 3 Engine-tankers, 4 Brush Trucks, a Chief, Communications Assets, NC USAR Task Force 3 for Logistics and Shelter Support

City of Greensboro: Engine, Mobile Shower Unit, Tractor-drawn Communications Unit, Special Ops/NCTF6 Units Assisting with Logistics

Henderson County: Sent 7 Companies to Defend Chimney Rock the night the fire went over Round Top

Lenoir County: 11 Personnel from Several Fire Departments and the Office of the Fire Marshal

Moore County: 2 Engines and 8 Firefighters

Pamlico County: A 20-man Strike Team and 4 Engines
Pitt County: 6 Departments and 13 Firefighters, 3 Brush Trucks, plus QRV
Wake County: 5 Engines, 10 Brush Trucks, 57 Firefighters and a Commercial Bus with Passenger Van

Forestry Crews

State Forestry crews from NC, OR, VA, AZ, and other loctions.
US Forest Service units from NM, AZ, AK, CA, FL, ID, MT, NC, OK

Wildland Crews & Apparatus from Out of State

Beaver Dam, Littlefield, AZ
Black Timber Wildland Services, Queen Creek, AZ
Central Arizona Fire, AZ
Chihuahua Fire Engines, Ruidoso, NM
Daisy Mountain Fire Dept., AZ
Eagles Engines, Mescalero, NM
Golden Valley Fire Dept., AZ
Guadalupe Fire Dept., AZ
Harquahala Fire District, Tonopah, AZ
L&A Wildfire, Sante Fe, NM
North County Fire & Medical, Sun City, AZ
Palomias Fire & Rescue, Hereford, AZ
Peoria Fire Dept., AZ
Shiloh, NM
Summit Fire Dept., Flagstaff, AZ
Sundance, WY
Superstition, AZ
Surprise, AZ
Taos Pueblo Fire Dept., NM
Taylor-Snowflake Fire & Medical, Taylor, AZ
Three Points Fire District, Tucson, AZ
Timber Mesa, AZ
Wildfire Support Team, Santa Fe, NM

Supporting Agencies

NC Forest Service
US Forest Service
NC Incident Management Team
Oregon Forest Service Incident Management Team
NC Emergency Management
NC Office of the State Fire Marshal (OSFM)
Rutherford County Emergency Management
Henderson County Emergency Management
Buncombe County Emergency Management
Emergency Management from the following counties: Bladen,
   Caswell, Cleveland, Craven, Forsyth, Gates, Granville, Hertford,
   Mitchell, New Hanover, Polk, Rockingham, Surry, Wake, Wilson
Southern Air Command of the US Forest Service (SAC)
National Weather Service
NC Wildlife Resources Commission
NC Division of Parks and Recreation
Virginia Department of Parks and Recreation
NC Department of Public Safety, NC HART – One helo
NC USAR Task Force 2 (Buncombe) – Various fire/rescue agencies
NC USAR Task Force 3 (Mecklenburg) – Charlotte FD, see above
NC USAR Task Force 6 (Guilford) – Greensboro FD, see above
Various Emergency Management Agencies from other NC counties

Humanitarian Services

American Red Cross
Billy Graham Rapid Response Team Ministry
Heart with Hands, Asheville
North Carolina Baptist Men and Women's Disaster Relief Ministry
Samaritan's Purse, Boone, NC
Bills Creek Baptist Church
Greenhill Baptist Church
Bat Cave Baptist Church
Grace Lutheran Church, Hendersonville

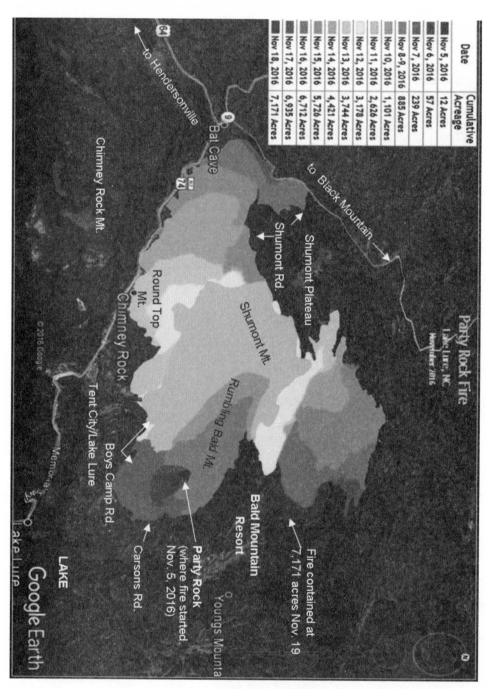

Date	Cumulative Acreage
Nov 5, 2016	12 Acres
Nov 6, 2016	57 Acres
Nov 7, 2016	239 Acres
Nov 8-9, 2016	885 Acres
Nov 10, 2016	1,101 Acres
Nov 11, 2016	2,626 Acres
Nov 12, 2016	3,178 Acres
Nov 13, 2016	3,744 Acres
Nov 14, 2016	4,421 Acres
Nov 15, 2016	5,726 Acres
Nov 16, 2016	6,712 Acres
Nov 17, 2016	6,935 Acres
Nov 18, 2016	7,171 Acres

This Plan of the Fire's progression can be viewed in color on the author's Website at: www.rosesenehi.com

BLUE RIDGE SERIES of Stand-Alone Books

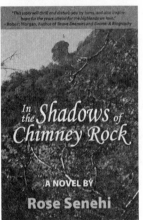

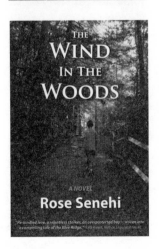

Winner of the 2012 IPPY Gold Medal Fiction-Southeast

Render Unto the Valley. *Karen Godwell isn't as much ashamed of her mountain heritage as of what she once had to do to preserve it.* She reinvents herself at college and doesn't look back till her clan's historic farm is threatened. She returns only to come face to face with who she was and what she did. Cousin Bruce sees life through the family's colorful two-hundred-year past; Tom Gibbons, a local conservationist, keeps one eye on the mountains and the other on Karen. Her nine-year-old daughter is on the mission her dying father sent her on.

In the Shadows of Chimney Rock. *A touching tale of Family and Place.* A Southern heiress reaches out to her mountain roots for solace after suffering a life-shattering blow, only to be drawn into a fight to save the beauty of the mountain her father loved. Hayden Taylor starts to heal in the womb of the gorge as she struggles to redeem her father's legacy, never suspecting the man who killed him is stalking her.

The Wind in the Woods. A romantic thriller that reveals a man's devotion to North Carolina's Green River Valley and the camp he built to share its wonders; his daughter's determination to hike the Blue Ridge—unaware that a serial killer is stalking her; and nine-year-old Alvin Magee's heart-warming discovery of freedom and responsibility in a place apart from his adult world.

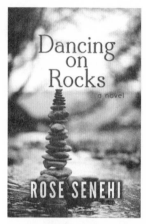

Dancing on Rocks. Nursing her mother back to health wasn't all that drew Georgie Haydock back to the little mountain tourist town. Hiding around every corner, are a family's painful memories of a child who disappeared in the middle of the night 25 years ago. The summer roils as her mother thrashes in her bed, insisting that the woman stalking her store downstairs is the missing sister. Meanwhile, Georgie aches to reunite with the hometown boy she never forgot.

Carolina Belle. Belle McKenzie is obsessed with finding the best apple anyone ever bit into and determined to rekindle the love this obsession destroyed. She risks her life rescuing four hundred antique apple trees her neighbor has collected from all over the South. Pap thinks of Matt as a son, but Belle thinks of him as the man she loved and who betrayed her. Rich in emotion and driven by suspense, woven throughout this story is the fascinating history of the American apple that started when settlers planted seeds all over the country and kicked off one of the biggest evolutionary experiments this nation has ever seen.

Other Novels by Rose Senehi

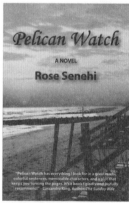

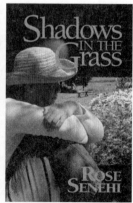

Pelican Watch   **Windfall**   **Shadows in the Grass**